JISHIN

JISHIN

Lives Shattered, Love Discovered
amid the Great Tokyo Quake

Lee Riordan

YENBOOKS

Published by Periplus Editions (HK) Limited
under the Charles E. Tuttle imprint

LCC Card No. 96-61136
ISBN 4-900737-40-2

First Edition, 1997

Printed in Singapore
Cover illustration by Dong Guangliang

Distributed by:

USA **Charles E. Tuttle Company, Inc.**
Airport Industrial Park
RR1 Box 231-5
North Clarendon, VT 05759
Tel: (802) 773-8930
Fax: (802) 773-6993

Japan **Tuttle Shokai Ltd.**
1-21-13 Seki
Tama-ku, Kawasaki-shi
Kanagawa-ken 214, Japan
Tel: (81) (44) 833-0225
Fax: (81) (44) 822-0413

Southeast Asia
Berkeley Books Pte Ltd.
5 Little Road #08-01
Singapore 536983
Tel: (65) 280 3320
Fax: (65) 280 6290

Tokyo Editorial Office:
2-6, Suido 1-chome,
Bunkyo-ku, Tokyo 112, Japan

Boston Editorial Office:
153 Milk Street, 5th Floor
Boston, MA 02109, USA

Singapore Editorial Office:
5 Little Road #08-01
Singapore 536983

Visit Tuttle Web on the Internet at:
http://www.tuttle.co.jp/~tuttle/

To the memory of my parents
Hugh Leo Riordan and Tatiana Lunskaya Bachmanoff
and the Japanese people
they came to know, love, and respect
during their time in Japan

To my wife

Barbara
whose editorial skills made the telling of this story possible
and so much more meaningful

Contents

Forewarnings and Forebodings
9

The Days Before
12

August 31, Afternoon and Evening
46

September 1, Early Morning
68

September 1, 11:58 A.M.
111

September 1, Noon
130

Miss Tatiana Lunskaya Walks to the West
152

Major Phillip Faymonville and
the Imperial Hotel
166

Raita Kanoh in the Yoshiwara
170

Shimaku Suzuki at Mitsukoshi
178

Yoshinari Yamamoto and His Family
182

At the Temple of the Goddess of Mercy
187

Sanji Nakamura and the Honjo Horror
198

Professor Hugh Riordan Walks to the East
210

Sifting Through the Ashes
254

The Kiss
271

PHOTOGRAPHS
137–144

Forewarnings and Forebodings

Although most of them were not seismologists or scientists, they all knew the earthquake would occur. They did not know the precise location or the exact moment, but—while for the most part they avoided discussing their personal fears at length—the average person in Japan was convinced it had to come soon.

Initially, not one of them admitted to being overly concerned. If they brought themselves to think about the subject, devoid of panic and with some intelligence, there actually were factors giving rise to a feeling of optimism. Shouldn't any long-range prediction of a large-scale earthquake be based, more or less, on the law of averages? The general Tokyo-Yokohama area, where all of them lived or visited often, had last suffered a deadly convulsion in 1894, twenty-nine years ago; thirty-nine years before that, in 1855, there had been another. Since thirty-nine years had intervened between the last two major upheavals, and now only twenty-nine had passed, perhaps they could count on that ten-year cushion.

Then too, only last year Doctor Omori, Japan's foremost seismologist, who had been making dire predictions for many months, stated that the recent fairly severe shock had, in all probability, satisfied the law of averages, bringing on a period of relative safety. Yes, there were encouraging signs. A smasher occurred every generation, according to learned Japanese, but a generation certainly was a flexible figure.

For a time, immediate concern faded into deeply veiled expectation. People living in Japan, where exact scheduling was relatively rare except for trains, classes, and Westernized businessmen, became used to waiting, and did not become impatient. Life was rather uneventful, so they delayed the thought of a potential incident as much as possible. Temples, shrines, and churches were more crowded than usual. Temple charms, strips of rice-paper with sacred prayer writing and symbols upon them, were posted on fences and poles all over Tokyo and Yokohama. Soon, their expectations started to fade. What was there to worry about? The ground shook a bit, indicating conditions were normal.

Then there was quiet, an ominous quiet that drove away the nascent feeling of relief.

Gradually, as signs were assimilated and interpreted, the prognosis became terribly grim. First of all, the quiet began to scream at them ever more loudly each day. The Tokyo-Yokohama region averaged at least fifty good shakes every year, or about one per week. Often the ground seemed to be trembling constantly. The consistent occurrence of minor shudders was regarded as keeping any area concerned in a comparatively safe condition, by preventing an abnormal accumulation of stress in the earth's crust. Some slowing down of this seismic activity was regarded as potentially lethal, and a harbinger of a destructive shock. Now, day after day, the earth on which they walked and rode, below the buildings where they worked and lived, and beneath their bodies, which slept for the most part fitfully, was perfectly still.

The second foreboding sign concerned Yamanaka, Kawaguchi, Saiko, Shoji, and Motosu, the five lovely lakes that surround Mount Fuji, Japan's sacred mountain. These lakes, whose reflections of Mount Fuji artists delighted in depicting, varied in maximum depth from about fifty-three feet to over four hundred. They were only seventy-six miles from Tokyo and, incredibly, they were beginning to dry up. According to all recorded history, this happened very seldom, but whenever they dried up, a crushing blow was imminent.

The local Japanese newspapers, under light but effective government control, did not actually predict an earthquake, but continued to print disquieting facts such as the fact that the priceless vases in the Okura Fine Arts Museum and the Imperial Museum were being loaded with extra shot and sand, or were having their lashings rechecked to prevent their being tipped over and broken.

The Osaka *Mainichi,* one of the most daring and liberal newspapers in Japan, came out and flatly predicted a severe earthquake. It outlined the telltale signs and also mentioned the old Japanese superstition that a giant catfish lived underground which, when disturbed by the chronic folly of the men who lived above, would heave its back in anger.
The *Mainichi* spread this seismic array before its readers and stated that the only question remaining was whether the lethal shocks would take place in the north or in the south of the country.

The most elaborate warning appeared on the front page of the Japan *Advertiser,* a resourceful American newspaper printed every morning in Tokyo. This article cautioned its primarily foreign readership to take the signs of foreboding seriously, to learn what they could do to protect themselves if they were not able to leave, and why one or both of Japan's two biggest islands, Honshu or Hokkaido, was sure to suffer a catastrophe.

While the admonitions were unofficial, nonetheless they were out. Many people living deep in the bowels of Tokyo and Yokohama had not heard or seen the warnings, but most upper class Japanese and members of the foreign communities did. They reacted in a variety of ways.

The Days Before

One subscriber to the *Advertiser* was Professor Hugh Riordan, an American teaching English at Tokyo's Imperial University. He had taken the warnings with utmost seriousness from the beginning. Although he was far from being a coward, having played as a guard on his college football team and been in the Marines in World War I, he was still terribly concerned. He fancied himself something of a naturalist, and, as the probability of a quake increased, his informal studies turned to the history of earthquakes. What he learned from his studies was far from encouraging. He felt certain that more substantial buildings would topple under the stress of a heavy shock, to say nothing of a great proportion of the flimsy residential houses that took up a great part of Tokyo. These homes were purposely built of light materials to enable them to collapse with minimum damage, but Riordan worried that the wreckage of these buildings would burn fiercely in the aftermath of an earthquake, killing thousands as the flames spread unstoppable. Any fire in Tokyo was difficult to contain because of the thin, kindling-like construction. In fact, throughout history, large fires in Tokyo had been so common they were referred to as the flowers of Edo, Edo being the old name for the city.

Classes did not meet during the summer months, though Riordan worked as a consultant at the university during the summer months. He took advantage of his partial vacation by making short trips away from Tokyo. Because much of his work was by its nature sedentary, he'd realized even in his early thirties that he must make a special effort to keep physically active. He had climbed to the summit of magnificent Mount Fuji and seen the emptying lakes at its base.

He was popular with his students, and many visited him during these days of comparative rest. They met at the foreign-style house he shared with its owner, a German professor named Werner Heise. The students came to drink green tea and talk about the subjects he taught them. It was a mark of great distinction to be a university student, so they wore their black serge uniforms with gold buttons and peaked caps even when school was not in session.

Eventually, their discussions always came around to the probability of an earthquake. His pupils and most of the other Japanese Riordan knew made it a point to bring up the potential disaster almost as an afterthought, and then to speak of it in a detached, unemotional manner. Public emotion of any kind was considered bad form among the Japanese. They agreed on a number of points. The best course of action would be to pitch a tent in an open field and stay there until the danger had passed. During the initial violent shocks, if you were inside anything but one of the heaviest, most reinforced structures, you stood a good chance of being killed instantly since it probably would fall down with a great thud. If near a window, you would be wise to dive out of the building immediately. Arthur Gray, one of Riordan's friends, who worked with an American importer, regularly practiced diving out of his office window. If there wasn't a window close by, you must dash for the strongest point of the room, the doorway, and stand in the open arch. The ceiling, floors, and roof above might miss you as you cowered in the portal. As a last resort, you could try flattening your body against an inner wall. Professor Heise's home was located on relatively high ground on the outskirts of Tokyo, within easy walking distance of the Shinjuku rapid transit station. From his extensive gardens, you could see over the sloping land all the way to the

Imperial Palace and downtown Tokyo. Directly across a wide road there was an attractive Japanese house that also belonged to Heise-san, as he liked to be called.

Many wealthy Japanese had houses that were a combination of styles, half-foreign and half-native. The German professor did them one better by having a Western-style house and a Japanese-style one across the street, to meet the needs of his amphibious existence. His pretty Japanese wife and five children usually lived in the house of native-style, while Heise-san preferred to reside in his foreign house with his colleague Hugh, whom he found an excellent conversationalist, though a good deal younger than himself. This did not imply that he did not love his wife and family, but while Japanese ladies looked very picturesque, they did not expect to be much spoken to. Sometimes, Frau Heise did not appear Japanese in her looks, her manners, or even her thoughts, but nothing could change her heart. She never considered objecting to this arrangement because Japanese wives had little right to complain about anything.

Heise-san took part in the tea-time conversations with Hugh and the students. His teaching demeanor was too rigid, his courses too subjective for his own pupils to visit him regularly. His lengthy service in Japan made him somewhat aloof. Yet, without a doubt, he felt great affection for his family. He became more and more apprehensive about the potential earthquake until, one day, he took his wife and children to Yokohama, and shipped them off to his native Germany.

When he returned to Tokyo, he told Hugh that the university held his signed contract saying he would teach there for two more years, and being a man of responsibility he must honor it, even if it meant being separated from his kin. His colleague patted him lightly on the shoulder. Only a few years before, Hugh Riordan had been fighting Germans, but this German, at least twice his age, had tears in his eyes, and was his friend.

This thought of leaving had entered Professor Riordan's mind, too. Saturday, September first would be his second anniversary in Japan. His three-year contract expired a year later, in 1924. Returning to the States and leaving all the earthquake worries behind was, he had to admit, an attractive idea, but he could hardly bear to think of breaking his contract. He was a representative of his country, and he greatly admired and respected many of his Japanese friends. Besides, he was in love with his French teacher. Yes, he thought of her as much more than his teacher, and he hoped she regarded him as more than a pupil. They had shared a number of rather informal dates, but he was not entirely sure of her feelings. He had learned that a flock of men were after her. He considered the suitors that he knew of: two Japanese, an Englishman, a Frenchman—all rich and influential.

He freely admitted to lacking wealth, but he had some influence. Teachers were much respected in Japan, and an American teaching at a local university was a showpiece. He'd hobnobbed with Japanese nobility, attended Imperial garden parties; met the Prince of Wales; and had luncheon with Professor Einstein. These obvious marks of distinction ought to impress his French teacher. Besides, he was pretty certain she liked him.

With his practical nature, however, Hugh realized that his background and hers were vastly different. Tatiana Alexandrovna Lunskaya was Russian. Her Tartar ancestry was evident in high cheek bones and mildly slanted, flashing green eyes, features enhanced by a frame of thick black curls. As a twenty-year-old member of the Russian nobility, she had escaped the 1918 Revolution by traveling across Siberia for thirty-five days during the worst of winter in a boxcar. Their religions were different too, he being Catholic and she a member of the Orthodox Church. But she was proud, stubborn, bright, well educated, and very pretty. At the time he'd first met her, about twenty months ago, she was literally starving to death, sometimes eating as little as a single banana a day. When he suggested, as diplomatically as possible, paying a little more for his French lessons, she had refused. Nor would she take an advance against future lessons. She also turned down any offer of a loan. Now, he was happy to observe, she was doing much better—in fact, comparatively well. She had more requests for private lessons in Russian and French than she could handle, and she was on the staff of the Athenée Français, a school primarily for Japanese run by the French government.

A constant source of irritation was the fact that she lived in a decrepit section of Hongo, all the way across Tokyo from him. Since cars were scarce and quite expensive, her location forced them to meet downtown most of the time, both for lessons and social purposes, and hardly helped Hugh with his romantic ambitions. After each encounter, they were forced to go their separate ways by streetcar. Miss Tatiana Lunskaya turned a deaf ear to any thought of moving.

She claimed she liked her hotel. He had seen the Matsunami Hotel a couple of times, and it seemed no better than a run-down Japanese boardinghouse on an alley, without a single foreigner around for blocks.

But, the important thing to Professor Hugh Riordan, former farm boy from Wisconsin, was that he could see progress in his relationship with this lovely Russian noblewoman. He no longer had to call her "Tatiana Alexandrovna," using her first name and the patronymic in the semi-formal Russian way. He learned there were many less formal, familiar forms of Tatiana, such as Tanya, Tanoosha, and Tanitchka. When they were together, he addressed her as Miss Tanya, hardly acceptable in correct Russian circles, but nevertheless a delicious familiarity.

Was the nagging fear of the coming earthquake always in the back of his mind? Of course it was. There were other compensations however, for he had not lived in Japan long enough to become weary of it. He felt a strange warmth toward this country of soft, polite voices and smiling faces. This was a place where, as shadows lengthened, a myriad of tiny shops spread their goods under the light of a thousand nodding lanterns, and where the soft glow of a teahouse blended with the geisha's song and the plucking of a samisen. For now, Japan was his home. He would not leave. To hell with the earthquake, Hugh Riordan was in love.

* * *

When Tatiana Alexandrovna Lunskaya first arrived in Japan, she had rather enjoyed the trembling of the ground, especially at night. With her head on a rolled-up towel—she refused the wooden pillow of native women—and her body cradled between two futons; she welcomed the gentle rocking of a mild earthquake. In reality still only a girl, this brought back memories of how her mother had rocked her to sleep during childhood illnesses at her home in St. Petersburg years before. She had no idea of what had happened to her family since the Revolution. While attending Tomsk University, she had been forced to flee the Bolshevik scourge across Siberia to Harbin, then under Russian control, then to Vladivostok, and finally to Japan. Her searing experiences were still fresh, although she tried to put them out of her mind. Oh good God, it had been so hard, so indescribable: people shot, bleeding, freezing to death, the narrow escapes, she herself almost burned alive. She starved in Siberia, and starved in Japan, but she had never given in to these conditions, never stooped to selling herself; she could hold her head up high.

During the past year, her life had improved immensely. There were many private pupils, a regular teaching job, and she began to earn an adequate amount of money. There even were a number of men, some of them wealthy, who were interested in her, not as a mistress but as a wife. They included both foreigners and Japanese. Another prospective husband was her American friend, Hugh. Neither of them had ever discussed marriage with each other, but she felt it possible. Hugh, it was such a funny name, with no close equivalent in Russian. If she had known the location of her family (assuming some of them were still alive), and could have written to them, she would not have been able to explain his name. There was a savory fragrance about him, the dry, heather-like smell of a clean man. His hair appeared to be thinning, and he wore glasses. His cheeks were so pink he looked as though he were constantly blushing. He had something she rarely found in men, an air of wholesomeness. There was a practical side to him, too. She got angry when he warned her about the probability of a severe quake, because the thought disturbed her bliss when things were going so well.

How could she prepare for an earthquake? During the Revolution, destruction and death came to be expected. During World War I, when her country suffered terribly, people determined to be brave, to fight until their dying breath. How could she prepare to fight an earthquake? Where could she go? There wasn't any place, except into a field for days, weeks, months, or even years. That was impossible. But, how to exist with an ever increasing, gnawing fear? The only answer she could see was prayer. Whenever Tatiana had a free moment, she would pray. She also sang the vesper service for Bishop Michael every Saturday evening in Yokohama and at Sunday masses, too. She felt some reassurance in knowing her friends, the Peacocks, had given her an open invitation to stay with them at their home in Yokohama whenever she wished. She planned to spend her weekends there.

Wednesday, August first dawned with the prospect of being a beautiful, warm, day. A strong breeze off Tokyo Bay kept the usually oppressive humidity from taking hold on the Kanto Plain on which Tokyo and Yokohama are located. It promised to be a good day for Miss Lunskaya because she should be paid for some of her teaching activities. "Should be" was, unhappily, the correct phrase to use, since private pupils sometimes hedged about paying on time. However, today she was optimistic. She could absolutely count on money from the French school and most of her private students, and she hadn't a single thought about the earthquake on her mind. Long ago, she had fallen into the general Japanese custom of eating only two meals a day, but this morning, full of the prospect of financial gain, she breakfasted on one of her ubiquitous bananas. She must remember to bring some to Klavdia Davidovna, who had been so depressed, and the Morozovs, with whom she lived.

Feeling pert in a light pink dress, carrying her notebooks, purse, and bag of bananas, she went downstairs and bowed to Mr. Saito, the hotel proprietor, and Michiko, the maid saying, "Good morning."

They both bowed, pleasantly returning her greeting as she went out the front door into the alley. None of the seven Saito children, who usually played outside the entrance was about, though there were plenty of other children. The second they spied her, they ran up laughing, yelling "Foreigner!", and began following her, though they kept a respectful five or six feet away. Tatiana didn't mind in the least, although in the beginning this kind of display had frightened her. The children were cute, and friendly, and "foreigner" was a factual, rather than a derogatory, term. Indeed, she suffered no inconvenience from the polite staring which often greeted a foreigner in all corners of Tokyo.

The street vendors were out early today. She bought half a dozen warm, hard-boiled eggs encrusted with salt for the less fortunate people she would be visiting in a few minutes. She presented a couple of the eggs to a pair of smiling children dressed in particularly shabby clothes. Both bowed deeply and thanked her.

It was only ten more minutes to the Morozovs' second-floor rooms. She had visited there many times before, so the way seemed quite familiar to her. Knowing the way was very important in Tokyo because the few buildings that had numbers were never in sequence, and the streets, except those downtown, had no names. About the only source of direction available, besides well-known landmarks, was the name of the ward in which one's destination was located. The Morozov's rooms were in Hongo, but so too was her hotel.

She arrived just as the bell of the nearby mission-church chimed 7:00 A.M. As locks were not generally used in Japanese homes, Tatiana was able to let herself in quietly. Ludmilla Efimovna Morozov and her thirteen-year old son were out, selling their newspapers. Every morning they could be seen hawking their papers somewhere in the vicinity of their residence, with bells tied to their waists announcing their presence and profession. Somehow, Tatiana had missed them this morning. They sold Japanese papers they themselves could not read. The Morozov daughter, who now called herself Pavlova, after the world-famous Russian ballerina, still slept soundly, as usual impossible to disturb. Tatiana knocked at the flimsy door of Klavdia's room. Once within, she saw that Klavdia Davidovna lay on a cot instead of a futon, looking drawn and tired.

"Are you feeling any better?" asked Tatiana.

"Oh Tanya, it is sweet of you to come. I've been so afraid. I was awfully sick last night, and again early this morning."

"Well, when you see what a nice day it is, you will feel better."

"Oh, I wish that I would, but I doubt it. Anyway, you probably came to see Ludmilla Efimovna and Shura."

"Now, you know they are always out selling papers this time of morning." She opened the bags of eggs and bananas and kneeled by the cot. "You see, I came to have breakfast with you."

In order to see better, the young Jewish girl turned on her side and leaned over the edge of the cot, whereupon it tipped over, depositing her and two ragged blankets on the tatami. She lay there in a crumpled bundle weeping fitfully.

Tatiana helped her to a sitting position, hugged her for a moment, and then began combing her hair with a large comb she took from her purse. "Now, now, did you hurt yourself?"

"No, but I wish that I had." She would not stop crying.

"Well, you must fix yourself up to be presentable on such a sunny day. Remember, you are a very pretty girl."

"Oh Tanya, I used to be, but now I am in such terrible trouble, I want to die."

"Klavdia, you mustn't talk like that. You have much to live for. We all have much to live for."

"No, I don't." Her weeping became hysterical. "No, no I don't. I didn't want to tell you. I'm going to have a baby!" Her sobs seemed to be tearing her apart.

Tatiana got up, looking at Klavdia, thinking *my God what can I do, what can I say now?* "You stop crying," she said sharply. "We'll talk about it as soon as I make some tea for our breakfast." She went out and found a small charcoal burner with a small pan of lukewarm water resting on it.

Klavdia Davidovna Appfelbaum was the daughter of a physician who served with distinction in the Czar's army. While the lot of Jews living in Imperial Russia was often a most difficult one, Doctor David Appfelbaum had been decorated by the Czar for meritorious service during the Great War. When the storm of revolution broke, he and his daughter headed east to the Siberian city of Irkutsk. He left Klavdia there with a Jewish family while he served with various loyalist forces, including those of Admiral Kolchak. After Kolchak was betrayed and executed, they fled further east and eventually made their way as far as Japan, arriving penniless. In Japan, Doctor Appfelbaum eked out a bare existence for them selling newspapers. Neither he nor his daughter spoke Japanese, and there were hardly any Jews who could help them.

One morning when Doctor Appfelbaum was to have started a new job, his daughter found him dead. Klavdia, shocked into insensibility by grief, took his papers and began selling them. The Morozov mother and small son came upon her and took her in. She was only seventeen. They wouldn't let her sell newspapers anymore, because, they jokingly told her, they didn't want the competition. But, she soon despaired at remaining inside. She had no skills of any kind, yet she wanted to contribute to her newfound family in some way. One afternoon, she spent five sen on a streetcar ride downtown. It did not take long for some unscrupulous foreigner to spot such an attractive young girl walking alone in the Ginza area. Speaking French, she innocently told him her story. He generously revealed to her how she could earn some money, and she followed his advice that same afternoon. It reviled and disgusted her. Nevertheless, she began to have a steady, if small, income. She paid for her food and room over the protestations of the Morozovs, but they never questioned her. The extra money enabled them all to rent a larger place. Tatiana had met her in the Maruzen bookstore, studying a book of French poetry.

Klavdia continued to be despondent as she and Tatiana ate their small breakfast. Tanya searched her thoughts for something to take her mind off her troubles. "What do you think of all this talk of an earthquake coming, Klavdia?"

"I'm afraid it doesn't concern me."

"Well, why not? It concerns all of us. It certainly frightens me."

Klavdia looked steadily out the open doorway. "Because I will be dead. I'm going to commit suicide."

"Don't be foolish. You're young and pretty and . . . "

"And pregnant!"

"Are you certain?"

"I am positive."

Tatiana, trying to appear unconcerned, finished the banana she was eating. "Well, women have been pregnant before."

"But, I sold myself. Did you know that?"

"Yes."

"You knew?"

Tanya sighed and drank her tea. "Yes, I did."

"Does Ludmilla Efimovna know? And Pavlova?"

"I suppose they do."

"But . . . but how would they know?"

"It became rather obvious. One had only to look at you."

She covered her face with her hands and gently sobbed into them. "But, I needed money. I had to have some money."

"Well, I think everyone would understand that." She reached forward with her handkerchief to dry the other girl's face.

"I remember you were hungry, once. You told me you were weak. Did you sell yourself?"

"No."

"Did you ever think of selling yourself?"

"No."

Klavdia drew back, pushing the handkerchief away. "Why not, was it your Imperial Russian pride?"

Tanya clutched her handkerchief, feeling the bite of the other girl's question. "No, I never thought of it. I may have had my pride, but I also could buy enough bananas to keep living."

"Do you think I sold myself because I am a Jewess?"

"No, I would least expect that from a Jewish girl."

"But why?"

"Because of what you said—pride."

She renewed her flow of tears. "Now you are saying I am a disgrace to my own people."

"Of course not. You are a human being who didn't know what to do. I understand, I have been that also."

"But, what can I do?"

"Well, you can pray."

She shrugged and turned her head, as if the thought angered her. "Oh yes, pray. Pray to whom?"

"To God."

"Your God or my God?"

"I think our God is the same."

They remained silent for a minute. Klavdia's tears slowed. Tatiana finished her tea, saying, "Eat your food. Remember what they used to say in Russia, to get children to finish their food?"

"No, no I don't."

"About the Armenians?"

Suddenly, she nodded. "Oh, I think I do—it was: 'Remember the starving Armenians.'"

The Jewish girl began to giggle. "You know what I think?"

Tanya began to return the giggle. "No, what?"

"I think the Armenians are big and fat, and we Russians have been starving to death!"

Their giggles turned into laughter, laughter they could not stop.

While sitting in the streetcar on her way downtown, Tatiana racked her brain for ways to discourage Klavdia's thoughts of suicide. She would make it a point to visit her as often as she could. She'd try to find out about a doctor. Perhaps she might ask one of the priests, or even Bishop Sergei, to go to see her. The Orthodox Church in Japan was extremely compassionate. Just meeting Bishop Sergei was an inspiring experience because of his profound kindness, and the fact that he looked exactly like a living portrait of Christ.

Across from her two Japanese ladies in colorful kimonos smiled while staring at her. She heard the word, "foreigner" repeated, and "very pretty."

Further down the line, her car stopped near a row of businesses with a couple of signs in English that had once made her laugh, after Hugh had explained them. The Japanese were excellent students, eager to learn, and fast to imitate. They were especially fascinated with the English language, putting it to use however possible. Many Japanese businessmen thought English signs would attract foreigners and add dignity to their shops. Consequently, a barber shop displayed a large, three-color sign proclaiming, "Head Cutter," while a tailor's sign announced: "Respectable Ladies Have Fits on the Second Floor."

*   *   *

At 9:30 A.M. sharp, Miss Tatiana Lunskaya arrived at the municipal office building to give one of her thrice-weekly French lessons to Mr. Raita Kanoh, an official in the Customs Department. By Western standards, many Japanese men were quite good looking. Tanya considered her Tuesday-Thursday, late afternoon pupil, Viscount Nabashima, to be one of the handsomest men she had ever seen. Alas, Mr. Kanoh was not so endowed, being a diminutive man, small even for a Japanese. He had a round, chubby face with dimples, and tiny, sunken, piggy eyes. His teeth glittered with dentist's gold, and his manner was one of polite self-importance. When the lesson ended, he approached a subject they had discussed previously.

"As I mentioned before, Mademoiselle, I have a very good position. If you marry me, I shall buy you the biggest diamond in Tokyo."

"I remember your saying so, Monsieur."

"Of course, the diamond would be completely yours. I would make no claim on it in the future."

She studied her notebooks, knowing she should not antagonize him. He paid promptly, and well. "I also recall your saying you wanted to marry me because I was intelligent and possessed a good knowledge of languages."

"Ah, yes, you remember correctly."

"But, aren't there any other reasons?"

"No, I think those are sufficient."

Tatiana could hardly restrain herself from becoming angry. The idea of choosing a wife like a governess, for her linguistic ability, seemed appalling.

Kanoh began to laugh nervously. "If I merely wanted a woman, I would go to the Yoshiwara," he said, alluding to the city's venerable red-light district.

His pronouncement hardly made her feel better. "I intend to marry for love, Monsieur."

"Ah, quite so," he said, nodding vigorously. "Do people always marry for love in your cold country of Russia?"

"Well, yes, most of the time."

"Ah, I did not know this," he said getting up from behind his desk. "In Japanese, there is no word which is quite the same as the French word 'love.' So foreigners say we do not understand what this 'love' is. Perhaps this is so. However, I am learning many new ideas. You might help me with some of them."

The conversation was becoming too sticky for the Russian girl. She wanted to extricate herself without causing him to lose face, but she wasn't sure how to accomplish a polite escape. "I would have thought a man with your important position would have been married already."

"Ah, yes, I am married presently."

"But . . . but what about your wife?" asked Tanya incredulously.

"She is easy to manage. She has a good disposition."

"But what would happen to her?"

"A Japanese wife does not wish to disobey. Divorces are easy here."

"How could you divorce her? How could you explain it to her?"

"No explanation is necessary. She has already given me children."

"But, she is your wife. Can you just put her out?"

"No matter, no matter," he answered, shaking his head; "We all have a wife. A wife is no matter in Japan."

Her head was spinning, and it seemed insufferably hot in his office. In order to change the subject she blurted out, "Are you worried about the earthquake?"

The question had a visible effect on him. He blinked twice, like an owl, went to his window and looked out, pursing his generous lips. "Ah yes, *jishin*. We have a proverb which says the four things we should fear most are *jishin, kaminari, kaji, oyaji*—earthquake, thunderstorm, fire, and father. It is perhaps significant that earthquake is mentioned first."

Tanya got up, and taking the white envelope that lay on his desk, which should contain her money, slipped it into her purse. He turned back toward her.

"All Japanese think about earthquakes. They are part of our culture. We usually do not talk about them."

"I see. I only wondered if you were making any preparations."

"What would be the sense in that? As the saying goes, *shikata ga nai*—it can't be helped. Au revoir, Mademoiselle," he said, bowing.

* * *

At 11:00 A.M., Miss Lunskaya began teaching the first of her two formal classes of the day at the Athenée Français. She had been happy to observe that the school was, at last, doing a booming business. In fact, the increase in the number of students was to be the subject of the first faculty meeting of the summer, scheduled for half-past one that afternoon. There were six instructors on the teaching staff: three foreign, and three Japanese. She was the only woman. Monsieur Côte, the director, had generously observed several times that the quality of teaching in the Russian schools for the nobility must have been superb to turn out such an excellent French teacher.

Nevertheless, the twelve o'clock class, with its air of confusion, often proved rather difficult for her. This time period drew the really eager, progressive Japanese, who attended it during their lunch periods, and sometimes utilized a lapse in recitation to swallow a rice cake, a bit of fish, or a sweet potato.

Everyone felt quite cheerful after the brief faculty meeting. Monsieur Côte announced a small raise in pay, owing to the new flood of students, and tea with cake was produced for a little celebration. Among the other teachers, Tatiana especially admired Yoshinari Yamamoto, a middle-aged Japanese who wore a Phi Beta Kappa key from an American university. Hugh had told her this key represented a high honor, and since she had once received a scholastic medal from the mother of Czar Nicholas, these trappings of accomplishment impressed her. She also adored Yamamoto's children, some of whom had studied at the school. It was a treat to hear these tiny Japanese speaking Parisian French. She questioned him about the health of his family.

"It is very kind of you to ask, Mademoiselle. They are staying with dear friends in the United States, in the state of Michigan."

"How nice, but you must miss them."

"Yes, I do."

"How is that called, Mitchi . . . "

He smiled, "It is a state name, Mich-i-gan." He drew out the word phonetically.

"Mitch-igan," she pronounced. "Well, my friend Professor Riordan is from Vis-con-sin. Is that nearby?"

"Why, yes, it is an adjoining state."

"How interesting, I must tell him! But, why did you send them so far away?"

"I attended university in America, as you know, and I have good friends who would welcome them. Besides, although we Japanese are supposed to be stoics, I wanted them to be away during any seismic disturbance."

"And, so far now, we have not had any."

"No, not even the slightest tremor. It is a bad sign."

"When will your family be returning?"

He sipped some tea and sighed. "The end of the month. They must return for school."

Monsieur Côte brought his cup of tea and sat down beside them, touching Yamamoto on the shoulder. "If you want my opinion, there won't be another big earthquake in Japan for at least twenty years."

"I pray you are right," said Yamamoto.

"Tell me, Mademoiselle, do you ever see those wonderful people, the Peacocks? I believe Mr. Peacock is with Revillon Frères."

"Why, yes, I do. I will see them this weekend, I'm going to Yokohama to stay with them."

"Splendid! Please give them my regards, particularly Madame Peacock. She is a perfect example of the charming women of France."

"Yes," agreed Tatiana sincerely, "she certainly is!"

*   *   *

At approximately the same time as the Athenée Français faculty meeting was coming to a close, some eighteen miles away the Peacocks were coming to an important decision.

Odylia and Herbert Peacock were pillars of foreign society in Yokohama, and Tokyo too, for that matter. As tall, fair and English as his wife was petite, dark, and French, Herbert commanded many people and a huge salary in his position as Far Eastern Chief of the Revillon Frères Fur Company.

Probably because of the city's great significance as a commercial port (Tokyo Harbor could not accommodate deep-draft ships), and their larger proportion of the total population, the ten thousand foreigners in Yokohama had more influence there than non-Japanese in any other Japanese city. The most affluent of this set lived on "The Bluff" overlooking Yokohama Harbor, a select spot designed by nature to catch the cooling breezes from the ocean. If not living on the Bluff, these expatriates could often be found living in the posh hotels along the waterfront of the city.

The Peacock's large, pastel green, English-style house stood out in a parade of impressive homes. This house was occupied by Herbert and Odylia; their twelve-year old daughter, Nanette; William, fourteen, called "Gee Gee"; and Henry Peacock, Herbert's thirty-nine year old younger brother. Henry also worked for the French Fur Company, as a traveling representative. Three displaced Russians also lived in the big house with the beautiful gardens: Zoya Semionovna, the governess; Paula, the cook; and Ivan, the butler. These three had followed Peacock to Japan when he left his post as English Consul at Krasnoyarsk in Siberia, and were intensely devoted to the Peacock family.

This delightful first day of August, the three Peacock adults were seated in wicker chairs around a marble-topped table deep in their fairyland of a garden. The noise and bustle of the city below rose muffled and distant, as eternally aloof as the sounds of the universe might reach the deities of heaven. Henry was in a foul mood, drinking his third scotch and soda. He had been, as he told everyone, in a funk for a couple of weeks, ever since that Russian girl, Tatiana Lunskaya, had turned down his proposal of marriage as though it were a joke. The damned "Little Bolshevik," a title she naturally detested even when he used it in a humorous way, had hardly taken him seriously. He wasn't certain, perhaps he had meant it as a joke, but it didn't seem funny now. Herbert and his wife were drinking green tea. In this idyllic setting they discussed a serious matter: the predicted earthquake, and what to do with the children.

Henry lighted a cigarette, expelling his first long drag violently. "Let's stop all this bloody haggling. There's only one thing to do, and that's to get them out of here."

"Of course, you're right," Herbert agreed. "I suppose Odylia and I would feel more comfortable if we had visited Canada at least once, and seen the school."

"Yes," said Mrs. Peacock, "we must be certain that Nanette and Gee Gee will be happy there."

Henry laughed, "Children are never happy in school, but Prescott's is one of the finest. You've both been to America, you know. You can take my word for it, Canada is like America, except the people are generally a bit more civilized."

"I do want them to study in England, eventually," said the elder Peacock brother.

"Yes, I'd feel more at ease if they were in England or France," acknowledged his wife.

"You know there isn't time to get them into a British school. Besides, they can be off to England next year," said Henry. When his brother and sister-in-law wrestled with family problems, Henry's mind sometimes slunk back to his cozy bachelor lodgings at Hakone, where wildflower-covered hills and a myriad of memories awaited him. Too little free time had forced him to rent out his digs.

Henry was a handsome man, with dark brown, wavy hair, and an athletic build. Women adored him. Why, right at this moment, hidden in his jacket pocket was a love letter from Zoya Semionovna, the governess. He wondered what new entreaties it contained, while Ivan placed a fresh pot of tea and dish of sweet cakes on the low garden table. Damn, one Russian girl adored him, and the other acted indifferently toward him. That Tanya, his bloody Little Bolshevik with the shining hair and proud green eyes, there was a woman to challenge a man! He made himself another drink.

With everyone's drinks replenished, the discussion continued. "Oh Erber," Odylia left off the consonants at both ends of her husband's name, in the French manner, "if Nanette and Gee Gee are away, what will we do with Zoya Semionovna?"

"We'll keep her on, of course. We'll find something for her to do."

Henry lighted another cigarette. "Good boy, Herbie, you can make a gardener out of her."

"Good Lord," said Herbert, laughing, "there's enough to do around here. She can help Paula a bit until we find her a new position."

"And, dear sweet Tanya," said Odylia, dabbing her tearful eyes with a flowered handkerchief. "She won't be able to give Nanette her lessons, or teach her dancing anymore."

"My dear, Tatiana is always welcome here. She can stay whenever she wishes. After all, she's a friend of the family, and she might even say 'yes' the next time Henry asks her."

"Oh 'Enri, did you really ask Tanya to marry you?"

"Why no, of course not, not in so many words at any rate."

Henry paused, momentarily studying his drink, "Well then, I should think it's all settled, Odylia. You leave with the children Saturday, on the *Empress of Canada*. It's a lovely trip, ten days over, a few in Canada, and ten days back. The ocean air will do you a world of good. You ought to go too, Herbie."

"Oh, yes, Erber—can't you come, too?"

"No, my dear, you know I can't— simply too much to do."

"Now, Herbie," said Henry, draining his glass, "it might be a good idea for you to go. Vacation would do you good, and you'd probably miss the 'big shake' over here."

"No, no, there isn't the slightest chance. Too much business. I don't really think the quake will be so awful, but I must admit I'm relieved you'll all be away for awhile. And, you're going to London, Henry?"

The younger Peacock chuckled a moment. "I'll be at Claridge's, sitting on my tail, reading in the *Times* how this whole bloody country blew up."

"Oh 'Enri, how terrible you are to say such things. I must take my children and yet I won't be with my husband." She touched the handkerchief to her eyes, again.

Herbert Peacock grasped Odylia's hand. "My dearest, you'll be back before you know it. You'll be here by the end of the month when Freddie and Ann come over. We'll have an enormous welcome home party for you, a super holiday, with the Suzukis, and Tanya, the Desjardins, and anyone you'd like to invite." He got up and gently raised his wife until she was standing, then bent down to kiss her on the forehead. "Let's go inside and tell Gee Gee and Nanette—and we'll let Paula clean up these dishes."

Henry stood up too. *Good God,* he thought, *what a relief to have that over.* He noticed Zoya Semionovna smiling at him from an upstairs window. He must get off by himself for a moment to read her latest letter and, depending on what she said, decide how to handle her.

Freddie Keefe, like his longtime friend Herbie Peacock, was a typical urbane Englishman of the old school. He resembled Herbie in that he was tall, slender, and fair with a medium mustache. They both wore glasses, loved their wives, and remained faithful to them.

Vladivostok had not been an easy post for Keefe, right from the moment he first arrived as the new English consul. He found a great deal of activity there, especially during the war, as it was the chief seaport of Asiatic Russia. After the war, and subsequent revolution, business slacked off a great deal. He and Ann, having no children, were able to travel around a bit and recharge a social life that was virtually nonexistent in Vladivostok because most everyone breathlessly awaited the arrival of the Communists. The Bolsheviks took their good time about coming. When they did, they weren't as cruel as anticipated—only stupid. Working with the commissars turned out to be a terribly frustrating affair.

The beginning of the month of August had sent Frederick

Keefe into a flurry of activity, not that there was any more conscientious servant to the Crown than he. It was primarily a case of trying to keep up with all the recent regulations, restrictions, and directives of the new Bolshevik government. Each new commissar decided to demand an extra set of reports from the British consular office, and the Bolsheviks had been changing commissars every few weeks. It was difficult to communicate with most of them since, being from the approved ranks of the proletariat, a number could not sign their names. Nonetheless, they could be extremely demanding. Keefe recalled with a taciturn smile how he and his clerks had worked overtime to compile a report for a recently arrived commissar, only to find upon delivery that the imperious gentleman had just been summarily executed.

Every six months or so, the Keefes made it a point to visit Odylia and Herbie, and spend a few memorable days in pleasant company, dining, dancing, talking, or taking those colorful side trips from Yokohama to Nikko, Nara, Mount Fuji, and other scenic places. Japan was a beautiful country. They enjoyed reminiscing about previous visits, and contemplating the next one, which happily would commence in less than a month, the twenty-sixth of August. The steamer trip took only forty hours, but to make sure the crossing would be devoid of anguish, Ann and Freddie decided to keep off the Russian ships.

Over the past couple of years, the service of these ships had deteriorated noticeably. The food was meager and of poor quality. The cabins reeked of disinfectant. There were all kinds of extra charges, and when arriving in Yokohama, you frequently had to pay a bribe before the Russian seamen would produce your luggage. By way of contrast, the Japanese service could be counted on to be first-rate, with excellent foreign food, clean, tidy cabins, and good porters to help while disembarking.

Keefe had written the Peacocks about the day of their arrival, but until the date on his desk calendar caught his eye, he had completely forgotten to make reservations. You could count on the ships being crowded at the end of August, too. His office boasted a telephone but since the Bolsheviks had arrived, it had been completely useless. He called in a clerk, and gave him instructions to obtain two reservations on a ship belonging to the Osaka Shosen Company for the twenty-sixth of the month. As the clerk was leaving his office, he stopped and turned around, slightly clearing his throat, and asked: "Sir, I do hope you won't take offense, but aren't you at all concerned about an earthquake occuring in Japan?"

"Earthquake? Oh yes, an earthquake."

"It's been in a couple of the papers, they're supposed to have a real smasher!"

"I know, I know. Of course, I was worried about it." Keefe leaned back in his chair. "But, we've decided if it hasn't come by the twenty-sixth, it won't come at all. People over there say it's business as usual, and they're right on the scene. You can't let fear rule your life, my boy."

"Yes sir, that's true, I suppose. I'll get over to the Osaka office right away. Thank you, sir!" The young clerk shut the door.

Keefe opened the middle drawer of his desk and pulled out a large Manila envelope. He leaned back in his chair again. What his clerk had said only a moment ago disturbed him. Yes, he was worried about the earthquake, but they had planned this holiday for so long. He couldn't disappoint Ann, or himself for that matter. Blast it all, they were always having a shake of some sort over there.

He opened the large envelope on his desk. Now, here he had something quite intriguing. He had worked on it for some months as a favor to Herbie and that pretty Russian girl, what was her name . . . Tanya . . . Tatiana Alexandrovna, yes. It had filtered down through his secret sources of information, but its validity could be counted on. Apparently, Tanya's mother and both her sisters were still alive. Anyway, they were a year ago. Keefe smiled with satisfaction. He knew Herbie would be awfully pleased.

* * *

At exactly half-past three by his pocket-watch, Major Philip Faymonville, the American military attaché in Tokyo, got up from behind his desk in the newly completed Imperial Hotel and announced: "It's half-past three, Miss Lunskaya, our time is up."

Tatiana taught Russian to the rugged major twice a week, while all her other pupils studied French. Faymonville expected to be transferred to Russia in a year or two. He looked down at his desk and snapped his fingers. "By gosh, I knew there was something. Today is the first of the month; I must owe you a pile of money. How much is it?"

This was a moment she dreaded with him, a moment that embarrassed her so much she found it difficult to speak. Americans were so brash and matter-of-fact with money. This was not the Russian, European, or Japanese way. She remembered that when the family doctor would make a call at their home in St. Petersburg, her mother put his fee in an envelope and placed it on a table in their foyer. Their physician usually picked it up on his way out. Neither he nor her mother looked at the envelope directly, but rather, seemed to pretend it was not there. People of good breeding never discussed money, and certainly avoided displaying coins or paper. To do either would be terribly bad form. Most of Tatiana's private students were from relatively high-born Japanese and European families, and they handled charges in the manner to which she was accustomed. She never even mentioned her fees. They paid what they thought was fair, in a small, discreet envelope, weekly or by the month.

"Come on, Miss Lunskaya," said the tall major, pulling a billfold from his uniform blouse. "What do I owe you?"

"Well I . . . I really don't know," she answered, avoiding his gaze.

"I'm sorry, I forgot that this embarrasses you. You see, you are a fine teacher, and you deserve to be paid well." He withdrew a bunch of one yen notes, displaying them on his desk. "There, just take what I owe you."

Without looking at them, she reached out for a few bills and crumpled them quickly into her purse, getting up to leave.

Faymonville laughed, not unkindly. "I'm glad that's over. Oh, by the way, from now on let's meet in the larger room next to this. My office is too small, and I don't want you sitting under that slab of Frank Lloyd Wright's with an earthquake on the way."

"Mr. Wright?" questioned Tatiana.

"Yes, he's the American architect who designed this place. It's his first hotel. We call him 'Frank Lloyd Wrong.' You can see," he said, pointing to a number of stone slabs, "he loves to use big pieces of rock. If one of those pebbles dropped on you, we'd need a toothbrush to clean you up."

She shuddered at the reference.

"I'm sorry, you'll have to excuse the American sense of humor."

"Well, I think it is a beautiful building."

"Yes, I guess it is," agreed Faymonville, "If you like tiny rooms, and don't want a drink of water, or feel like taking a bath. Anyway, I wish they had room for me at the Embassy."

"Are you worried about the earthquake, Major?"

"Worried?" he chuckled, "Not much, but you see I have arranged a clear path to my window. There's nothing in the way, and it's always open. At the first little shock, I'm going out, head first."

*   *   *

A short distance to the west of the Imperial Hotel lay a hilly residential district, where Tatiana had lived over a year before. She'd been forced to move to her present lodgings in Hongo because the rent was cheaper. She still had a number of friends in her old neighborhood, and seeing the day had turned out so well, she decided to visit one of them—Mrs. Webb, the manager of Tatiana's former rooming house. A maid informed her that Mrs. Webb had left for the afternoon, and would not return until after seven o'clock. Across the street and up a hill, behind a formidable iron fence, stood the impressive house of Shimaku Suzuki; or rather that of her father, Bank President Suzuki. While there were impressive residential sections in most Japanese cities, including Tokyo, it was not unusual for a palatial residence and spacious grounds to be set right among blocks of very modest, flimsy native dwellings. The houses of the rich were generally fenced off and often cleverly hidden. Such was the location and condition of the Suzuki home.

When the Russian girl lived across the street, Shimaku used to wave at her from the garden, and eventually they met and talked for hours on end through the locked iron gate. They were about the same age, but no high-born Japanese girl so young would ever be allowed out alone. She had to be accompanied by at least a maid.

Banker Suzuki had heard about their encounters, but being somewhat Westernized, he allowed Tanya to visit his daughter. Two rooms of his stately house were done in foreign decor, with tables, chairs, and even thick rugs for the floors. The girls enjoyed rolling them back when Tanya gave Shimaku a dancing lesson. She also taught her French. As far as circumstances would allow, the girls became close friends. Shimaku's father noticed a subtle change in his daughter, a slight shift toward more independent, foreign ways, brought on by her friendship with this Russian girl. As the banker was somewhat progressive, he thought it quite charming, and decided having Tanya visit, now and then, was a splendid arrangement.

Shimaku saw Tanya leaving the old rooming house, and walking quickly for a girl dressed in a tight, sky-blue kimono, waved her yellow parasol through the gate to attract her attention. Soon, they were chattering excitedly through the bars. Shimaku apologized for the fastened gate, to which she had no key. Tanya said it made no difference since she had to return to the Matsunami Hotel by five o'clock for a lesson.

"I wish you did not have to leave so soon, Tanya. When my father comes for tea, we could take up the rugs and dance."

"We will another time, soon."

There was disappointment on Shimaku's face, which was the color of a magnolia petal. It could not be judged overly pretty, but perfectly oval, smooth, and sweet. She had deep brown eyes like those of a kept deer, full of warmth and affection. "But, ever since you moved away, you have not visited me so much."

"Well, I have wanted to, but now I have more pupils and less time. I have missed you."

Shimaku sighed, "Do you earn enough money to move back? I wish you would."

"I might be able to," said Tatiana, giving the Japanese girl a wrapped hard-candy from her purse, and taking one herself, "but I better wait and see if I can hold on to my students."

"Tanya, you should keep the candy for yourself. Oh, I worry so much about you."

"Why? You mustn't, you know."

"Because you don't have enough money. If I had any, I'd give it all to you. And, now there is the earthquake . . . "

"What does your father say about the earthquake?"

"He never tells me anything about it. But, I have heard him tell my brother it will be very bad. They have made preparations at the bank. Oh, what will you do if it comes?"

"Well, I don't really know, run into the street, I suppose," answered Tatiana.

"Do you remember the people who were killed only a little way from here last year?"

"Yes, I remember very well. I ran out into the street then."

"And, how is your American?"

"Well, he isn't mine. However, I still like him very much."

"Maybe you will marry him one day."

Tatiana blushed, "I don't think so. You know there are always many problems with foreigners," she said with a laugh.

Shimaku began giggling, and couldn't stop, even as her friend waved goodbye. The idea of having a boyfriend was almost too much for the Japanese girl to contemplate, much less the idea of seeing a man from a different country.

*　　*　　*

Mr. Saito, the owner of the Matsunami Hotel, bowed and handed Tatiana a letter when she returned. It was from Monsieur Saburo Fuji, a young businessman who had taken many lessons from Tatiana, but who had yet to make any sort of payment. Fuji traveled extensively around Japan, often sending her post cards from interesting places. This was the second letter he had written her, and it made her angry. The text, polite and respectful, said she was an excellent teacher, and it pained him not to pay her, but he needed every extra sen to spend on his new motorcar. Motorcars were rather rare in Japan. Unfortunately, he found the upkeep much more than he had anticipated. He used the car quite a lot for business trips. Now, it was particularly useful to transport him around the countryside, beyond the more vulnerable earthquake areas. Trains would be swept off the tracks when an earthquake struck, so he admonished Mademoiselle Lunskaya to stay away from them. A car should be quite safe. He assured her that he would drive right through the narrow alley to the entrance of her hotel when he returned to Tokyo and give her a pleasurable and lengthy ride in his motorcar.

He signed the letter, "respectfully and sincerely, your devoted student." Tatiana wanted her money, not a memorable ride in an automobile.

At five o'clock she ushered Monsieur Toshi Sugawara, a lawyer, into her room. After a couple of polite bows, they each sat on a pillow, placed on the tatami, with a low table between them, and opened their notebooks.

Sugawara, who had played tennis for his university, was tall and handsome. He had an air of quietude and refinement, but smiled easily, seemingly from a deep goodness within him, rather than from a sense of polite decorum.

Certain members of the foreign community raised eyebrows a little when they heard that Miss Tatiana Lunskaya gave language lessons to men in the privacy of her room. Some said, behind her back to be sure, she did not seem to be "that type of girl," cleverly implying the impression of there being some possibility. Obviously, these gossip mongers did not know, or perhaps did not want to know, the facts.

Of course, it was more convenient for her to give lessons at her hotel. She saved time and travel expenses. The truth was that she taught only *Japanese* men in the privacy of her room. Since the Revolution, she remembered having "difficulties" with a Czechoslovak, a Hungarian, two Canadians, an American, a Belgian, two Englishmen, and more Frenchmen than she could count in Japanese. She had never had any trouble, at any time, with Japanese men who, no matter what their station in life, were always polite and respectful. For this, she admired them tremendously, and felt enormous gratitude.

In another regard, Tatiana was not so impressed with Japanese etiquette. When she first arrived in Japan, she had been appalled that most Japanese toilets were not furnished with doors, quite often without walls, and were sometimes open to both sexes. The Japanese showed no distaste for the human body, nor did they manifest a particular interest in it. She made special arrangements for bathing, for baths were also often open to both sexes, and sometimes frequented by jovial family groups. At least she could easily plan her baths ahead of time. The toilet in the Matsunami Hotel could have been called typical, and it presented many difficulties for Tatiana. Adjoining a frequently traveled hall, it consisted of a porcelain-lined hole in the floor with thick screening on three sides. The fourth, open side fronted directly on the public hallway. One straddled the hole and did the best one could while people—men, women and children, sometimes even dogs and cats strolled by, two or three feet away. Under circumstances like these, she was very appreciative of the lovely manners of the Japanese.

Sugawara had once met Fuji, because one had his lesson immediately after the other. When their hour of study was over, Tatiana showed Sugawara Fuji's letter, and asked him for his advice. He said, "As a lawyer, I should be happy to sue him for you, Mademoiselle. It would make an interesting case for a Russian to sue a Japanese in Japan. I have some little influence, which might be of help."

She said she had better wait. She did not want to start any trouble. He agreed that waiting, for now, was probably a good idea.

He grew thoughtful for a moment, then said, "I see he says he is worried about the earthquake. You know, I used to worry too, but I do not anymore."

"Well, how encouraging. Why is that?"

"I have become a Christian. I have joined the Methodist Church."

Tanya did not know much about the Methodists, except that they were Christians. In Russia, the Orthodox Church had been the one, official, religion. "I am happy for you, Monsieur."

"Yes, thank you. I attend the Ginza Methodist Church. Have you seen it?"

"Well, yes of course. It's a beautiful church."

"May I ask, without offending you, if you are a member of the Russian Orthodox Church?"

"Yes, I am. I sing in my church in Yokohama every Saturday evening, and Sunday morning."

"Ah, sometime I should like to see an Orthodox service. I am told the music is very different and impressive."

"Well, I hope you will have a chance sometime soon. I am sure the music is different from that at the Methodist Church, but I am not sure that it is impressive."

They both rose from their cushions and picked up their notebooks. On hers, the small white payment envelope had appeared as if by magic. She closed the notebook, placing it in her left hand.

"We Christians," he said, "do not worry about an earthquake, or the future."

Tatiana was not certain just what he meant. Before she could ask he bowed, saying, "God's will be done."

She repeated, "God's will be done," crossing herself, from right to left, the way she had since childhood.

* * *

Professor Hugh Riordan knew it would be impolite to take out the gold pocket-watch in his vest and check the time, but he reckoned by the angle of the sun's rays as they glinted off the gold buttons of his students, and the time they had taken in conversation, that it must be after six o'clock. Heise-san, who was working in his garden, always insisted on dinner exactly at half-past six. He would have to find a way of courteously indicating that they should leave.

The four of them had arrived about half-past three to drink green tea, which he hated, and engage their professor in a discussion of the problems facing the world, and Japan. Riordan thought them a handsome lot, with their closely clipped black hair, and intelligent, eager expressions. He greatly admired the overwhelming majority of his students, most of whom had had strict upbringings in good families.

This afternoon, the son of a baron gave the opinion that world racism and its consequent effect on Japanese world trade was Japan's primary problem. Toji Nakamura, whose background Riordan didn't know, said Japan's future expansionist policies, forced by its burgeoning population and lack of space, would be a source of major difficulties during the next decade or two. Naga, the son of a general recently deceased, mentioned the possibility of an earthquake, saying "The government knows it is coming, and yet little is done."

His cohorts pointed out that there was little to do except wait. "Oh yes," he protested, "you can say it can't be helped, but our fire-fighting forces could be increased; extra water could be stored in strategic areas; pamphlets telling the people what to do could be distributed by the tens of thousands; disaster teams could be formed; food could be stored; there is so much that could be done!" His friends disagreed, saying some of these steps no doubt were being taken quietly anyway. A full scale effort might cause panic.

"But," Naga continued undaunted, "these steps would be important to our people, it would show them the government cared for them. Education could save lives. Most of our uneducated people still believe an earthquake comes from the wiggle of an enormous catfish." He took a deep breath before concluding: "We, those of us in the ruling class; our intellect runs on ahead, but our heart loiters in the Dark Ages."

Another of the pupils, the son of a viscount, at least agreed more must be done for the people. Helping the farmers to keep agricultural prices up, and supporting the city workers in their trade unions was his top priority. Otherwise, he felt the seeds of revolution might very well be sown.

Heise-san entered the room, making them realize the lateness of the hour. They got up right after Riordan told them that a month from today, September first, he would begin his third year in Japan.

On their way out onto the front porch, he found himself next to Nakamura. He liked to know something about his students, so he asked, "What does your father do, Mr. Nakamura?"

"My father is Sanji Nakamura, a policeman, Sir."

"In my country, policemen are very much respected. Here in Tokyo, they do an excellent job."

"Thank you for your kind words."

Once again, Riordan had reason to appreciate the democratic Japanese university admissions system. Here were the sons of a baron, a general, a viscount, and a policeman, representing a cross-section of Japanese society. "Do you live nearby, Mr. Nakamura?"

"No, my family lives in Honjo, across the city."

He repeated the name, "Honjo?" He had not been in that ward, to his knowledge, but it sounded so much like "Hongo," the ward where Miss Lunskaya lived. "That would be in the southeastern section of the city."

"Yes," agreed Nakamura, "we live not far from the Dai Nippon Brewery and Azumabashi.

Hugh almost forgot himself, and came close to shaking his departing students' hands. These students had been exposed to Western customs for a sufficient length of time to do that, if he had wished. Nonetheless, he knew that the Japanese preferred not to shake hands. Instead he bowed, and they followed suit.

Suddenly, Naga bent forward and placed both of his hands on the ground. He said, "Our catfish is still sleeping." The young men laughed, while Riordan wondered how much longer the recumbent beast would remain quiet.

August 31, Afternoon and Evening

Tanya glowed with anticipation. Hugh had suggested she call on these wealthy Americans today, and not wait until next week. He understood Mrs. Armstrong was already considering a teacher for her daughter, making an early interview imperative. So, she had rushed after her last class to catch the interurban train to Yokohama. Because she was in such a hurry, anxious to make arrangements for a weekly, Saturday morning pupil, the ride of eighteen miles seemed longer than ever.

When she arrived in Yokohama, she walked rapidly for twenty minutes, directly to the Bund, a wide, attractive ocean-front boulevard. Here, the Grand, the Oriental Palace, and most of the luxurious foreign-style hotels were situated. A number of supremely impressive private residences also looked out on the comings and goings of yachts, ocean liners, warships, and picturesque fishing fleets. It was just five o'clock. The beautiful street appeared more colorful than usual, with the house flags of steamship companies snapping in the salt-tinged breeze; crowds of brightly dressed Chinese and East Indians, who had finished work for the day, were leisurely enjoying the seascape.

The Armstrong house was not far from the new Yokohama United Club. Tanya recognized it immediately from Hugh's description. Built of brown stone and brown wood, with a large second floor porch, it had the appearance of a huge Swiss chalet. As she rang the bell next to the brass-hinged door, she had no doubt the Armstrongs were extremely wealthy people. She would be safe in asking for two yen per lesson.

A Japanese houseman, dressed in an over-large black

jacket, ushered her down a long tiled hallway flanked by marble busts on pedestals, to a thickly carpeted drawing room. There she found a profusion of chairs, love-seats, and flowered sofas. Tatiana selected an overstuffed chair next to a low table. Another Japanese servant brought a tray with tea and tiny rolls, placing it on the table in front of her. She wanted some tea desperately, but felt she must wait for her hostess.

The walls of this spacious room were covered by a number of genuinely awful paintings. An easel and paints in an upholstered alcove explained the dreadful pictures. Mrs. Armstrong must fancy herself an artist of sorts, assumed Tanya, one immune to embarrassment, or, perhaps more likely, protected from an honest appraisal of her work by her social standing. Nearby stood a grand piano lacking any sheet-music, covered by knickknacks of various sizes.

Into these gauche surroundings strode Mrs. Armstrong, one hand clutching a large flowered handkerchief, the other, outstretched. "How do you do Miss Lunskaya, I'm Abigail Armstrong. So nice of you to come."

Tanya rose and took her hand. For some reason, she felt happy that Mrs. Armstrong, though tall, expensively dressed and well-structured, was quite plain.

"Sit down, sit down, we'll have some tea. You're here about French lessons for my daughter, Abigail, aren't you?"

"Abigail won't be back until tonight, but Professor Riordan recommended you very highly. Bill and I saw him at a garden party about a month ago. Here, have a cup of tea and a cake."

Tanya took the proffered tea and roll.

"Abigail is a rather slow learner, takes after her father I am afraid, but she is a good girl and she simply must learn French."

"I see. I am a very patient teacher."

"Good. But tell me, weren't you—or aren't you the daughter of the Russian Czar, or something like that . . . ?"

The Russian girl almost choked. She began coughing.

"Here, have some more tea to clear your throat. I suppose I have some of the details mixed up—but, you are from the royal family, aren't you, or something . . . ?"

Tanya described her background and teaching experience. Mrs. Armstrong kept pouring tea, seemingly convinced.

"All right then Miss Lunskaya, you can have the job. You can start at ten o'clock in the morning next Saturday, not tomorrow but a week later—let's see, that's September eighth—and every Saturday morning thereafter until further notice."

"Thank you!"

"I do hope Abigail likes you."

"I think we will get along. As I mentioned, I have taught many young girls."

"Yes, good . . . oh my, I completely forgot . . . what do you charge? We may not be able to afford you." She lit a cigarette.

"Well," said Tanya, flushing, "I charge two yen for each lesson."

"Two yen," repeated Mrs. Armstrong, "now let's see—I can never figure these things out—that would be one dollar, American?"

"Well, yes, I believe that is correct."

"But you must realize Miss Lunskaya, I would see to it that you had tea and cake during the lesson." She stubbed out her cigarette. "Let's say the tea and cakes would be worth 50 sen. So, I could pay you one yen and 50 sen. After all, I would furnish you tea and cakes."

Tanya flushed an even deeper red. Her hands shook just a little. "Would you judge the amount of tea and the size of the roll to be about the same as I have just had?"

"Why yes, approximately the same."

The Russian girl opened her purse and gingerly extracted two silver twenty-sen pieces, and one ten-sen piece. "You apparently need these more than I do." She closed her purse

with a click, got up, left the drawing room and walked reso-
lutely down the hall.

Mrs. Armstrong, flabbergasted, quickly went into the hallway. "Wait a minute. I know you Russian refugees need
money." There was no response. "I know some of you Russians have starved to death." Still there was no response.

When Tanya got to the ornate outer door, the Japanese
servant in the black coat opened it for her, bowing, it seemed,
more deeply than normal. As she walked out, she could hear
Mrs. Armstrong yelling, "I can't understand you foreigners.
What the hell is wrong with you people?"

After he closed the door, the Japanese manservant continued to face it for a moment. He waited to turn around
until that trace of a smile had left his lips.

*   *   *

For a month, Klavdia Davidovna had been contemplating suicide. She did not mention it to the Morozovs, in fact,
she tried to be quite cheerful in their presence. She felt certain Tanya had not exposed her plan to them because if they
had known, being very open, honest people, they surely would
have been unable to keep such a secret to themselves, and
would have confronted her with it. Just to make certain, for
the past two weeks she had avoided talking to Tanya about
her death wish.

Still, there could not be the slightest doubt that Klavdia
was pregnant and terribly depressed. She had refused Tanya's
many offers of counsel with priests of her church; nevertheless, she spent much time analyzing her circumstances. These
all boiled down to the fact that she did not especially want to
die, she only wanted to shut out the pain of living.

During one of her money-making trips to downtown Tokyo
a few months ago, she had befriended a lonely half-Japanese
girl named Midori, who supported herself through a number
of liaisons with foreign businessmen. Now, late this last after-

noon of August, in Midori's room at a foreign hotel, she discussed her plans quite freely with her confidante. As she expected, Midori did not seem at all shocked.

"I too have thought of suicide many times. My life is not easy. Two years ago, my lover and I almost did this together."

"Were you very much in love?"

"Hai, I was no longer a virgin because of him. But, love is not important in Japan. He is a banker's son, and I am a half-caste. So we had no chance from the start. I knew this."

"How terrible."

"It would have been *shinju*."

"Shinju?"

"Yes," Midori smiled. "It means double love suicide. Have you heard of such lovers' suicide?"

Klavdia shook her head.

"When a boy and girl fall in love, and objection to the marriage comes from one of the families involved, or both, the young couple sometimes commit shinju. They usually tie themselves together with the girl's obi—you know, the long sash of the kimono—and then they enter the portals of the palace of death as one."

"It sounds very romantic."

"I think it is," agreed Midori. "But, you must have more tea to keep your strength up. This is from Uji, the best tea in all Japan."

"Thank you, it is very good. Thank you. How did you and your lover . . . decide to . . . where did you . . . ?"

"I understand what you are asking. The chosen spot for this lovers' suicide is usually a high and lonely place. We thought of a beautiful waterfall, or the edge of a volcano, or the deck of a sea-going steamer. All these involved too many difficulties and preparations. We decided on a bridge, a very high viaduct over a busy rapid-transit line. It embarrasses me to tell you I waited there but my lover did not appear. When I finally realized he was not going to come, I wanted to jump alone, but two policemen stopped me and took me away. The police watch it very carefully."

"Where is this bridge?"

"Only a little way from Shinjuku Station on the train line that goes around Tokyo. It is easy to get there."

"Shinjuku!"

"It is on the northwest side of the city, but the police watch this spot closely, night and day."

Klavdia drank her tea, thinking deeply. "Would you mind if I asked you how you felt . . . after . . . after you tried . . . "

"No, not at all. I think you will understand." Midori poured more tea. The cups were pretty and quite small. "I was sorry to be unsuccessful. Sometimes, I am still sorry."

"Oh, Midori-san, I do understand, really."

"Of course, it would have been better had my lover joined me. We Japanese have a secret admiration for the actors in a shinju tragedy. We know that there are times when it is the only thing left."

Klavdia nodded vigorously, even though Midori stared at one of the walls, not looking at her. Her brain was brimming with joy at the thought of shutting out the pain of her life. Yet, being a highly intelligent girl, she could not miss her friend's emphasis on the words "we Japanese." For she knew that in reality, Midori was not entirely Japanese, but entirely alone, having few friends, and fewer distractions. The Europeans had no use for these children of two cultures, and the native Japanese looked down upon them.

The polite word for these people of mixed heritage is, of course Eurasian. Klavdia wondered, for a moment, if being a Eurasian—citizen of a country with a musical name, but no earthly existence—were even worse than being a Jewess alone in Tokyo. She felt enthused, however, at the imminent prospect of death improving her condition.

"Midori-san, have you thought of suicide again since you were on that bridge in Shinjuku?"

"Yes, a number of times."

"How would you do it?"

"Oh, I think my bridge is best. But, I might slash my wrists. There are other bridges, too. Many jump from Ryogokubashi. It is long, and high, and well known because of the fireworks displays. From there you can easily jump into the funnel of a passing steamship. Whatever method I used, there is one detail I would insist on though . . . "

"Yes, what is that?"

Midori thought for a moment. "If there were a chance for my body to be found, I would tie my legs together, at least loosely, to keep them from opening too much. It is important for you to die honorably, not immodestly. That is the reason the police caught me on the bridge in Shinjuku—with my legs tied, I could not run fast enough to escape them."

It was a complication Klavdia hadn't thought of. However, it seemed like an excellent idea, one that appealed to her innate sense of decency.

* * *

Saburo Fuji had been carefully watching the young boy for over two hours, as he washed and waxed Fuji's motor car. At first, this had proved a difficult task, because Fuji was terribly nearsighted and the dampness in the garage continually misted over his thick glasses. Presently, with the hose shut off, and the boy rubbing paste-wax onto the black finish of Fuji's automobile, he noticed everything. There, he spotted a scratch, probably produced by a stone, on an otherwise gleaming fender. He grimaced in pain at this discovery, as though the wound, instead of being to his car, were to his own body.

In truth, he might have preferred this injury to be to himself, because it would probably heal without the services of an auto repairman, these being even more scarce than the cars themselves. That nick in the thick paint, surely hardly discernible to anyone else, bothered him. Would his French teacher notice it, on their ride to Yokohama tomorrow, and think less of him? Presumably not. She should be far too overwhelmed at the magnificence of his vehicle. Still, he knew it was there, and it troubled him.

Saburo intended tomorrow's trip to cover half of what he owed his teacher. The other half he would pay to her, when they arrived in Yokohama, with the draft from The Yokohama Specie Bank which he had in his pocket. He figured to come out ahead by quite a bit on the deal, counting on her not to notice because she would be flushed with excitement from the thrill of the almost twenty-mile ride. After all, how many poor foreign girls got a chance to motor along the ocean in a new car handled by an expert driver? Actually, there was a possibility he was being generous. Perhaps, the trip alone might suffice. He could still change his mind about giving her the draft when they arrived in Yokohama. He must remember to point out the extra expense of a round trip, because he would return directly to Tokyo.

All his young life, Fuji could be classified as a man striving for distinction. He had no university degree, but his job as a traveling salesman of mineral water earned him enough to live in comfort if not with the respect he so coveted from his peers, most of whom held desirable government jobs. None of them owned a new motor-car however, and few of them knew more French, or read English better than he did.

He belonged to the *Nippon Automobile Association*, which was headquartered in Tokyo and had many foreign members. He enjoyed talking about delightful motor trips to Yokohama, Kamakura, Kyoto, and Kobe, and the hazards of muddy rock-strewn roads and inadequate bridges. In a way, he was an adventurer. Among his friends, his automobile set him apart, and brought him the attention he craved, and knew in his own mind he deserved.

Fuji was the most mobile and most successful of the salesmen in his organization. Improving highway conditions, coupled with his audacity, had brought him many new accounts. The last few days, with little rain to muddy the outlying roads, had been particularly successful for him. While his overt ambition was not especially characteristic of the Japanese, he believed himself to be different. He felt a good deal of satisfaction in the recognition he received.

He understood the importance of his car in gaining this recognition. A wealthy Englishman once told him, "Every rich and well known personage owns a fine automobile." He had been right!

Finally, the boy finished with his waxing, and began refueling the car out of five-gallon gasoline tins. Surely it looked a magnificently impressive machine, somewhat more like a monument than a motor-car.

The young man gave the empty tins to Fuji, who stacked them on the floor of the rear seat. He knew where they could be resold for 10 sen each.

It was almost time for his dinner. He got in and drove until he was in the Ginza area. He surveyed the throng which pulsated along the street from dawn until well after dusk. He passed pushcarts, bicycles, rickshas, but only one other motorcar. By the time he reached Shimbashi Bridge he felt pretty good. He smiled inwardly, for himself alone. His car had never furnished transportation for a foreign woman before. It would be yet a new distinction. Tomorrow promised to be a memorable day.

* * *

Tomorrow, besides being the start of Professor Hugh Riordan's third year in Japan, would mark the beginning of the Labor Day weekend back home in America. That usually signified the end of summer, when people tried to crowd the last of their warm weather activities into three frantic days. This weekend, he hoped to see a great deal of Miss Tatiana Lunskaya. In fact, he counted on celebrating with her. After all, it marked his second anniversary, and was important to him.

While he walked through the Ginza, on his way to meet her at the Fugetsudo Restaurant, he thought over the plans he had made. After dinner tonight, they would go to the cinema and see a Japanese movie with English subtitles. He couldn't recall the name of the picture, but a couple of Japanese professors had recommended it highly. Then tomorrow, they'd begin by eating lunch in the picturesque café on the Mitsukoshi Department Store's fourth floor, where many foreign delicacies were served by delightful Japanese girls, many of whom spoke English. Riordan felt certain he would enjoy Mitsukoshi's with Tanya far more than any luncheon celebrating the official opening of the Imperial Hotel, also scheduled for Saturday noon.

They might spend the afternoon strolling around Ueno Park, and through the Imperial Museum at its center. After a swift, pleasant interurban ride to Shinjuku, should come the pièce de résistance—a superb German dinner conceived by Heise-san and his well-trained cook. Professor Heise promised "*sauerbraten* to remember for at least a decade." Based on past examples, Riordan did not doubt his word. The meat had already been marinating for a full day. And Sunday? Well, Sunday they could plan later, perhaps tonight.

With the coming of dusk paper lanterns were being lighted in front of the various shops. They swayed in a fresh, cooling breeze off the ocean, that blew away stench from the canals and the Sumidagawa River. Lights sprang up everywhere in the Ginza. The double line of streetcars moving along the center of the street looked like an endless procession of friendly, glowing, one-eyed caterpillars. The entire scene pleased Riordan immensely. Even though the hour was somewhat late, he could still hear that unending patter of hundreds of wooden clogs in the background. It sounded like heavy rain on the barn roof back home.

He felt quite cheerful as he walked through the entrance to Fugetsudo's. When he saw the expression on Tatiana's face, he knew immediately her mood must be quite different from his.

Could he be late? No, he was right on time. Yet she greeted him with sparks in her eyes. They were seated on the second floor, next to a window overlooking the street, colorful with paper lanterns.

"Miss Tanya," he began, "you don't look very happy."

"I'm not!" she answered, staring away from him, deliberately avoiding his eyes. "I'm beginning to dislike Americans. They think of nothing but money, money, money—at least your dear friend Madame Armstrong does."

"Why, I had forgotten. You called on the Armstrongs this afternoon."

"Well, in Russia we have a proverb about the absent-minded professor."

"Yes, we have a similar saying in America."

"When you aren't counting money, I suppose."

He decided to humor her and not defend his countrymen at the moment. "I've never had much money to count. Please tell me what happened."

Slowly, bitterly, the Russian girl related her experience in every detail. All Hugh could do was apologize, explaining that while he was acquainted with the Armstrongs, he did not actually know them very well.

"When I meet people like that, even I begin to understand why there are communists in the world," she observed.

"Don't tell me you are thinking of joining the Bolsheviks?" By her reaction of disgust, he realized immediately his joke was inappropriate for the present moment. Still, Riordan tried to make light of it, repeating the old saw: "It takes all kinds of people to make the world."

Not even an excellent dinner could bring her completely out of her lingering depression. They had glazed sweet potatoes, curried rice, and cooked fish. Neither of them had been able to develop a taste for raw fish, a favorite amongst the Japanese.

A couple of distractions interrupted their leisurely dining. While Tatiana transferred sweet potatoes from the serving-dish to her plate, there occurred a deep rumbling that shook the entire building. She dropped a potato on the table exclaiming, "Is it the earthquake?" Her eyes were wide with fear.

"No, no," said Hush, taking her hand. "It's just a heavy truck . . . or do you call them lorries? I haven't seen many in Japan, but they can make a lot of noise."

A few minutes later the proprietor of the restaurant appeared, and quickly lowered all the window shades, shutting out their attractive view. He bowed, explaining that the crown prince would be driving by in a few minutes. Of course it was understood no one could look down upon such a royal personage. So, for the entire length of his announced route, on all floors above the first, shades were drawn, by imperial order. By the time they finished eating, the windows were uncovered again.

After leaving the restaurant, they walked a couple of blocks toward the movie theater. On the way, Tatiana asked if they could stop and sit down for a few minutes on one of the benches in a tiny park.

"Are you especially tired tonight?"

She sighed. "Yes, I suppose I am. It has been an exhausting day."

"And seeing Mrs. Armstrong didn't help."

"No, it didn't. I won't be able to forget Mrs. Armstrong for a while."

"But, you should."

"I can't. I won't," she replied.

He had not known her long enough to realize her temperament was far different from his. He possessed a quick, sometimes almost violent temper which cooled down quickly. Something might bother him terribly at two o'clock, but often by three, he had forgotten it. In contrast, she was usually slow to anger. Her resentments, however, simmered over long periods, and were in most instances, not soon forgotten.

"We can skip the movie tonight, if you prefer," he said.

"No, you are counting on seeing it."

He took her hand in both of his, being careful not to caress it. "Not at all. It might be better if you went home early tonight and got a good rest, because I have a big weekend planned for us."

She reacted quickly. "What do you mean about this big weekend? I can't meet with you this weekend."

"But, you have to, Miss Tanya." He forgot and caressed her hand. "I want you with me—especially tomorrow, because it is my second anniversary in Japan, and we can . . . "

"No, no I cannot." She withdrew her hand from his. "I must go to Yokohama tomorrow. I always sing the vesper service on Saturday night, and mass on Sunday. Besides, the Peacocks are expecting me."

"All those problems can be solved quite simply. You can go to church here at the Cathedral, and even see Bishop Sergei. He likes us. And, you can telephone the Peacocks. I'll pay for the call."

She got up and began walking away, the perversity of her mood contributing to her anger. "No, no I can't. I've never used a Japanese telephone . . . I don't know what they are saying."

Riordan followed her closely, perhaps too closely. "I'll make the call for you . . . I know I should have told you ahead of time, but I wanted to surprise you. Anyway, this is a very special occasion. Heise is going to . . . "

"No, no I can't. Even if you told me before, I couldn't. I have promised to sing vespers and mass every weekend." She quickened her pace as though to escape him.

"But, this is such a special occasion. I thought you'd want to help me celebrate."

"I wish I could. I cannot, though."

"Of course you can, if you really want to . . . "

She walked rapidly, shaking her head. Some of the people passing began to stare at them curiously. A few laughed, lightly. Riordan knew that any street argument would be considered terribly bad form, and he tried to keep his rising temper in check.

"Miss Tanya, don't you see it won't be a special occasion if you aren't with me."

"I wish I could. I cannot."

They were now at the corner where the streetcars to Hongo stopped.

"If you really wanted to, you would change your plans . . . just this once . . . "

"No, I have promised to be there. They are counting on me . . . I also am paid a little for singing."

"So," he fought to keep is voice down, "who is thinking of money, now? Not a nasty American, but a Russian!"

"It's not the same, you're not being fair. I am poor. Oh well, let's not argue about it. It is no use." A Hongo-bound tram approached.

"Now, there isn't any good reason why you can't change your plans for this one, special weekend."

People were boarding the streetcar, which had stopped in front of them.

"Professor, I don't feel well, and I am tired. I am going home." Halfway into the car she turned and called: "Arigato" (thank you).

Before Riordan could properly react, the tram started down the street, spitting sparks.

He stood there dumbfounded. He couldn't move. "Well, I'll be damned," he said to nobody in particular. For a moment he considered running after her car, but his pride made him think better of it. "What a hell of a note," he muttered. Disappointment flowed through him as he walked along the Ginza. Even though his heart ached, he headed for the theater where they were originally going to see a movie. Might as well forget Russian girls for an hour or so. It was constructed Western style, and patrons were seated in a fashion he was accustomed to.

The show had begun. After settling in his seat, becoming accustomed to the glare of the projector, and the hush inside the theater, he thought he heard something unusual. Someone was sniffling, crying. Soon the crying became louder, a noisy, almost uncontrollable weeping. The sound emanated from directly behind him. *Could it be Tanya? Had she gotten off the streetcar, followed him, and now be about to tearfully ask his forgiveness?* He stole a hopeful look behind him. There sat a huge sumo wrestler, with long top-knotted hair, body overflowing his seat, trying to wipe his eyes with two small squares of soft paper, which represent the Japanese version of handkerchiefs.

It must be a terribly sad picture, thought Riordan. Somehow the wrestler's blubbering summed up the prospects for his anniversary weekend.

* * *

Captain Yoshida appeared quite drunk and Faymonville was not at all surprised. The Gods who created Japan were extremely fond of drink. Yoshida had followed this divine example by downing four scotch and sodas. Here in the American major's room before a proposed late dinner at the Imperial Hotel, he found himself out of his element, which was customarily warm saké.

No matter, since among Japanese men, a drunken guest was usually much more esteemed than a sober one. Many Japanese, however, are easily affected by strong drink, and Yoshida, an exceedingly charming fellow under most circumstances, was becoming surly. He unbuttoned the choker-collar on his blue uniform blouse.

"I suppose you will attend the grand opening luncheon here tomorrow, Major?"

"Yes, I guess I'll have to. Are you?"

"No, the army is sending a general in my place," he said, laughing. Faymonville thought this a shame, because he usually enjoyed Yoshida's company.

The captain took a long drink from his fifth Scotch, studying the American through the bottom of his glass. He sucked in his breath. "Even if I were a Japanese general I would not go tomorrow."

"Why?"

"Because the hotel is designed by this Wright, an American. It is located in Tokyo, and should be designed by a Japanese."

"Well, what difference does it make?"

"It will fall like a house of cards during the first big earthquake. What American architect can understand the power of a Japanese earthquake? Besides, this hotel caters to foreigners . . . foreigners and especially you Americans, do not belong here."

Faymonville lit a cigarette. He was somewhat taken aback at this change from Yoshida's usual Japanese politeness. "Are you mad at us—Americans?"

"Yes, all thinking Japanese are."

"Why?"

"Because of the Five Power Naval Treaty of last year . . . through which you are trying to keep us from reaching our destiny."

"I guess I can understand your feelings, although I don't share them."

The Captain got up unsteadily, and made himself another drink. His face was fiery red as he downed the Scotch. "And, you are talking constantly about limiting immigration. Our population is very dense in the fertile regions, and increases so rapidly that emigration from Japan is absolutely necessary. You Americans know this."

Yoshida gulped, coughed, then gestured with his glass, "You refer to us, the descendants of God, as the 'yellow peril'. Isn't that true?"

"No, I do not. However, I have heard the term." The American felt irritated even though he liked Yoshida a great deal. "I have been referred to, behind my back, as *'ketojin.'* That means 'barbarian' or 'hairy rascal' doesn't it?"

An infuriating Japanese smile spread over Yoshida's crimson face. "The term is hardly used anymore. It refers to all foreigners, not only Americans." The smile disappeared abruptly. "But one day soon we will have to fight you Americans, and we will win, do not doubt that for a moment."

Faymonville snuffed out his cigarette. "I wouldn't count on that if I were you. But, why are you telling me this, Captain?"

The Japanese sat down on the bed, momentarily sorting out muddled thoughts. "I tell you this because I am your friend, Major." His eyes closed. He fell back, keeping his glass upright, and soon began snoring, with his mouth wide open.

Damn it, thought Faymonville, *I probably won't be able to get him out of my room until the luncheon at noon tomorrow.*

* * *

Before Mr. Raita Kanoh left the Customs Department earlier than usual, he had explained to his superior that he would not be at work Saturday morning, because it was necessary for him to attend to some urgent personal business.

Upon his return home, he delighted in a relaxing bath and shave, and now was enjoying a short nap. He dreamed of the Russian girl, and of the pleasant night that lay before him with all its potential for unbridled excitement.

When she enters the room, Mrs. Kanoh thinks of the coming night too, but not with the joyous anticipation of her husband. She carries a red lacquer tray. On the tray is a small teapot, a tiny cup without handles, and two rice-cakes. She puts the tray down beside her husband, and makes a deep bow, ending with her forehead touching the floor.

Mr. Kanoh stirs, stretches and yawns, rubbing his small hands over his dimpled cheeks and deep-sunken little eyes, almost lost in fat. He pointedly takes no notice of his wife's presence. She pours the tea for him with a pose of timeless grace, and respectfully bows again.

Kanoh yawns again. A little spiral of steam comes from the diminutive cup. Then, he sucks in the weak green tea with a deep whistling sound. He ignores the rice cakes, rises from his couch, and leaves the room.

A maid quickly appears and lays out his clothes for the evening while Mrs. Kanoh supervises. There is a black Western-style suit, white shirt with French cuffs, gold cuff-links, navy blue tie, and a pair of heavy black shoes, imported from England. The maid bows, and disappears without a word.

Kanoh re-enters, still clad in his kimono of light gray silk. His black hair shines with an expensive pomade; its fragrance saturates every corner of the room. He undoes his sash, letting his kimono drop to the floor. He is wearing a set of American underwear, shorts and shirt. His wife quickly picks up the kimono and folds it carefully.

Mrs. Kanoh helps her husband with his dressing, holding each garment, waiting for him to slip into it, like a well-trained valet. Mr. Kanoh does not utter a word to her, but completely ignores her. After his tie has been adjusted, a gold watch placed in the pocket of his vest, and its chain draped across his middle, he strolls out into the hallway, carrying his shoes.

Mrs. Kanoh bows deeply in the manner of the dutiful wife she is. Perhaps she is a bit more sensitive than most Japanese wives, however, because as she makes her obeisance a tiny almost reluctant tear drops to the straw tatami at her feet.

* * *

In truth, Tatiana did not really want to get off the street-car near the Morozovs. She felt tired and depressed, after a day that had been lengthy, hot, and disappointing. The visit with Mrs. Armstrong continued to vex her. She longed for the cool sanctuary afforded by her room, and the soft security of her futon. Nonetheless, she knew she should drop in on Klavdia.

Was that why she boarded the tram to go home, leaving Hugh standing on the corner, an expression of shocked amazement covering his face? Was it her concern for Klavdia? No. Yes. She really didn't know for certain. She had been exhausted. It was so impossible to disagree with him. Small wonder he had become a professor. Whatever argument she could have used, he would have destroyed with his logical approach. She didn't intend to quibble. Her plans had been made, and she could not change them. Promises must be kept.

But, now she might have offended him too deeply. Perhaps he would stop coming to his class at the Athenée Français. Oh, what if she never saw him again!

The Morozovs were not home. Ludmilla Efimovna and Shura were watching Pavlova perform in a ballet. Klavdia appeared to be in an unusually cheerful mood, a fact that worried Tatiana because the Jewish girl's pregnancy had begun to become more apparent. She knew the Morozovs avoided discussing this development with Klavdia. Tatiana had been careful not to mention it either.

"I am happy to see you smiling this evening," said Tatiana.

"Oh, Tanya, I am glad that you came to see me. I was hoping that you would. You haven't been here for at least three days, and Ludmilla Efimovna asked if I had seen you."

"Well, I have been giving my lessons and spending some extra time at school, but I have been thinking about you."

"I'm happy you have so many pupils. Would you like some

tea?" She referred to the battered metal pot standing on a rather smoky *hibachi*, a small brazier commonly used in Japanese homes of the time.

"No thank you . . . well, yes I would like some very much."

Klavdia quickly filled two cups, much larger than the usual Japanese version. They both sipped the hot, strong tea with pleasure.

Tatiana said, "At first I forgot your tea would be good and strong. Most everyone here makes it so weak it tastes like warm water."

"Yes, I know. This is the way I like it, too."

"Well, what have you been doing?"

"I had some weak tea this afternoon with my Eurasian friend, Midori."

"Midori?"

"Yes," answered Klavdia, "she is a very pretty entertainer I met some time ago, a very lovely girl."

"Is she a dancer?"

"No, but she could be. We discussed the earthquake."

"And, what did she say?"

"Only that it will come, soon."

"Is she taking any precautions?"

"No, she thinks there is nothing to be done."

"Once this evening, when a truck went by, it shook the building, so I thought the earthquake had come," said Tanya.

"Sometimes, I wish it would come quickly and then you could all stop worrying. Ludmilla Efimovna makes me practice running down the stairs with them."

"Aren't you frightened, too?"

"No, not for myself. Of course, I don't want others to be hurt."

They sat quietly, both drinking their tea. Even considering Klavdia's unworried exterior, Tanya felt distressed about what might be the girl's innermost thoughts, her lack of concern over imminent peril.

"Have you found a rabbi to talk to?"

"No, I haven't even found another Jew, although I haven't looked very hard."

"You aren't thinking anymore of doing anything foolish?"

"No, Tanya," she smiled, "nothing foolish."

"Klavdia, why don't you come to Yokohama with me tomorrow? We can stay at the Peacocks. They are such nice people and they told me to bring you anytime."

"Oh no, not this weekend."

"We could have a special treat. One of my pupils is driving me in his new car. Doesn't that sound like fun?"

"Do you mean your American friend?"

"Well no, one of my Japanese students, who owes me a lot of money."

They both laughed.

"Oh, it does sound like fun, but I might go with you another time. Anyway, do the Peacocks know I am Jewish?"

"Klavdia . . . they don't know . . . I didn't have any reason to tell them . . . and if they did, it wouldn't make any difference. They are wonderful people. I'm sure you'd enjoy them."

"Thank you, Tanya . . . maybe another time. This weekend I have some important things to do, but the ride does sound exciting. When are you leaving . . . how long will it take?"

"I don't know how long it will take. He's calling for me at the Matsunami, at noon."

By that time tomorrow, Klavdia expected to be on her way to the bridge in Shinjuku.

* * *

Raita Kanoh caught a streetcar headed for Asakusa Park. Though the tram might be somewhat beneath his dignity for this night, he always appreciated the value of a yen and never felt prone to waste them even if he held a secure, permanent position. Of course, he had made this trip many times before.

The park was only half-a-mile from his ultimate destination.

While he rode, he thought about the Russian girl. He seemed to be making some progress with Mademoiselle Lunskaya, but he could not be sure. He mentioned "love" at least twice during his lessons for the month of August. True, whenever he did, she changed the subject, but he thought she must be considering marrying him.

Probably, he surmised, it was hard for her to contemplate a union with such an important person as himself. After all, she was only a refugee even if, as rumored, a high-born one. Marrying him should be the epitome of good fortune for her. She would aid him greatly in his ambition to be appointed to the Foreign Service. Later he might have a good chance to become a Cabinet Minister. She possessed all the necessary qualifications to be his new wife: poise in foreign society, knowledge of Western dress and customs, and great fluency in a number of languages.

He must tell her his ambitions in explicit terms, so she could better visualize how bright the future would be. Naturally, she must agree to tutor him every evening, when he was not otherwise occupied. Later, if things did not work out, she always had the diamond. He smiled as he thought about it. How could she possibly resist?

A short while later, he got off the tram near the main entrance to Asakusa Park. There was a huge crowd around the park, enjoying a pleasant evening. Kanoh could see the Kannon Temple, dedicated to the Goddess of Mercy. For a moment he thought of going in to buy a picture of Kannon as a talisman against sickness. Instead he hired a ricksha whose runner knew without being told where he wanted to go.

Quietly, the rubber-tired vehicle sped down dusty, narrow, twisting streets, past huts and tawdry houses with glowing paper doors, and bright gate lanterns. Where the ricksha slowed because of the constricting pathway, or a particularly sharp turn, the smell of native cooking became overpowering; acrid, humid, and heavy, like wood-smoke from damp logs. Kanoh also noticed the sour, rotten odor of pickled radish, so popular with the Japanese masses.

Kanoh felt impatient. He yelled at his driver to speed up, even though the runner was more elderly than usual. Their pace, to Kanoh's dismay, slowed. They were climbing the Emonzaka or "Dress Hill" where men traditionally adjusted their clothing to make the best impression. He smoothed his coat and tightened the knot in his tie. He wished the evening were a bit cooler. He licked his lips in anticipation.

Now, the narrow streets became quite crowded. There were shops, tea houses, and beer halls. On the right stood a small Shinto shrine called the Yoshiwara Shrine, dedicated to a special God, who brought rich lovers for the girls who prayed to him. The ricksha slowed, conforming to the slow forward movement of the tide of people being drawn to brilliant, vari-colored lights, and the pleasures of the "Nightless City."

Kanoh's ricksha stopped to one side of the O-mon, the great gate, where four policemen were standing. Only physicians were allowed to enter while riding or being carried. All others had to be on foot. He stepped down and handed his driver fifteen sen.

Then, he walked quickly through the wide iron gate, gratefully noticing a light breeze of perfumed air. Finally, he had arrived at the Yoshiwara. He could hardly wait to sample the tantalizing delicacies so readily available within.

September 1, Early Morning

Until 1614 there had not been any definite place set apart in old Tokyo, or Edo, for sexual commerce. That year, a red light district was founded in a marshy area of the ancient capital, one covered with rushes and reeds. Because of the abundance of these grasses, the place was called *Yoshiwara*, or rush-plain. Later, in order that the locality might have a more pleasingly appropriate name, the Chinese character for rush was replaced with one with a more auspicious meaning, but the same pronunciation, and the prostitution quarter became known as "good-fortune plain."

Over the more than three hundred years since its founding, the Yoshiwara had expanded tremendously, so that on the evening when Raita Kanoh entered the main gate for yet another time it was a walled city of pleasure housing some five thousand grand courtesans and lowly prostitutes.

Few of these women came from Tokyo. Most were recruited from rural provinces where living conditions could be terribly difficult under poverty caused by personal misfortunes, overly large families, crop failures, and other unhappy circumstances. A large proportion had been sold into servitude by their destitute parents. Many Japanese considered it an act of heroism for a girl to sell herself for a few years in order to help her poverty-stricken family. Indeed, a number of Japanese authors have written tenderly romantic love stories about the inmates. Unfortunately, venereal disease, premature aging, or a shame-motivated suicide often awaited these girls, some of whom were quite beautiful.

During the numerous years of its existence, this compound had burned to the ground thirty times, having last been swept by fire in 1911. This was the latest of many *shin*, or "new" Yoshiwara. Its wall was surrounded by a shallow moat that ran into tidal pools, enclosing an area roughly a quarter-mile-square. The wide main street, *Naka-no-cho*, tonight crowded by throngs of men, with some women and children, ran for 716 feet from the broad entrance gate, through the settlement to the large stucco hospital housing the Medical Inspection Bureau.

Throughout Tokyo, it would have been difficult to find a

section outwardly cleaner, freer from obscenity and outward signs of moral degradation than this quarter devoted to the enjoyment of the senses. It was too late for the blossoming of the many cherry trees, but their branches were covered with thousands of tiny electric lights. Garlands of flowers, both real and artificial, were visible everywhere. Paper lanterns in trees, on stands on the ground, or hanging from windows gave off a blaze of variegated light in every corner, brightening the people's faces with a pleasing medley of color. The iniquitous crowd exuded an atmosphere of controlled joy and gaiety. If a drunk raised his voice, his friends quickly quieted him. It all appeared a familiar and much loved sight to Raita Kanoh.

As quickly as possible, he elbowed his way through the teeming humanity. The going, of necessity, was slow. He bumped into two monks wearing rush baskets over their heads to keep from being recognized while they visited the brothels. One frantically grabbed at his basket to keep it from falling off, grunting, "Fool." Kanoh said nothing, and continued moving along.

On both sides of the main street near the entrance gate were rows of two-story teahouses called *hikite chaya,* or teahouses that lead by the hand. These establishments served as go-betweens for better-class visitors, who often ate meals there. The teahouses could also have a particular geisha summoned for their customer, and if she met with his approval, they might retire together to her bordello. The wealthiest men might join the *oiran* or "grand courtesans" in private rooms in the teahouse itself for more complete privacy.

Now, to Kanoh's right and left were buildings of varying architectural styles; all excessively ornate with plaster or cheap marble statues, flower-smothered balconies, colored tile inserts, and other diverse devices to achieve an outer distinction for their temple-like facades. Many entrances were elaborate and memorable. Golden dragons, fish, and pheasants embellished the ceilings. They mingled with the ever-present fruit blossoms, real and manufactured, to lend an aesthetically jumbled, yet pleasing effect.

Raita Kanoh thought all these entryways quite beautiful. He did not possess a particularly developed artistic sense, but he appreciated the heavily polished brasses, rich bronzes, gold, mother-of-pearl, marble, and jade figurines. Red, black, and gold lacquer ware of considerable craftsmanship caught his eye, as did huge inlaid Italian vases, and flowered Limoges plates set in the walls.

The customs officer stopped before one of these palatial entrances, looking past the red satin draperies into the fascinating interior. He could see a restful, cool, perfumed inner sanctum of flowers, green grasses, softly rushing fountains, and murmuring lotus-pools. This place was not his destination, he merely gazed inside to remind himself of the type of garden he would build for his house when he married the Russian girl.

Still, he took the time to linger and stare at the rows of colored, full-length pictures showing the girls who could be bought within. These likenesses were brightly lighted, mounted behind plate glass, and stood on either side of a sort of box office. It had the air of a theater.

Kanoh grinned knowingly when two young fellows in student uniform paid their fees after studying the pictures. They entered the house quickly, leaving the crowd outside to wonder which of the beauties they would visit.

Those young boys must have money, thought Kanoh. At that age he had not been able to afford an upper-class house like this, one so select it displayed its delightful inmates only photographically.

As he pushed along further, inwardly cursing the multitude that slowed his progress, he passed lower-class houses with their inmates on display. Here, he had to move inside the entrance to see a gaudy collection of women, not visible from the street, seated on silken pillows in front of flat gold screens containing large mirror inserts. Dressed in sensuous robes of silk and satin which covered them from neck to ankle, they were elaborately coifed—their glistening black hair held tortoise-shell hairpins and elaborate combs. With their eyebrows heavily penciled, lips painted crimson, and impassive faces under their white powder, these dignified ladies of pleasure waited quietly for the call to service.

Outwardly, there was nothing to disturb even the most prudish person. Kanoh blinked his small eyes, and again licked his lips. Reflected in a mirror behind a girl covered with white satin, he could see a perfect image of the nape of her neck. It was the most important fetish of the Japanese male, and hers disturbed him greatly. But, he forced himself to look away. He had an even more breathtaking destination.

When he returned to the street, he found the throng packed together even more tightly. Two efficient policemen were barking sharply, "Now move along, step quickly." He proceeded past two small crossroads, stopping only to survey the women at a third-class house—there were five classes or levels—he used to frequent before he became relatively wealthy.

Like other establishments of this class, it had a cage-front consisting of vertical bars, behind which the women were on display. Horizontal bars denoted an even lower class house; thus a prospective customer, even in a drunken condition, could tell the relative cost of the woman he desired.

Bright lights seemed to thrust the charms of these women, encased as they were, right out into the multitude. Full length background mirrors added brilliance to the dazzling exhibition, seeming to double the number of girls silently staring between the bars. They wore lavish kimonos of red, gold, green, and blue, embroidered in gold thread with dragons, fish, and flowers. One affected a Victorian appearance, wearing floor-length black lace, black gloves to her elbows, and her hair combed straight down to her hips.

A foreign passerby observed that it looked like an aviary full of beautifully feathered, black-eyed birds, most of them delicately diminutive, but a few plump as chickens. His companion was not so kind, and referred to the women on display as a menagerie, a zoo. Whatever the outside opinions, Raita could have loved all these women; in fact he wanted to—however, he had almost arrived at his objective.

He turned down a side street near the end of the compound, past a particularly brightly-lit corner house where the women in their barred, glassless windows were plaintively singing some old love song. A bit unusual, he thought, but anything could be expected in the Yoshiwara, the nightless city.

From somewhere nearby came bursts of gay, unbridled laughter. In one of the many houses, a group of women were chanting in unison, and this chanting was accompanied by the clapping of hands, a samisen, and a drum. These sounds, Kanoh guessed, were from a kind of musical striptease that sometimes ended in an orgy. Yes, Kanoh used to participate in such debauchery, enjoying it immensely. But, his present position would no longer permit such open display. Besides, he found the memories of discreet, rather more tasteful pleasures, lingered longer.

Quickly, he moved along a quiet byway, off the side street, so narrow that the balconies of four-storied European-type buildings on either side almost touched. The air seemed cooler, somewhat fragrant here. He adjusted his tie, took a deep breath and mounted the few steps to a gray stone house with a pink glow emanating from its windows. A well-built, bald-headed man clad in a black kimono, standing in darkness on a lower porch, bowed to him. The door opened as if by magic.

There, bowing low, all wearing bright kimonos, stood the hostess and four maids in a semicircle, squealing happily with obvious sincerity, "Welcome, welcome."

One of the maids took his shoes; the others led him upstairs to a lovely room with new, clean-smelling tatami on
the floor. Rapidly and effortlessly, continuing to squeal happily, two of them undressed him to his shorts, and helped
him into a cool gray yukata, the light, cotton kimono. After
he kneeled on a cushion before a priceless lacquered table,
the remaining maid began serving him a cup of tea and some
cakes. Kanoh pushed the tea utensils away, muttering one
word, "saké."

It appeared instantly in a tall white filigreed bottle, with a
set of small matching cups, all on a tray having a similar motif.
As fast as the little maid poured saké, he sucked it down. The
rice-wine was at a perfect, delightfully warm temperature.
Raita Kanoh began to relax. He noticed, in the *tokonoma*, or
alcove, a vase of beautiful flowers; and above, on the wall, a
rare, rather indiscreet print. The subject of the print brought
a smile to his homely features, and desire to his loins. First,
he must eat however, and enjoy the singing and dancing of
the geisha.

While he continued to down more saké, a number of dishes
were arranged before him. There was a red lacquer bowl brimming with fish soup, and several individual trays containing
pickled seaweed, mushrooms, clams, and in the middle of the
table, on an inlaid silver platter, *fugu*, or blowfish.

If it were incorrectly prepared, fugu could easily kill a diner;
in fact it is estimated that an ounce of its poison might kill
many thousands of diners at a single sitting. Carefully prepared in a number of ways by an expert, however, it had a
reputation for being both delicious and an aphrodisiac. This
latter attribute held no interest for Kanoh. Rather he savored
its taste, and especially its reputation as a *must* food for the
adventuresome. He fancied himself one of these adventur-
ous types.

The customs official ate rapidly and well. The moment he
finished a dish, it disappeared, removed quickly by one of the

barefoot maids. Another maid constantly refilled his cup with the warm, clear saké. When the small jug was emptied, another of like design took its place, and the drowsy wine poured again.

In some unseen place, a *samisen* began to tinkle, accompanied by a muffled drum. Suddenly, with a diminutive burst of laughter, two pretty young girls entered, made the usual prostration of greeting, and began to dance gracefully. They were dressed in layers of diaphanous silk kimonos that seemed to float in the air at each step and gesture. Their large black wigs were laced with colorful flowers, combs and pins, and flashing ornaments of gold.

This pair of unusually nimble geisha first performed the slow dance of the young girl of the wisteria, with exquisite grace. Kanoh watched sullenly, somewhat bored. He had seen it many times before, but he knew he must go along with the traditional progression of events. After all, he should act as a Japanese gentleman of position, and most of them supposedly enjoyed this sort of thing. At least his saké cup never stayed empty for long.

Now, the girls picked up dancing fans—considered good luck pieces. Every movement of their heads, bodies, and of their pointed fans had a meaning. They told an ancient story with their dance.

When they finished, they dropped down on either side of their honored, well-paying guest, and pressed close to him, pushing their knees against his thighs. They took turns telling him funny, erotic stories. Kanoh laughed uproariously, finding it difficult to keep from grabbing at them both. The heat of their knees, the fragrance of their musk-covered bodies, and the effects of warm saké began to cause him to lose the poise of a Japanese gentleman. His groin ached.

A jester appeared, began singing, and invited all those present to join in. Everyone did except Raita Kanoh, who roared his displeasure. With a wide swing of his arms he swept the bottle and saké cups off the table. They flew, crashed and broke against a nearby wall.

Both geisha gasped in astonishment. The jester turned and ran out, forgetting his customary bow. An embarrassed, absolute silence hung over everyone. Even the samisen had quieted its incessant twanging. Such undignified behavior was hardly expected and inexcusable in this high-class establishment, no matter how much saké had been consumed.

Kanoh awkwardly scrambled to his feet, pushing himself up from the table. He came close to falling, but stood, almost upright, swaying first one way, and then another. The room seemed to reel around him in a slowly turning circle. Immediately, a pair of maids were at his side, supporting him. They held him up momentarily, hoping he would gain his balance. Both geisha picked up their fans and left noiselessly.

The hostess appeared, smiling broadly and bowing deeply. While the disturbance must have summoned her, she made no mention of it. If she had, Kanoh would have lost face.

"It is late," she announced. "It is time to drink nectar from the 'Blooming Blossom.' "

Both maids began to giggle softly at first, then loudly, joined by the hostess. He blinked his eyes and started tittering too. All four of them, in a tightly bunched knot, left the room and slowly advanced down the hall, laughing foolishly.

They went up a small flight of stairs, the women constantly pressing close to him. This house supposedly contained almost a hundred rooms, and twenty-eight oiran, girls who were at the top of the Yoshiwara hierarchy. They bestowed their favors infrequently and with some discrimination.

Over the period of a number of years, this boorish, drunken customs official had sampled many flowers of the nightless city, but tonight, Miss Blooming Blossom was to be his for the first time. Until now, she had always been busy, so Raita Kanoh arranged this visit to her abode many weeks ago in June.

Her apartment consisted of four rooms on the top floor, a reception-room, a parlor, dressing room and bedroom. Under usual circumstances the maids served tea and cake, and sometimes saké, in the reception room; however, the hostess wisely decided that Kanoh could not wait. She good-naturedly directed the still giggling girls to take him directly to a large, soft, luxuriously thick, red futon. Bowing low, they quickly departed, giggling their way out of the sleeping room.

Some minutes after they left, Kanoh's head began to clear. He sat up, red-faced, eventually rising to his knees, and looked about the room. Never before had saké so adversely affected him. He wondered how long he'd been in a stupor. A rustling sound from the direction of the dressing room caused him to turn his head.

There, framed in the entranceway stood Miss Blooming Blossom, holding a saké cup of greeting for her honored guest. She bowed slightly, without obeisance, and advanced slowly, extending her arm with the cup before her. She stopped in front of the customs official, her look disdainfully proud, rigidly arrogant. He ignored the proffered cup, staring at her with his mouth wide open.

Her face seemed an expressionless mask of thick, pearl-white powder; her tiny mouth a crimson bud. She had an exquisiteness of features that was completely feminine. She wore a long, loose-fitting, richly embroidered purple satin robe. Her heavy black hair was crowned with an array of gilded pins and shining ornaments that caught even the subdued light.

To Kanoh, she appeared to be the most desirable woman he had ever seen, far beyond his wildest, most sensuous dreams. He sucked in his breath appreciatively. All at once, he felt the saké cup become a barrier between them. He grabbed it out of her hand and gulped the liquid, spilling most of it on his chin and neck. He hurled the cup into a corner of the room.

Miss Blooming Blossom slowly leaned forward and sank into the thick futon until she was kneeling in front of him. Her robe dropped from her shoulders with a whisper, revealing a plain white satin undergarment held up by two straps that accented the warm body underneath. Again, Kanoh sucked in his breath appreciatively. He felt about to explode.

Then, he had to blink his eyes in disbelief. Her one remaining garment plummeted silently to the red futon. Wherever she had applied the dead-white makeup, on face, neck, hands and forearms, she appeared to be made of ivory. In all the other areas however, her skin was a pale color indicative of a life lived mostly indoors and after dark.

While most women Kanoh had been with thus far had possessed small flat, rather shapeless breasts, not so Miss Blooming Blossom. Hers were quite large and somewhat conical, the glowing violet nipples seemingly pointed away from each other. Her bottom was pleasingly curved and well-rounded. All these treasures Kanoh evaluated in a rapid glance. But his eyes moved quickly to the most sensuous area of all, the painted nape of her neck, and area traditionally of much appeal to the Japanese male.

She leaned forward, still unsmiling, so he could observe it more closely. Yet again, he sucked in his breath, this time until he almost choked. The back of her carefully shaved neck had a slight indentation running down its middle, a shallow seam between two soft pulsating mounds of pleasure. Never before had Kanoh gazed upon a feminine neck so maddeningly erotic. He could not tear his eyes away from it. The strong fragrance of musk engulfed him. His fists clenched and unclenched spasmodically, in unison with those awful, pulsating, demanding aches in his groin.

He could restrain his desire no longer. Indeed, there was no reason why he should, her services for the entire evening had been paid for. He clumsily but firmly grabbed her naked shoulders with his pudgy hands. She did not move, nor change her disdainful expression. After all, she had served many hundreds of men, who had expected a multiplicity of skills from her. It was not likely that she would be surprised.

Perhaps this seemed a challenge to Kanoh. Suddenly, not even taking time to suck in his breath, he lunged forward and sank his teeth into the soft nape of her neck. He clung tenaciously there, repeatedly biting, tasting her blood.

Miss Blooming Blossom screamed, indeed, she emitted a series of shrieks that stopped all activity in the house, and were heard throughout a goodly part of the Yoshiwara.

* * *

Paula, the Peacock's rotund Russian cook, took great pride in every meal she prepared for them. Her culinary artistry caused the English family to be envied by even the more affluent people who lived on the Bluff, a number of whom had tried to lure Paula into service in their own kitchens. But Paula would never consider leaving the Peacocks, as long as they wanted her. She had been with them since their days in Russia. They were the only family she had, and probably were kinder to her than her real family would have been.

The good-humored Ivan lightened her limited chores around the house with his congenial kidding and storytelling. It was hard to believe all of his family, back in Russia, were dead. She felt sorry for Zoya Semionovna, who was now a governess only four houses away, because Gee Gee and Nanette were attending school in Canada. Nevertheless, she was close by, enabling her to visit often. Paula could not determine if the root of Zoya's sadness lay in her change of households, missing the children, or the traveling Henry Peacock, or all of those factors combined.

Living on the attractive Bluff with its magnificent view of Yokohama Bay, in the beautiful Peacock house, serving a family to whom she felt utterly devoted, Paula was happy and content. As far as reasonably possible, life was good.

This morning she prepared a special breakfast for the Peacocks and their friends the Keefes, who had recently arrived and were staying at the Belmont Hotel. Her breakfast featured *blini*, the light, medium-sized Russian pancakes with plenty of sour cream and black caviar.

"Paula, I jolly well think I would walk all the way from Vladivostok just to have some of your blini," said Frederick Keefe.

"Thank you, Sir."

"They are superb, simply superb."

Odylia said, "She made them just for you and Ann. Of course 'Erber and I love them, too.

"You know," observed Keefe, "I never could understand why the Russians eat them only before Lent. I'd like to have them every day."

"Then you shall have them again tomorrow, Freddie," said Herbert Peacock. "Can you arrange that, Paula?"

"Yes Sir, I would be happy to—thank you." Paula bowed slightly and returned to the kitchen with a look of proud contentment on her face.

"I love this black caviar," said Ann Keefe. "We can find only a little of the red, and that is always fishy tasting."

"Yes, I'm afraid the Bolsheviks do not cultivate epicures among their ranks," said Keefe. "We are often lucky to get the basic essentials for eating. Everything is still terribly disorganized. So, dear friends, we will doubly enjoy this wonderful food while we are here. But, tell me, will we be seeing that nice Russian girl, Tatiana Alexandrovna?"

"Oh yes," answered Odylia, "dear Tanya will be here this afternoon, and will stay with us until tomorrow." Sometime during the years she had been married to Herbert Peacock, Odylia had acquired a precise ease of movement as she made tea that caused people to watch her without really knowing why. She recognized this, and when guests were about, she relieved Paula of her tea-making duties.

Not a drop of hot water spilled onto the lace-covered mahogany table as she worked. With deft strokes, she dropped the China tea into her pot, then filled it to an exact level with hot water from the whispering brass samovar. One graceful sweep of her arm placed the teapot in position atop the samovar, where the added heat would maintain a more precise temperature. She smiled, folded her hands, and waited for the tea to steep. "Tanya comes every weekend now, to sing the vesper service Saturday evening, and the regular mass on Sunday."

"Yes," said Mr. Peacock, "I understand that Bishop Constantine will not begin a service without her."

"You know, I really like that man," observed Keefe. "You are aware I got know him rather well in Vladivostok. Some people say I helped arrange his escape."

They all laughed.

"I didn't, of course, but I know the poor fellow refused to leave, at first. Lucky he did, though."

"He hasn't been here in Yokohama very long. He serves as a simple priest," said Peacock.

Keefe finished an extra helping of Blini. "I'd love to visit with him a bit. Wouldn't you, Ann?"

"Yes, although I only met him once at a reception."

"Perhaps we can all go to mass with Tanya," said Odylia, beginning to pour the tea. "She sings divinely."

Keefe took a cup after his wife was served. "Thank you, Odylia. Back in our rooms, I have some information that should interest Tatiana Alexandrovna. I believe it is certain her mother and two sisters are alive . . . or were a little while ago."

"Oh, how wonderful!" said Odylia.

"Good boy, Freddie," said Peacock. "I was hoping you could run something down."

"I'll show you the reports when we get back to the Belmont, for tiffin."

"Wonderful—really excellent, Freddie, old boy. That is good news. You are to be congratulated. Now, I have some more good news. I've hired a car for the weekend. I've had a deuce of a time getting one, but Porter, my secretary, is bringing it. He should be here straight away," said Herbert Peacock.

"Good show, Herbie. It's going to be too hot to do much walking, today."

"Yes, Odylia and I know how much you two adore fine porcelain—as we do—so let's finish up and drive to the Mokuzu Kozan Works. We can see the kilns, the workshops, and they have a number of showrooms . . . possibly even buy a few things."

"Isn't Mokuzu famous for blue and white pieces?" asked Ann.

"Yes, and they are probably as well known for their apple green glazes. Odylia, where do we have that green Mokuzu ware?"

"Oh 'Erber, I'm not sure. Remember, I just returned from Canada. We can ask Ivan. He'll know, I'm sure."

"Yes, of course, my dear. If Ivan doesn't, Paula certainly will."

Keefe drained his teacup. "May I have a spot more, please, Odylia?"

"Why, of course."

"Thank you. After being deprived in Russia, I'm still not accustomed to the wonderful food you have over here. I must confess, I'm already looking forward to tiffin at the Belmont."

"Fred, I'm afraid you're going to put on a great deal of weight, between Paula and the Belmont." observed Ann.

"That may well be, but I'm willing to stop eating for a little while. I'm ready to stroll around this porcelain factory."

They all laughed with him.

"Good," said Herbert, "we'll make plans for the afternoon during tiffin." He rose, dabbing his lips with his napkin. "I believe I just heard Porter drive up. Now dear people, shall we continue our 'rememberable' day?"

"Good Lord, Herbie," said Keefe. "What a perfectly apropos word, 'rememberable.' I don't believe I have ever heard it before."

"Well fine," said Peacock, "I must confess I just made it up."

*   *   *

"I believe that is set-point," called out Toshi Sugawara just after his opponent missed a difficult backhand.

"Yes," yelled the winded Kojuro Nabashima, "you have beaten me again." He kicked at the gravel of the court in disappointment.

The tall, good-looking Sugawara did not leap over the net in victory, rather he walked around it and shook his friend's hand. "Your rallies were good, but your serve is a little off, and I think you are a bit out of condition." He spoke in English.

"Toshi, I must admit you are right."

"You see what happens when you get married." They both laughed.

"I haven't had enough time to practice."

They sat down on one of the benches that were located around the courts and towelled themselves off.

"It feels good to raise a sweat," observed Sugawara.

"It does," agreed his friend, dropping the towel around his neck. "It's easy this morning—terribly hot and humid. So, when will you get married Toshi?"

Toshi smiled, "Oh, I don't know—when my parents find someone suitable for me."

"Is that so difficult?"

"It seems to be—besides, I'm thinking of asking my French teacher."

At first incredulous, Nabashima reacted by bellowing with

laughter. "Your French teacher? You mean that Russian girl?"

"Why yes—and she is no mere girl—but a Russian noble-woman, a real lady!"

"Now, don't be irritated with me, Toshi. I know my uncle thinks a great deal of her—but you can't be serious—actually thinking of marriage."

"I don't know, I might."

As it approached mid-morning, the courts became completely full. Only about a quarter of the players were Japanese. The rest were Westerners, though they displayed no more skill at the game than the Japanese.

"Toshi, you always were full of wild ideas." Nabashima hesitated a moment. "I have heard you even became a Christian."

"Yes, that is right. I am a Methodist."

"But, why? I am surprised. Did some Christian missionary get hold of you? Did the Russian lady talk you into it?"

"Oh no, we have spoken of religion but once, and I brought up the subject. She is of an entirely different sect."

"Well, what are all these different sects about? I cannot understand there being so many. Buddhism accepts good and bad. There is no conflict, nothing to fight against. It provides you with complete emotional security. What more could you want?"

"Answers, Kojuro—I wanted the answers to questions. Who am I? Why was I born? Why must I die? What are death and life all about? What . . . or who, makes it happen?"

Nabashima nodded his head a couple of times vigorously and began to untie his tennis shoes. "We all think of these questions at times, but do you have the answers . . . as a Christian?"

"No, I don't, however I am on the way to finding out." He thought for a moment. "Some of the answers are coming to me."

"Give me an example."

"I will quote the Gospel according to Saint John: 'I am the way, the truth, and the light. No one comes to the Father but by me.'"

"And what exactly is that about? What is the Father?"

"God is the Father."

"Just one Father?"

"Yes, there is but one God."

"But, Toshi, how could there be only one God? We have *Amida, Jizo, Kannon,* and so forth. Many Gods are required to take care of many things."

Sugawara stood up and looked kindly at his friend. "There is but one God."

"All right, why did he make you?"

"God made me to love and serve him in this world. He also made me to be happy and content with him forever in the next world."

Nabashima rose, shaking his head, trying to think of a new argument, but feeling he had inadequate knowledge to do so. "I'm not offending you . . . ?"

"No, my friend, not at all. I am happy to talk about it with you."

After changing shoes, they began walking together, away from the tennis courts, hardly noticing a couple of close matches being contested energetically and skillfully. Under usual circumstances, they would have watched, but they were both deep in thought about their discussion.

"Can your God do anything, Toshi?"

"Yes, He does anything and everything."

"And, you call him Father?"

"Yes, my friend, He is the Father of us all."

"But Toshi, through Buddhism I expect to attain nirvana. Can you find peace, freedom from pain, worry, and the external world through Christianity?"

"Oh yes, Christianity is the supreme experience of transcendence—liberation from the concerns of everyday life and union with ultimate reality—where suffering is eliminated and compassion and wisdom are attained."

"I see, and you find all this through God?"

"Yes, yes through our heavenly Father."

Nabashima, though enlightened, remained unconvinced. His friend Toshi, while far from being a radical—as long as he had known him—had an unusual way of thinking, often far from the established norm. This afternoon, they were planning on luncheon and a walk through the attractive grounds of Asakusa Park. The magnificent Kannon Temple, dedicated to the Goddess of Mercy, stood nearby. If they spent some time there, near the big bell, the red pagoda, the revolving sutras, the Fox Shrine, and the Inner Shrine—maybe, just maybe, Toshi would come to his senses on this question of religion. *It certainly would be worth a try,* thought Nabashima.

* * *

In downtown Tokyo was the huge Mitsukoshi Department Store, the finest and largest in Japan. It stood six stories, concrete over heavy brick, designed in a stately Renaissance style with two-story columns and massive stone lions at the main entrance. From miles away, people could see its tall, ornate cupola towering above the extensive roof garden.

Inside, Mitsukoshi offered the greatest selection of high quality merchandise in the Orient, along with a staggering assortment of the products for which Japan was famous, porcelain, art objects, lacquerware, fabulous silks, and all the rest. Its clientele included the top members of Japanese aristocracy, representatives of the working class on a spree, and particular Westerners who appreciated that English was spoken in every department and that foreign delicacies, including ice-cream, pie, cake and excellent coffee, were served at lunchtime by comely Japanese waitresses in the delightful café on the fourth floor.

Shimaku Suzuki and her mother planned to eat in the

café at noon today. Now, about quarter-past eleven, accompanied by a maid, they were both studying the most expensive ready-to-wear kimonos Mitsukoshi had to offer. These garments were to be for Shimaku's trousseau, although there were no definite plans for her marriage as yet. There had been some talk with other families, and a go-between, however, and her prospects were beginning to brighten. Shimaku, of course, would not be consulted about the matter. She would, as was expected, abide by her father's decision in the choice of her husband.

This morning, Mrs. Suzuki wore a plain kimono, dark brown in color, with a simple gold sash. It was considered good taste for Japanese ladies of middle age to dress modestly, with restraint. She was tall for a Japanese woman, yet small-boned, with a pure oval face, rather lacking in expression. Her small mouth, which unlike her daughter's seldom smiled, seemed drawn and cramped. She wanted Shimaku wed to be sure, yet she did not want to hurry. Being a married woman in Japan presented many difficulties; nevertheless, being an unmarried one was a tragedy.

Shimaku had her mother's figure, with a face of the much admired melon-seed shape. Her eyes, slightly tilted, moved like shining, animated currants as she surveyed the colorful kimonos brought before her. They were so pretty, she wanted them all.

When she tried them on, she hardly noticed the oppressive heat, which was only faintly dissipated by the constantly moving fans of admiring store attendants specially trained in the art of showing approval of a customers' purchases. The sight of bright colors and flowery patterns, the feel of Japanese silk, kindled in her the aspirations Japanese women had held for generations.

She must have this pink one with red and white storks; and that sky-blue one, lined in red, covered with pink chrysanthemums; and the orange version patterned in flowers along with a yellow sash; and certainly the gray highlighted with cherry blossoms; and positively the one in plain white moonglow.

Shimaku could not really be classified as beautiful, but in this country of great uniformity she desired to be attractively different. Her straight black hair was parted on one side in the foreign style Tanya had introduced to her. She wore it that way with her father's approval, a distinct contrast to her mother's more conservative, conventional, helmet-like coiffure.

The closest Mrs. Suzuki came to a smile was when they decided to buy all of the kimonos Shimaku had tried on. Truly, it was a happy moment for both of them, one reserved only for the very rich.

Now, they must consider material for her formal, ceremonial kimonos, that were usually of a single color, and had to be tailored with the Suzuki crest in white on the sleeves and back.

Shimaku examined cloth in gray, magenta, and navy blue. She asked to see more colors because these darker hues, although customary, did not excite her. She loved bright multicolored things.

As she let the cool silk slip absent-mindedly through her hands, she began thinking how nice it would be to have luncheon in the café in only a few minutes.

* * *

Yoshinari Yamamoto, having been educated for the most part in the United States, ran his family with a combination of Japanese paternalism, and American democracy. He listened to the wishes of his four charming children, but not overly. He even considered the opinions of his lovely wife, but not too much. So, this Saturday morning, when he decided to go to downtown Tokyo in order to buy presents for them, and they all expressed a desire to accompany him, he had decided against their wishes. The gifts he planned on buying should be considered surprises, thus the members of his family were required to stay at home.

While the family accepted his decisions without question, Yamamoto was far from being a typical Japanese husband and father. On occasion, he played with his children and helped them with their lessons. He often displayed visible affection toward his wife.

In general, the usual Japanese male believed that the more he showed tokens of love, or talked about it, the weaker he became. Wives were not treated as equals or as companions by their husbands, who were often taught that marriage was to be arranged in the interest of forming the right business or family connections, and not for pleasure. Hana, Yamamoto's wife, certainly was not treated as his equal; however, she enjoyed being much more equal than other Japanese women, and lived with that rarest of gems, her husband's sincere love.

It was hot, and the earlier, abbreviated rain had raised the humidity, nevertheless it appeared a beautiful day to Yoshinari Yamamoto. He liked nothing better than buying gifts for his family. Truthfully, he should have done it before they arrived only a few days ago, but he had been busy at school, and he really wanted to see them first and get some hint as to what they might want.

Initially, he checked the small open-front shops, off the main street of the Ginza, with their goods displayed on shelves slanted toward the street, so prospective customers could see all the merchandise at a glance. Many of these shops were so small their wares overflowed into the thoroughfare.

These goods had no firm price, but were subject to bargaining between the buyer and the proprietor. In one such store, he found, under a large glass case-front, a small doll dressed in complete kimono to delight his younger daughter, Kiku.

Yamamoto had taken great care in naming his children.

Because his wife's name was Hana, meaning flower, he chose Kiku and Tsubaki for his daughters, meaning chrysanthemum and camellia respectively. He planned on adding more blossoms to his family bouquet. So far, there were two sons, Yoshinari Jr., a naming custom he learned in America, and Koshiro. He loved all his children equally, not believing in the old Japanese saying that daughters were only better than no children at all.

The little doll with its friendly brown eyes, chubby pink cheeks, dressed in a dark blue kimono and silken sash, seemed to hold out her arms to him.

"How much is this one?" he asked, indicating the exquisite doll. There were four others near it under the glass.

"Truly on such a hot day, when crowds are small, we must consider selling all our goods cheaply. Ten yen is asked for such a lovely doll for an honorable daughter."

Yoshinari smiled broadly. "But, the day is not too hot for making jokes. Only three yen is possible."

The merchant turned away from such foolish talk and busied himself with sprinkling down the dusty street around his place of business with water.

"Three yen," said Yamamoto, holding up the bills. The shop keeper shook his head and shrugged his shoulders to indicate the hopelessness of such an offer.

Yoshinari turned into the stream of people passing by. He had gone only some twenty paces when the merchant confronted him with the doll in a bag. "Truly it is necessary to reduce the price. Five yen, take it please." He placed the bag in Yamamoto's hand.

"Four yen," he bargained, holding out the bills. The proprietor shook his head sadly. "Truly it is only because you have the look of a samurai that I sell to you at a loss."

They went their opposite ways, both well satisfied.

Next, he stopped at Miyamoto Shoko and Company, Gold and Silversmiths, and splurged on a tiny silver tea set for his wife. He actually wanted one with jade accents, but as he had supposed, it proved too expensive. He loved this store with its gold and silver art objects, its ivories, bronzes, and jade jewelry.

Another store he favored was the Mitsukoshi Department Store. He took pride in thinking that it was just as good as Wanamaker's or Marshall Field and Company. Last Christmas, surely just to please the foreign element and sparse Christian population, Santa Claus appeared in one of the Mitsukoshi windows, all in red, with his white beard, and a bag full of presents. Santa had shared the window with Hotei, the happy God of Plenty, noted for his bald head, laughing face, and huge stomach. Yamamoto felt this display had exemplified the tolerant religious attitude of the Japanese.

In Mitsukoshi, where prices were definitely set, he purchased a fine quality shuttlecock and battledore set for his sons, who had avidly played with a broken set before their summer trip to America. He had thought of buying them books on some intellectual subject, yet he acknowledged they would better appreciate the game equipment. If only they had more room to play.

It took him some time to decide on a present for his elder girl, Tsubaki. She was very serious, an excellent student of languages, and quite artistic. He wanted to cater to her love of fine things, for while most Japanese women were inexorably destined to be wives and mothers only, she could be brought up as a repository of ancient arts and creative talent. He spent almost an hour admiring an eighteenth-century medicine box that was beautifully finished in black and gold, however it cost much more than he could afford to pay, even though he felt the necessity of occasional extravagance. His family's trip to America had almost bankrupted him. So, he settled on a larger, more modern, yet less beautiful, red lacquer case that was tasteful in appearance, with her namesaké, a camellia, on its lid.

All his presents were carefully wrapped, and tied with a special type of string, known as *mizuhiki,* in a decorative knot. In Japan, it was considered vulgar, sometimes insulting, to offer a gift that was improperly tied. It pleased Yamamoto to think only his wife would really care how the gifts were wrapped. She was, naturally, more bound by tradition than the children.

His shopping done, he thought of yielding to one of his own desires. As a student in America, he had developed a taste for sweet foreign desserts. The café in Mitsukoshi, like the store itself, catered to many foreigners, and was one of the few places in all of Japan where you could order pie and ice-cream. For months, he had been thinking of this pie a la mode.

He went to the fourth floor and was about to enter the café when he thought better of it. A nearby clock gave the time as quarter-to eleven. He should be getting home with his gifts. The prospect of seeing his wife and children's happy faces overcame his strong desire for pie a la mode. Denial is good for the soul, he reflected to himself—so near, and yet so far.

Outside, he searched for a home-bound streetcar. There were none to be seen, in fact at the moment there weren't any trams at all in sight. It seemed unusually quiet without the jolting and grinding of their wheels. Few people appeared to be about for this time of day. *It must be the sultry weather,* he thought. There wasn't the slightest breeze. The skies had cleared and a hot sun blazed down on him. His shirt and light silk suit were damp with perspiration.

A weird, choking, unpleasant feeling had come over him. The air felt as though it were an invisible wall closing around him, squeezing his breath away. He took out a handkerchief and wiped his face. Strange, he should be feeling on top of the world—his arms were loaded with gifts for his beloved family. He hoped he wasn't getting ill.

Soon, a single tram came in sight, showing his destination. Yamamoto boarded it gratefully. For some reason, the usually polite conductor did not smile, or even look at him, when he deposited his money. Grabbing on to the hangers with his free hand, he stumbled to find a seat. It was like an oven inside.

*   *   *

Suicide is an important part of Japanese culture. By Western standards, self-destruction is considered a futile submission to despair, and is generally condemned. Japanese respect for suicide permits it to be thought of, in some cases, as a virtuous and purposeful act, often regarded with approval and sometimes even worthy of adulation. A great proportion of Japanese feel, in certain situations, it is the most honorable course to take.

Of course, ritual suicide had always been well known among Japanese. *Seppuku*, suicide by disembowelment, or its vulgar synonym, *hara kiri*, meaning to cut one's stomach, happened often enough to keep the practice familiar to the vast general population. In theory at least, the performance of this particular type of suicide was limited to members of the upper classes. The operation consisted of deeply slashing the abdomen from left to right and from bottom to top, with a short sword. When the act was not performed successfully, the victim signaled a friend or relative waiting with a longer sword to finish the job by chopping off his head.

There were many popular, if less ceremonial, ways of taking one's life. Jumping from bridges came first in popularity because of its simplicity, as was jumping in general—deep into the bowels of an active volcano; from one of the many suicide-cliffs into a river, the ocean, or boiling sulfurous springs; or from the top of incomparably beautiful Kegon Falls near Lake Chuzenji.

Most of this was vaguely familiar to Klavdia, who took the

main point to be that the Japanese populace often admired a suicide victim, even if, as she had learned, the police usually tried to prevent the act. Based on her conversation with Midori, she had decided to jump from the bridge in Shinjuku this afternoon. She had chosen this day because it had been her father's birthday.

She once thought of shooting herself, a nice quick way, but no gun was available. She had decided against slashing her wrists, because it would be too bloody, too painful, and too slow. She did not want the disposal of her body to be a bother for the Morozovs either.

Yes, leaping from the bridge seemed most appropriate— her faithful love for her father, coupled with taking the life of the unborn baby along with her own—her quick solution to these conditions seemed ideal to Klavdia's currently distorted sense of values. She did not covet death, only she could not face life. Life had not given her a fair chance, and so she was leaving it.

All these ideas she put down in a note addressed to Tanya and the Morozovs, which she left on the battered leather suitcase in her room. She carefully neglected to mention the location where she planned to commit this act of self-sacrifice. The few bits of identification she owned were included in her farewell envelope. The sash she would use to tie her legs together, she wrapped around her waist under her dress.

Mrs. Morozov and her son squatted near the hibachi pre-paring lunch. Pavlova was downtown, teaching her Saturday ballet class. Most Japanese used *shichirins,* or small charcoal-burning stoves, for cooking and *hibachi* for heating, but these living quarters only had hibachi. The Morozovs had just fin-ished a long morning when their newspapers hardly sold at all. A couple of bundles remained, piled in a corner of the room. They would have to try to sell these during the after-noon.

Shura cut some dried daikon into small pieces, while his

mother prepared rice in an earthenware bowl, sliced a tiny bit of salted cod-fish, and brewed a pot of tea.

Klavdia walked in and without saying a word, and took a cup of tea. Mrs. Morozov noticed the tension about her. "Klavdia Davidovna, you are very pretty in your white dress, isn't she Shura?"

Her son nodded, smiling.

"Thank you."

"Lunch will be ready in a little while."

"Oh, Ludmilla Efimovna," said Klavdia, gazing into her cup. "I must meet my friend, Midori, at half-past twelve."

"But, we have some salted-cod today. You like it, and you can't go away without eating."

"Oh, I should have told you earlier, Ludmilla Efimovna. Midori will give me some lunch."

Mrs. Morozov stood up and looked at her suspiciously. "Do you feel all right? You really don't look well."

"Yes, yes, I feel fine."

"Do you have enough money, dear?" asked the kindly, middle-aged Russian woman, rubbing her hands on her tattered apron.

"Oh, yes, thank you. I don't need any now." Klavdia quickly finished her tea, and said, "It always takes me more than a half an hour to get there. I must be going."

She gently embraced, for a longer than usual time, Ludmilla Efimovna, who hugged Klavdia in return, kissing her cheek. She bent and kissed Shura on the top of his head, noticing the oily hair-preparation he had used ever since his birthday as a touch of boyish vanity.

The whole scene made Mrs. Morozov uneasy, but she could not understand why. "Go with God, Klavdia Davidovna."

Klavdia slid the door open, looked back saying, "Sayonara," and closed it. She ran along the hall, and down the stairs. She felt as though a massive rock were crushing her chest, keeping her from taking a breath.

She ran until she got to the street, then paused and put on her shoes, staring back at where she had lived, if not happily, at least comfortably, with the Morozovs. Klavdia walked a few steps, and stopped again to look at the home she had shared with Pavlova, Ludmilla Efimovna, and young Shura.

She closed her eyes, tottered down the street, feeling a little faint in the sun. Oh, how Ludmilla Efimovna had hugged her! She sensed the love that this woman had for her for the first time. Yes, it was true, Ludmilla Efimovna actually loved her. And, she had a friend in Tanya . . . why, she had wanted her to go to Yokohama, and spend the weekend. She licked her lips, tasting the sweetness of the flower-scented brilliantine from Shura's hair . . . and Pavlova liked her . . . and, Oh God, today was the Jewish Sabbath . . . Klavdia's father would never forgive her for taking her own life on the Sabbath . . . never!

Tears streaming down her face, she retraced her steps . . . she would return to her home, to her room, to those who loved her. Now, she felt weak from her overpowering happiness as well as from hunger. Of course, Ludmilla Efimovna had bought the salted cod-fish just for her, and probably spent much more than she should have . . . oh, it would taste delicious, and after lunch, she planned to destroy the suicide note on her suitcase.

* * *

Tatiana felt as though she had not slept the entire night. Of course, she was worried about Hugh, and thoughts of him kept her tossing and turning on her soft futon until light began to show through the rice-paper-covered windows of her room. She had dozed off, but she was far from rested when she got up.

It was too early. She would go back to bed, and try to relax before her busy weekend. But first, she opened the paper bag on her tiny dresser and ate a banana. It made her happy that this was the last banana, just as she had planned, and none were left to spoil over Saturday and Sunday. She would buy more on Monday.

Before relaxing again, she lifted the futons and sprinkled yellow flea-powder under them. Like most Japanese houses, her floor was covered with tatami, soft mats woven of shiny straw, fixed to the floor. Also as in many native residences, these tatami were full of fleas. Sometimes a bold one crawled up into the futon to make sleeping difficult for her. She hated the yellow powder, which she now sprinkled over her body, but it appeared to discourage the fleas temporarily at least.

She knew she had been foolish to walk away from Hugh. She could see that, from her calmer perspective this morning. His factual, demanding way had been too much for her to cope with—she simply could not accompany him, but she had not been able to explain her reasons adequately enough to convince him. Even if she had tried harder, their knowledge of languages probably was insufficient for them to communicate with each other when such delicate problems came up. He did not know enough French and Russian; and she did not know enough English. Neither of them had yet learned enough Japanese.

She recognized she had acted badly, even if she had felt discouraged, aggravated, and exhausted. Although his dogged insistence had made her feel trapped, still she should not have run away. Would he feel, like a Japanese, that she had caused him to lose face? Someone once told her that Irish-Americans were very proud. Now, she might never see him again. As children began to play in the dirty alleys around the Matsunami Hotel, Tanya cried herself to sleep.

She slept fitfully. She dozed, and dreamed, then woke, then dozed again. Behind her closed lids she could see Hugh's face with disturbing clarity. His image would fade, and in a few minutes, return. She realized, in her slumbering state, that he represented someone to be counted on in her troubled world, and someone who had become increasingly important and dear. Oh, how angry he must be with her this morning.

And then, Klavdia's pretty face, with its inner torment, hovered in Tanya's subconscious. Oh Lord, how could she help her? How could she give her hope with which to live?

She moved about restlessly on the futon, barely asleep, seeming to see Hugh's healthy face before her. She sighed and cried out, for now she could see herself narrowly escaping from the Bolsheviks in Siberia. Again, in the box-car, her coat was on fire, and suddenly, far away, she could just make out Klavdia, about to jump from the Nihonbashi Bridge. What a terrible dream! It must be a dream!

The distant tolling of a remote temple bell awakened her completely. She sat up. Her futon and her nightdress were wet with sweat. Somewhere, someone played discordant notes on a samisen. How gloomy and desolate it sounded to her musically trained ears.

She slid open her paper and wood door and called down the hall for Michiko-san, the maid, who came running lightly, and brimming over with morning cheer. Tatiana asked if there were anyone in the bathroom, and was relieved to hear that it was deserted. Tatiana enjoyed her morning bath, but was not entirely comfortable with the Japanese custom of sharing a bath with others.

After a quick dip in the piping hot water—she always feared some other tenants would arrive unexpectedly for a bath—the Russian girl felt somewhat refreshed. Her natural optimism and self assurance returned slowly. She wished there had been one more banana left because she was hungry.

She made a mental note to ask Monsieur Fuji to stop his motor-car near a street-vendor so she could eat a small snack. Of course, she would pay for her own food.

Last night, weariness and disillusionment had made her discouraged and apprehensive even before she met Hugh. This morning she was finally rather rested, and she told herself that her depression of the night before had been senseless. But what about Hugh? Would he understand?

She decided to wear her white dress. She didn't have many clothes, but she knew that this was Hugh's favorite and she would wear it in honor of his anniversary even if she might never see him again.

In a corner of her simple, windowless room there was an alcove with a raised sill where most Japanese would have kept a small Buddhist altar. Over it, on the wall, hung a decorative scroll, which supposedly should be changed, to mark the current season. Hers never changed, however, always showing two fish in gold and black. Tanya used the raised portion as a base for a mirror, and kept her makeup articles below it. She knew this would shock many Japanese, but with so little room she had to be practical.

While she kneeled on a cushion before the mirror, brushing her hair and applying makeup, Michiko-san came to the door and, after some strenuous effort, made her understand she had a telephone call on the first floor.

She bowed to Mr. Yoshida before picking up the receiver. Somewhat awkwardly she said, in the Russian way, "Hallo! Hallo!" She looked at Mr. Yoshida, pointed to the phone and shook her head. He bowed, smiling, and gently took the receiver.

He shouted into the mouthpiece, "Moshi, Moshi," and listened. He clicked the phone a number of times and talked heatedly, apparently with an operator. He shook his head sadly, hung up and bowed.

The incomplete phone call disturbed Tanya. It was not the call itself, but the disruption signified a change in her mood. She hurried through her makeup, and the packing of a small wicker weekend case.

If he were on time, Monsieur Fuji should arrive shortly. An ominous sense of foreboding was creeping over her like an evil spirit. The intuition, that sixth sense that had warned her of disaster so many times before, gripped her entirely. It had saved her in Tomsk and Irkutsk when the train was frozen, but what did it mean now? She recognized the feeling too well to ignore it.

She sat down quietly on her pillow, in the old Russian custom of relaxation before a trip. She took a deep breath but could not smell anything out of the ordinary. She listened carefully, the children playing and shouting, people passing, Michiko-san tripping lightly in the hall, but heard nothing unusual. She looked upward at the ceiling, and at her single hanging lamp with its flowered porcelain shade.

The only unfamiliar aspects of the entire scene that Tatiana could recognize were her trembling hands and her wildly racing pulse.

* * *

Earlier that morning Sanji Nakamura had gone downtown to the impressive red-brick and granite headquarters building of the Metropolitan Police Board, which stood near an outer moat of the Imperial Palace and overlooked Hibiya Park. There he had taken the examination for sergeant. He found it extremely difficult, but he was a good policeman, he had studied hard, and he expected to pass and be promoted. Besides, today marked the fourth time he had taken this particular examination. He felt it would be impossible for him to fail. If he had to take the exam one more time, it would be hard for him to stand the dishonor; however, he was confident he had done well.

He liked being a policeman in the ranks, but he earnestly coveted the promotion. After all, he was forty-seven years old and had been on the Tokyo force for twenty-three years, ever since his discharge from the army. He usually worked near his home in Honjo Ward, a dull, quiet, heavily populated area of many odors, where little happened to draw the attention of superiors.

He, his wife and four sons, lived close by the Dai Nippon Brewery, the Azumabashi bridge, and the Sumidagawa River which flowed under it. Sanji often drank the excellent beer that could be purchased in a corner of the landscaped garden fronting the Brewery. Admission to the garden cost ten sen, but Sanji had not been charged the entrance fee in fifteen years. It was not a bribe, only an act of friendship.

Now and then, Nakamura took his sons to the beer garden. Even Toji, the youngest, began to acquire a taste for beer.

All his sons were grown, and all were still at home. They simply could not afford to marry, or live somewhere else. There was no escape from the neighborhood smell of open drains, partially exposed sewers, and the stench of the river.

The elder three sons all worked at menial jobs. None of them had ever been able to pass the entrance examinations for any of the local universities, even though they had tried repeatedly. The competition for acceptance into such institutions as the Imperial University and others was so intense that only about one in twenty were admitted.

Many aspiring students went through this entrance exam hell, year after unsuccessful year. Their intense efforts were sometimes worth it. Admission to a good university just about guaranteed an attractive job with the government, or a large first-rate business establishment, therefore promising a lucrative and secure career for the rest of one's life. No one doubted that the testing procedures, though brutal, were impartial.

Toji passed on his first try, the sole Nakamura ever to have a chance at the fruits of higher learning. Sanji, a well-read man, took particular pride in his youngest son, and perhaps for that reason, drew closer to him than to the others.

Another, more subtle factor, might have been that they both wore uniforms—Toji the black serge of a student starting another term, and Sanji the clean white duck of a policeman. This morning, after the elder Nakamura had returned, the son had watched his father while he prepared with evident pride for his mid-day assignment at the Ryogokubashi Bridge. Of the five substantial bridges that crossed the Sumidagawa River, about every half mile on its way to Tokyo Bay, this was the middle one, where fireworks displays could best be seen on summer nights.

First, he wiped the foggy perspiration from his spectacles, then from his balding head. Second, he carefully polished his sword and scabbard with cloth and a small square of rice paper, constantly checking his efforts.

As if in a ritual, Mrs. Nakamura held out the parts of his simple yet immaculate white uniform—the trousers, the tunic with gold buttons, and the pith helmet. On the wall, in one corner of the room they were occupying, hung a mirror at face level. Sanji carefully avoided looking into it because this might be construed as an unmasculine gesture, especially embarrassing in front of his youngest son. When he was completely dressed, he strapped on his sword and picked up his white gloves, lantern, pencil, and notebook. At the outer door, he put on his military shoes.

Toji had to attend a meeting at the Tokyo Commercial University scheduled for one o'clock. The school was a couple of miles away. He would walk across the Ryogokubashi Bridge on the way, so he asked his father if he might accompany him. They made a pleasing contrast walking together, but people refrained from making comments as they passed. Everyone respected the police and knew they were not to be trifled with under any circumstances.

Father and son enjoyed discussing worldly matters, the man somewhat cynically, the boy with touches of idealism. One of their favorite topics concerned Japanese-American relationships. Toji had made a study of American history since the time of Perry's visit to Japan, and pursued a continuing interest in things American. His father, repeating what he often heard at meetings of army veterans, constantly took the view that Japan must fight America in the near future. They talked on the same general subject this morning.

Toji was nodding his head. "True, we need additional land, but I think we can be expansionist without being warlike. We must try to work through negotiation."

"Oh my son, *bushido*, the way of the warrior, teaches justice, and benevolence, but not negotiation. And, our country is gradually falling under control of the militarists."

"But, it does not mean there must be war."

"Eventually it will be a choice between war and revolution, and there isn't any doubt what the choice will be."

They crossed some train tracks, turned a corner to the right, and passed by Ryogoku Station. Smells emanating from the river intensified as they approached the large, wooden bridge. "Yes, my son, one day we must fight the Americans. They have been unkind to us. They are our natural enemies, more so than other foreigners."

"I hope not Father, because not everything foreign is bad. One day I should like to go to America for a visit. You know, my English professor is American, and I admire him. I think he is a good man."

"He has poisoned your mind."

"No, I have asked him questions. Their country is more progressive than ours. I am sure of it."

That was too much for the older man. He stopped on the approach to the bridge and looked at his son. "Do not speak of this to others. Remember, you are Japanese. You are descended from divine ancestors, and ruled by the Son of Heaven."

His son moved closer to him, so as to emphasize his point and avoid being overheard. "Father, I am proud to be Japanese, only I am sure some things in foreign countries are better."

Sanji turned away from the boy, and walked stiffly to the *koban*, or police box, at the end of the bridge. When the policeman standing inside saw him, he bowed slightly, handed him a large notebook and swaggered rapidly into Honjo Ward, saber swinging to and fro. Sanji checked the notebook for a moment, put it on a shelf in the "koban," and turned to his boy, who stood nearby. "I am glad you are a student, my son, for you have much to learn."

"Yes, Father."

Twenty or twenty-five minutes before, the skies had cleared. The paved approach to the bridge reflected the streaming rays of the sun. It was insufferably hot. Little pads of wetness appeared under Sanji's eyes, misting his glasses. He took out his watch, turning it a bit to view it better. He absent-mindedly wound it as he proclaimed to himself, "Noon, already noon."

For the majority of Japanese, exact time was relatively unimportant. This did not apply to railroad conductors, policemen, or students.

The younger Nakamura examined his own watch saying, "I believe the time is still at least three minutes before noon."

This irritated the elder Nakamura, who felt upset with his son anyway. "What makes you believe that your watch is accurate, and that mine is not?" Toji did not wish to antagonize, but he thought he must be truthful. "It is because, Father, my watch was manufactured in Switzerland."

* * *

As far back as he could remember, to the time when he was a young boy growing up on the farm, Hugh Riordan recalled only a few nights during which he had difficulty sleeping. A good night's rest could be counted on as an expected reward for a full day's work. Last night however, marked his first sleepless night since his service in the Marines. Certainly, he might have dozed a bit as morning approached, but thoughts of the Russian girl played havoc with his nerves, and kept him tossing, turning, and talking to himself.

Heise-san's house was located on higher ground, overlooking Tokyo, where night breezes often dissipated the warm air, making sleep fairly comfortable. This night, however, Riordan thought he had never known anything so unpleasant as this moist drenching heat. Wide awake, he mulled over its effects. It sweated the wallpaper off the walls of his room. It saturated writing tablets and newspapers. It rotted books and spread mold on shoes and clothing. Worst of all, his bedding was soaked with perspiration making rest even more difficult.

He arose early and went out into the garden. It looked like rain with dull overcast skies, but outside the air seemed drier and the birds were chirping. For some reason, even without any breeze, the smells of the remote city—cooking, sewage, and humanity—permeated the neighborhood.

September first. According to recorded Japanese tradition, he thought, *it should be a day of disagreeable events, one to be cautious about.*

After he took advantage of one of Heise-san's most precious possessions, the tiled shower, he felt better. He decided to visit Maruzen to buy some books. The maid whom he had hoped not to awaken, would not let him leave before she presented a Japanese breakfast on a black, lacquered tray. There was a large bowl of rice, a dish of grilled, salted fish, and a small bowl of squash with pickled cucumber. The ubiquitous pot of green tea stood alongside. Hugh thanked the maid profusely, grateful for her persistence—he was hungry.

Why had Tanya been so cold to him the night before? Why had she steadfastly refused to join him today, to celebrate his anniversary? Did the church services in Yokohama mean more to her than his love? No, he never had told her he loved her. Should he have? Or was she simply too tired after an exhausting and difficult day? He knew how Mrs. Armstong's stinginess must have irritated her. Perhaps he should have been more considerate, and not insisted so much.

But, he knew she liked him a great deal—or did she? Had she found some other interest? After all, he did hear she gave language lessons to other men in her room, but never to him. No, that was impossible. But, how about the married Japanese official who offered her a large diamond to marry him? He tortured himself with questions. Questions, and thoughts, questions, and answers, and none of the answers meant anything definite because they could all be wrong. And, what would their relationship be from now on? Did this mark the beginning of the end? What should he do?

His head ached with unsolved questions about this Russian girl he adored. His stomach, even though full, pained with such gnawing despair and doubt that he almost wished he had accepted the invitation to the opening of the Imperial Hotel. At least, it would have distracted his anguished thinking a bit.

By the time he approached Maruzen, he felt even more depressed. A misty rain had begun coming down, making the hot, muggy morning even worse. The dense crowds hardly appeared to notice the precipitation. Their faces were all set in one melancholy expression. No one even looked at him with the usual curiosity reserved for a foreigner. He almost missed the attitude of petty conspiracy that often followed him. Today, no one seemed to care.

Being something of an intellectual, Riordan greatly enjoyed Maruzen. Along with almost every piece of Japanese literature published, and hundreds of rare and out of print volumes, there were English and American magazines, phrasebooks, maps and guidebooks, calendars, postcards and stationery. An entire busy floor was devoted to books in foreign languages. This morning he wanted to find *Don Quixote* by Cervantes, in Spanish.

Even at this fairly early hour, the bookstore appeared crowded with people of all ages. The generally well-educated Japanese loved books, and were eager to read. Riordan had difficulty getting through the aisles. A tacit general agreement permitted you to glance over any book or books you liked, for as long as you wanted, or even to read it from cover to cover, provided you remained standing. If you sat down, or leaned against something for support, you were asked to leave. Poor but determined students often took advantage of this convention to get through an entire semester of studies without buying any textbooks. Many avid readers enjoyed the complete works of Dostoevsky or Tolstoy while remaining upright and motionless.

After some browsing, and finally making his purchase Hugh went for a stroll. He did not know what course of action to follow next. Perhaps, he should hop on a streetcar and barge in on Miss Tanya at the Matsunami Hotel. She might be in a better mood this morning. No, that would probably only embarrass her. What if he bought her an impressive present? No, she almost certainly would not accept it. Well, he usually paid for their luncheons, and dinners and theater tickets—but those were intangibles, according to her way of thinking. What should he do?

On one of the side streets he observed a bunch of beggars clustered near a willow tree. This surprised him, because the police had a policy of keeping them away from downtown Tokyo. He dropped a few one-sen pieces into the crooked outstretched hand of a sightless unfortunate.

A passing Englishman shouted, "I wouldn't touch them. I wouldn't go near them. They're lepers, you know."

Riordan had been so preoccupied in his thoughts he did not notice the awful shape of these wretches. Some of them had lost arms, or utilized ragged stumps which terminated in reddish, revolting knobs, like a bone on which a dog had been gnawing. A few without legs were pushed around by companions in better condition, on small, multiple-wheeled dollies. There were a number who had lost their facial features. Where a nose once had smelled the fragrance of blossoms, there were two elongated holes; where eyes once had feasted on the sight of Mount Fuji, there were two putrefying sockets.

One with the remnants of a nose, but lacking lips or teeth, whose body was covered with dirty sores and lice, approached the American professor extending his hands and gurgling pitifully.

Hugh, heeding the Englishman's warning, recoiled from the leper, at the same time tossing a couple of coins into his hand. The approaching apparition dropped them, shaking its hairless head, and stretching its arms wide as though to closely embrace him.

Hugh recognized the threat immediately. He turned and ran, heading for the Ginza, about five minutes away. He could hear the leper pursuing him. He speeded up, losing his straw hat. It flashed through his mind that back in 1917 he had won the one hundred yard dash at the Marine Base in Quantico, Virginia wearing spiked shoes on a cinder track. Today, he certainly ran faster.

When he finally reached the Ginza area, somewhat winded from his exertion, the leper was gone. Now the Japanese in his vicinity were staring at him, no doubt wondering why this crazy foreigner had been running down the street at top speed. A couple of policemen eyed him suspiciously, but said nothing.

Riordan felt shaken, tired, and depressed. His hat was gone. At least he still had his books. He was far too sweaty to entertain the slightest thought of calling on Miss Tanya, keeping her company for the train ride into Yokohama, and visiting the Peacocks. He sighed, grateful that his breath had returned, and beckoned a ricksha. Might as well splurge a little, and try to enjoy what definitely did not appear to be one of his better days. He told the driver, "Shinjuku."

A ride in a ricksha never failed to be a pleasant experience for Riordan, provided the driver did not try to cheat him when he alighted. He always enjoyed riding in the man-drawn carriages, delighted in watching the runner wearing his dark blue coat and tight trousers in a matching shade, with his large, round mushroom-shaped hat, that bobbed as he ran. These boys were really in shape, having seemingly indefatigable legs. Hugh understood that some of them ran sixty to seventy miles a day.

This particular conveyance was beautifully dark-lacquered with nickel-plated metal parts. Its large pneumatic tires looked practically new. He wondered if the story were true, as many believed, that this was not an ancient and peculiar Oriental vehicle, but an 1871 invention of an American missionary in Japan. No matter, the ride was refreshing and pleasurable, certainly the best part of his day so far.

Under most circumstances, so as not to be woefully over-charged, he would ask the driver on his infrequent ricksha trips, to stop close to his destination near a policeman. In case of argument over the charge, the Japanese police could be counted on by foreigners to intercede on their behalf and come up with a fair decision of what should be paid; a deter-mination the runner seldom disputed.

This morning, as the sun came out, Riordan did not care. The ride had been somewhat uphill a good part of the way. He paid what the ricksha-puller asked, without question, and an unexpected tip, too.

Once inside the house, he related his morning's activities to Professor Heise. He also told him about his misunderstand-ing with Miss Tanya the night before. Heise-san listened at-tentively. He genuinely admired Hugh, and he liked the Rus-sian girl, although he had met her on only two occasions. Deep down, the gruff old German believed he had a way with women.

"I think you should talk to her as soon as possible and apologize."

"But why should I apologize?" asked Hugh.

Heise lighted his pipe, clouding the air. "Because you took her for granted, or rather you took her company for granted."

"But, I thought she liked me."

"I think she does, nevertheless, you can never make a woman think you might be taking her for granted. What time is she leaving for Yokohama?"

"Around noon."

"Come, you don't have much time," he said checking the clock. "You can call her on the telephone. I'll get her hotel for you."

Heise knew the language far better than Hugh, so he stood a much better chance of getting through on the unreliable telephone network. Besides, he was quite accustomed to using this instrument, having had one in his home for years.

After a number of minutes, and much chattering in Japanese, he handed the receiver to Hugh. "Here, the Matsunami Hotel, they are calling her."

Hugh held the phone gingerly. He sort of wished Heise would leave the room. What should he say? He'd begin by apologizing and wishing her a good trip. (A loud squawking noise issued from the telephone.) "Hello. Hello!" he said. All he could hear were about a dozen garbled voices speaking in Japanese. They sounded quite distant. "I think we have lost the connection."

Heise grabbed the receiver, pouring forth a torrent of Japanese. He waited. He could not contact anyone. "I'm sorry. I cannot even reach an operator. The line is out of order. Did you hear Miss Lunskaya?"

"No, we lost the connection before she got on the phone."

"Yah, we had bad luck," said Heise relighting his pipe. "You know that phone. It's no use trying again until things get in order. Remember, you can tell her you tried to call."

"Yes," replied Hugh, "that's a good idea." He did not feel at all relieved. She could be leaving at the present moment—without him.

They went out onto the porch and gazed at the tiled roofs of houses marching like stepping stones down the hill in front of them, the damp heat clutching both men like a smothering hand. The sun blazed down, not a pleasant golden sun, but a white orb forcing its discomforting rays through a hazy overcast.

Hugh could see all the way into central Tokyo along the wide street that separated Heise's two houses. It was the only thoroughfare of any consequence around, and it ran all the way to the Imperial Palace. There were few people in the vicinity, no doubt because it was almost lunch time. Memory, pain, and yearning swept over him suddenly. Where was she now? Did she miss him?

"Ach, it is too hot out here. Let's go into the study," said Heise, heading for the door chuckling, "Only mad dogs and Englishmen enjoy this sort of thing."

When they entered the study Heise patted Hugh on the shoulder. "It is almost time for lunch. A fellow always feels better after he eats."

Under other circumstances, Riordan would have agreed. He was about to say something to Heise about Miss Tanya, when he stopped, sensing a difference in their surroundings. Then, with the instinctively attuned ear of a former farmboy, he knew. The sparrows in the garden—they had suddenly stopped chirping.

September 1, 11:58 A.M.

I don't know why I am so nervous, thought Tanya, as she sat on her large pillow, tense with listening, it must be the automobile ride with Monsieur Fuji.

She was still staring fixedly at her ceiling lamp with its

flowered porcelain shade, when it began to swing, back and forth. Her eyes bulged as she followed its movement in an ever-widening arc. She screamed the moment it hit the wall showering her with jagged pieces of broken china.

"Oh my god, the earthquake."

At first her pillow had cushioned her from the short initial tremor. Now, the vibrations were so strong her entire body shook. The inside wall of her room buckled with a crack. She heard things rattling, falling, shouts and yells of terror, and the building coming apart.

The floor kept lurching as she quickly crawled through shattered porcelain to her doorway, where she lay huddled in fear. A rumbling noise was getting louder by the second.

She turned over and crossed herself. "My God!" she said in her native Russian as terror took hold of her. The ceiling of her room began to rip open.

* * *

Both Major Faymonville and Captain Yoshida were in uniform, just before noon. The Japanese officer had slept until almost eleven, and though he was nursing a hangover, he seemed his usual polite self this morning. The American, forced to sleep in an overstuffed chair because Yoshida had passed out on his bed, had risen much earlier. He'd breakfasted, done some paper work, taken a walk, then finally returned to change into his best uniform for the banquet luncheon celebrating the formal opening of the Imperial Hotel.

"Thank you for the use of your shaving equipment," said Captain Yoshida, as he sat on the edge of the bed, sipping a Scotch and soda.

"Well, I hope you had some hot water."

"No," smiled Yoshida, "not a drop."

"I'll have to admit my bath wasn't hot either, only rather tepid."

"The simplest Japanese inn always has sufficient hot water for all its guests, and you know how we love to bathe in hot water."

"Yes, well I guess you've got me there," observed Faymonville stubbing out his cigarette. "Mr. Wright provided a bathtub for every room, but hot water is hard to come by."

"A Japanese architect would have made certain there was sufficient hot water."

"You're probably right," said Faymonville. Yoshida was beginning to irritate him again. He moved in front of his dresser to check his uniform in the mirror. "Damn this heat," he muttered. Then, turning toward Yoshida, he said, "I'll have to be going down to the luncheon now," and moved to the door. "Help yourself to the Scotch, Captain."

Yoshida lifted his glass, then stood up and smiled, saying "Thank you very much."

"Perhaps we can . . . " began the major, as the building heaved under his feet. He grabbed for the doorjamb. It writhed in his grasp. He tried to speak, but he felt as if all the wind had suddenly been knocked out of him.

Yoshida, though having difficulty keeping his balance, was standing. "Jishin," he proclaimed loudly. "We will now see the Imperial Hotel fall like a house of cards." His voice sounded as though he were talking under water.

"Let's get out of here," bellowed the American. The floor bucked wildly under his feet. The door rattled and shook. He pushed his body forward, flinging it open, and leaped through it.

"I prefer to finish my drink," said Yoshida smiling. "I am a true samurai." His words were lost in the distant roar.

Faymonville ran down the undulating hallway, bouncing from wall to wall.

* * *

Saburo Fuji drove carefully off the wider street and into the narrow alley in front of the Matsunami Hotel. It was crowded with people, carts, and many children at play. He sounded his horn authoritatively and delighted in seeing the awed and respectful stares his car evoked. Skillfully avoiding a telephone pole, he stopped at the small entranceway and shut off his motor. Immediately a large group of children surrounded his automobile. Fuji opened the door, and stepped down onto the alley.

He felt terribly hot in his woolen foreign suit, tie, and spats, and the thick dirt of the alleyway worried him; it might dull the finish of his car. He was irritated to see a group of children playing the ever-popular local version of the scissors-paper-stone game, instead of admiring his shiny vehicle. He made a tentative bid for attention by scattering a bunch of copper coins, but there was no scramble over this generosity. Gravely, each child picked up a coin, but they regarded Fuji with a wary and suspicious eye.

It must be my expensive English clothing, he thought, pushing through them, toward the entrance of Mademoiselle Lunskaya's hotel. A sudden swaying movement of the ground beneath his feet startled him.

"Earthquake," he said aloud, "not a bad one, I think."

The earth surged up, and dropped down, knocking him off his feet in the open entranceway. *The Catfish is really wiggling its tail,* he thought, trying to hold onto his glasses. He attempted to get inside the hotel but could only collapse against it. Everything shook and vibrated rapidly. The children were screaming in terrified bursts.

Is the disturbance subsiding? No, he felt a sudden jolt as though the whole building had met with a violent collision. Now there were more screams, the splintering of wood, and the crash of building materials. A cascade of tiles poured into the alley, some of them just missing Fuji's head. *Will they hit my automobile?* He shivered in fear, but could not move because the earth shook him even more than his terror.

Gradually the seismic waves seemed to lessen, although

the ground still shook. Pushing his glasses on more securely, with sheer will and determination, Fuji got up and ran to his car. He grasped the starter crank, working it furiously. It would not start. He hardly noticed the injured and dying, in the brown pall of dust that clouded and thickened the air. He saw only the gleaming black body, as yet unscathed.

At last the motor caught. He jumped in and raced the engine, mistakenly throwing the car into reverse. It lurched backward, smashing against a leaning telephone pole. Fuji hoped only the bumper was damaged. It could easily be straightened.

He shifted into forward gear, and drove wildly toward the turn that would bring him to the main street. His motorcar smashed a cart, bounced over, and brushed aside bodies, both living and dead. He tried to swing his automobile sharply right, to negotiate the acute turn, but he could not. Something must have jammed the steering mechanism.

He stopped, jumped out, and ran around the stricken vehicle like a man possessed. A shock-wave knocked him against a front fender. Momentarily stunned, he could hear the cracking and tearing of the closely packed houses, and the rattling and crashing inside them.

I must save my motorcar, he thought wildly. *There, there is the trouble!* Large pieces of a cart and the body of a child were jammed between the fender and the right front wheel. Frantically, he clutched at the wooden pieces, pulling some free and breaking others. He flung them aside.

The child, a rather plump girl, hung limply, her legs and lower body firmly wedged at the very top of the wheel. Fuji pulled her head to no avail. He tried to drag her out by the armpits, exerting extra leverage by bracing his leg against the wheel. She wouldn't budge. He pushed from the front, hoping she might slide down the rear of the tire. This didn't work either.

Now in a towering, frightened rage, he crouched down,

and grabbed one of the dangling arms, yanking with all his strength. When nothing happened, he twisted and turned until it snapped. He pulled savagely. With a jerk, the arm came out of its sleeve.

Saburo Fuji straightened up, staring dumbly at the torn limb. He held it up for examination not seeming to know what it was, or how he happened to be holding it. With his free hand, he adjusted his thick glasses, but he was still too nearsighted to notice the telephone pole as it began to fall toward him.

*　*　*

Klavdia stopped a little way from the Morozovs' building. Was she dizzy because of the sun's heat? Her body swayed. No, the ground itself was moving. The unexpected pulsations under her feet startled her. She had difficulty standing.

Suddenly the undulating earth caused her to lose balance. She fell heavily on her knees and face, tearing the lower part of her dress. Shock after shock ripped through the ground, driving her down until she was prostrate; her arms outstretched, embracing a planet gone mad.

She wanted to get up, but she couldn't. The motion, instead of decreasing, grew wilder. All she could do was let out a long wailing moan, and dig her nails into the earth. After about a minute, the vibrations stopped momentarily. She was about to lift her head when the ground again leapt with tremendous force, as if to throw her body into the air.

Klavdia Davidovna began wailing again. Her knees and chin were pounded raw against the convulsing ground. Above the mounting roar, and closer now, came the sound of an enormous crash. Her upper body was showered with splinters of wood and bits of masonry. All around people were screaming in anguish. She dug her fingers more deeply into the earth.

For the next few minutes, she lay pinned to the ground by the severe undulations. Human screeches and cries tore at the girl's soul. Yet, she could not raise her head to see from where they came. She continued to moan, hardly conscious of the roar that had become part of her world.

*   *   *

Yes, it must be this sweltering heat, Yamamoto thought, *unbearable even for Tokyo.* He considered removing his suit-coat, but that would be "bad form" as the English said, especially since he was an educated, though not wealthy, man of position. Instead, he checked his watch. It read 11:58. He should be home, with all his presents by half-past twelve, then he could relax and cool off.

Or at least that was his plan. Fate, along with the pent up stresses within the earth dictated that events would take a different course. Jumping and swaying, the tram began lurching from side to side. Riders were flung back and forth in their seats and hurled into the aisle.

Yamamoto lay under three or four shouting, struggling persons, still clutching his packages.

The tracks spread apart as the ties between them cracked. The car bounced up and down, crossed over the street and crashed into a telephone pole, splitting in half.

Yoshinari Yamamoto and many others were dumped onto the pavement. Although stunned, and held down by two unconscious people on top of him, he could hear cries and screams and the awful rumbling of what he now realized was the earthquake. He no longer thought of the presents for his loved ones. Instead, there under the broken tram, he was only concerned about the safety of his precious family. Over and over in his mind flashed the terror-stricken faces of Hana and the children.

Now, crackling and hissing, a new sound intruded on his private horror. He searched for its source. There, two feet from his head and to the left lay a broken power line sizzling in a shallow pool of water.

*   *   *

Raita Kanoh's head ached, awfully. It was almost noon, and he still languished naked on the futon of Miss Moonlit Water. The hostess and maids had brought him to her apartment after Miss Blooming Blossom was taken away to receive medical attention. Miss Moonlit Water had proven a proficient substitute.

Usually, guests were expected to leave earlier in the morning. Kanoh, however, had drunk so much saké and expended so much energy that the maids found it impossible to awaken him. Miss Moonlit Water had already been to the hairdresser, and the bath-house. She sat in front of her mirror, applying makeup, pointedly ignoring the open-eyed customs official. Never had a guest stayed so long, it was contrary to Yoshiwara etiquette.

Kanoh's behavior did not go unnoticed by the brothel keeper. He took it into consideration when making out the bill. Too much wine last night, with the anticipation of a huge bill this morning, had caused his terrible headache. The bill was presented to him by a charming little attendant, who bowed and retreated quickly, before he could read the figures.

These were daintily inscribed with great detail on a long roll of thin white paper. The total almost shocked him out of his hangover. It listed the expected charge for the oiran, the maids' and attendant's services, the geisha, the jester, the food and wine; along with a bunch of vague extras including, in his case, emergency medical fees. Added to this already considerable amount were wages of various unseen workers: guards, clean-up people, upstairs and downstairs men, overseers, and many others. It was the largest bill Kanoh had ever run up. He lay there stunned, still watching Miss Moonlit Water.

With a freshly-washed face, the girl stared into a cluster of mirrors, studying her features. Already she had applied a base of camellia oil, and pink undercoating. Now, she used a flat brush to cover everything with a mask of thick, white, liquid powder, until no evidence of her own skin remained. She looked like carved ivory.

Suddenly, just as she began to rouge her cheeks, the house leaped to one side, and then back again. Miss Moonlit Water was knocked off her knees and onto her side. The building kept jumping. Her mirrors came crashing down, cutting her ankles savagely. She screamed and screamed, trying to get up, but the wild swaying made it impossible.

Kanoh, reclining on the thick futon, was somewhat insulated from the shock waves. He rolled over on his side, sucking in his breath when plaster came down from the ceiling. He stared at his bleeding concubine and said, "Ah, jishin."

During a slight pause in the massive tremors, Miss Moonlit Water stood up and headed for the door. She was knocked off her feet, as an invisible fist pushed the Customs Official deep into the futon shaking him violently at the same time. The residents of the brothel cried and shrieked. In the background Kanoh heard a mighty roar.

After a few minutes, the roar had almost disappeared as the vibrations diminished. Miss Moonlit Water ran out, leaving a trail of blood.

Kanoh rose, quickly put on his shorts, gray yukata, and grabbed his clothes and shoes in the dressing room. Large undulations again seized the building, which now leaned at a dangerous angle. The floors and walls had broken apart.

As Raita Kanoh made his way down the twisted stairs, he noticed that the house appeared deserted. *Perhaps*, he thought, *the earthquake was an act of providence.* He might well be able to leave without paying his bill.

* * *

Shimaku Suzuki, her mother and the maid were seated at a table in the café on the fourth floor of Mitsukoshi waiting for their luncheon to be served. They seemed more relaxed than many of the other Japanese patrons who perched rather stiffly on the unfamiliar Western dining chairs. Accustomed to Western style furniture in certain rooms of their home the three women were as gracefully positioned around the table as they would have been during a formal tea ceremony.

Mrs. Suzuki was reassuring her daughter that she would be, when the time came, a good wife. "You are a very sweet girl, you have a good disposition, your father says you are easy to manage, and do not tell lies without a good reason. He says it's the husband who must form the character of the wife."

Shimaku, began to look, with particular interest, at a pretty foreign lady wearing a pink hat. She remembered that Tanya wore them often. She loved her Russian friend, and tried to adopt some of her Western ways, but, like generations of Japanese women, who never covered their heads, she disliked hats.

"A wife is plain paper," her mother continued, "a husband takes his brush and writes on it what he will."

Shimaku nodded, inwardly unconvinced. The idea of being a piece of paper waiting to be written on disturbed her deep-seated, though heavily-veiled, wish for independence. She reached for her tea cup but it jumped away from her hand. The saucers and cups hopped about the table like so many frogs. The ladies stared at them in disbelief. One pair crashed to the floor.

"Jishin," exclaimed Mrs. Suzuki. Shouts and cries rang throughout the café as the building began to dance. Shimaku and her maid were knocked off their chairs. Mrs. Suzuki dived under the table and pulled the girls close to her. She wrapped her arms around Shimaku. The maid hugged both of them and they remained there vibrating for what seemed like hours, listening to screams and the chaotic roar of much of downtown Tokyo falling apart.

In a while, the shaking became less severe. Mrs. Suzuki

crawled out and dragged the terrified girls from their protective shelter. Pieces of shattered plaster and crockery lay all around. Some tables and chairs had splintered, but surprisingly few people seemed to be seriously hurt. An ominous cloud of smoke however, billowed from the kitchen area.

"Come," shouted Mrs. Suzuki, "we must get out." Others too were yelling in the confusion.

They ran, with short steps, as quickly as their tight fitting kimonos would allow them. "This way to the stairs," urged Mrs. Suzuki. Now they became part of a milling, actively pushing crowd.

A man, dressed in a Western suit and tie, obviously a Mitsukoshi executive, kept admonishing the crowd, with a broad smile telling them not to rush—there was no danger, the building would remain standing because it was strongly built, and there was a main staircase "just ahead."

Suddenly, from where he indicated, "just ahead," came a muffled crash, screams and a few piercing shrieks. Shimaku, her mother and maid joined hands, so as not to be separated. Word came back to them rapidly and they tightened their grips on each other out of fear.

The stairs were no longer there.

Paula's hands were occupied with washing the china, but her mind was elsewhere. Slowly, almost dreamily, she carefully washed each plate, cup and saucer. They were quite beautiful, reflecting another example of the wealth and class of the people she served.

The Peacocks and Keefes had left earlier in the morning and by now had probably visited the Mokuzu Kozan Porcelain Works. She hoped they had enjoyed it.

As she worked she hummed an old Russian folk song, "Down Along the Mother Volga." *How good it is*, she thought, *to be appreciated*. She still felt a glow from Frederick Keefe's compliment about her blini. *He is so kind*, she thought, *but of course so are all the people invited to the Peacocks'*.

Today she could take as much time as she wanted with her chores, for even Ivan was off on an errand to downtown Yokohama. Even so, she began to hurry just a bit so she could leave the hot kitchen and work in a cooler part of the large house.

She wondered what Zoya Semionovna was doing today. Her duties probably wouldn't be occupying her on Saturday. It was painful to think of her working for someone else, and Paula knew how she must miss Gee Gee and Nanette.

How lucky she and Ivan were not to have the worry about a new employer, in fact it would be impossible for her to imagine being a part of any other family.

From past experience Paula had decided few things in life were or could be permanent. Her exposure, even for a short time, to the Revolution in her native Russia had taught her that money, property, even social standing could vanish or be destroyed overnight. People and their sense of devotion and duty were all that really mattered. Those who could, helped one another. Adversity had made many friendships stronger and more binding than family ties.

Though her thoughts were far away, she was still acutely aware of the smothering heat. She worked slowly, but she still was quite wet with perspiration. Finally the dishes were finished and carefully put away. She longed to put her feet up and relax with a cup of tea, it was nearly time for lunch, or Tiffin as the Peacocks called it. But no, she decided, her dusting must be done and the bedrooms tidied before she could think of relaxing or eating.

As she passed from the stifling air of the kitchen into the hallway leading to the bedrooms at the back of the house, there was no change in temperature. It was almost always cooler here where the breezes swept up the Bluff from Tokyo Bay. But, there seemed to be no breeze at all.

The bedrooms were no cooler and as she made the last bed she noticed again that the sheets felt wet and clingy. How muggy it was! *The first of September,* she thought. In Russia the days would be getting shorter and the air cooler with the delightful wine-like fragrance that only the air of a northern country could have.

Finally, her cleaning finished, she thought of having lunch. Perhaps she'd make some lemonade; the Peacocks and their guests would certainly enjoy it whenever they returned. She took one last look around the room to make sure she hadn't forgotten anything. Satisfied, she moved toward the door. Suddenly, the floor moved beneath her. For a fraction of a second she thought she might be faint from the heat, but then with an almost detached horror she realized what it was—the earthquake!

She was knocked to the floor as if by a giant's fist. She lay on her back, stunned, and could only watch, as the walls and ceiling folded in upon her as if in slow motion. There seemed to be a moment of trembling hesitation until everything crashed into the basement.

The indescribable pain never reached its climax in her brain, only a single crystal clear thought floated to the forefront of her mind. *It has been good, I regret nothing,* then the darkness became absolute.

*　　*　　*

Ann Keefe, Odylia, and Herbert Peacock sat sipping wine around a table in the bar of Yokohama's Belmont Hotel. Even though the Belmont was two blocks from Tokyo Bay and somewhat less imposing than the Oriental Palace or the Grand Hotel, the Keefes usually stayed there because of its excellent food.

"Oh I'm so glad we decided to have tiffin here," said Odylia. "We enjoyed it so much during your last visit."

"It always is quite good," agreed Ann. "I do hope you won't mind waiting while Freddie has his tub."

"Not at all," replied Herbert. "This wine is excellent, and

we both know how Freddie can't seem to tolerate much heat."

"It's the humidity that's so awful," observed Odylia fanning herself. "I think we all envy his quick tub."

"Well, it's bound to be a bit cooler in the dining room," comforted Herbert. The grandfather clock near the entrance to the dining area began to chime. Peacock took his gold watch from his vest and checked it. "I say, their clock is a bit fast." While he absently wound his watch, he noticed the assistant manager, an old friend, standing in the dining room, wearing a red carnation boutonniere. Herbert loved carnations. *No doubt fresh from the greenhouse,* he thought.

"Oh 'Erber," began Odylia, "this wine . . . " Her eyes widened as she felt a slow, feeble, yet definite movement, beneath and all around her.

"Good God!" exclaimed Peacock, feeling the hotel lurch.

There was a single scream from the dining room. He looked toward its source in time to see the assistant manager buried under a huge crystal chandelier.

Peacock wrenched his chair backward over the parquet floor and sprang to his feet grabbing Odylia by the arm. "It's the earthquake!"

Anne sat transfixed, too terrified to move. Odylia was half out of her chair when the upper floors came down upon them.

* * *

Frederick Keefe stretched out in the steaming water, thoroughly enjoying his bath. *Nothing like a hot tub,* he thought, *No matter how short the break, how elusive but sacred is the chance to relax.*

He loved these trips to Japan, but how he detested its hot humid weather. He'd perspired so heavily during the tour of the porcelain factory in Yokohama, both his shirt and jacket were soaked through. Excusing himself, and leaving Ann in the company of Herbert and Odylia downstairs, he'd gone off to refresh himself.

They understood, even admired his meticulous habits, and his aversion to perspiration. They'd drink some wine while he "dashed" to the third floor, had a "quick tub," and changed. He'd join them for tiffin in a few minutes.

Yes, he was hungry even after Paula's huge breakfast. *The food here at the Belmont is wonderful even with American management, but one simply must be clean. Mustn't forget the Bay Rum.*

The bathtub was somewhat short for him. He couldn't see his flat stomach of which he was justly proud. *Never seem to gain weight no matter what I eat.* His toes gripped the top of the tub. How he'd always hated his skinny legs. Suddenly, the bathtub and his feet began to vibrate. A progression of tiny waves marched across the water, lapping against his chin. He stared, "Good God," he exclaimed, "the quake!" Like a plunging curtain, the outer wall dropped out of sight, revealing the bright water of Tokyo Bay. Before Frederick Keefe could even begin to scream, he and his bathtub were propelled out into the sunlight.

* * *

Toshi Sugawara sat quietly in the streetcar, smiling while his friend Kojuro Nabashima, tried to find flaws in his newly found Christian beliefs.

"But Toshi, as I have said, Buddhism accepts both good and bad. There is no conflict."

"And how about Shinto?"

"Yes, we have Shinto," said Nabashima becoming enthused, "how else could we explain our origins and our continued existence as a divine country. We need only look into our souls to know the emperor is a direct descendant of the Sun Goddess. It logically follows that his rights are divine and his reign must be absolute."

Sugawara noticed they were only a short distance from their stop. "That was well put Kojuro, but there is conflict between Buddhism and Shinto. Shinto teaches the present is the most desirable and wonderful of worlds, and that the next world is a bad place, cruel and terribly evil."

"I don't feel any conflict."

"I know, old friend, but I do. Buddhism says this world is a foul thing, and the next will be fine and wonderful."

Most of the other passengers stood up as their tram came to a halt near Asakusa Park. Some of them stared at the two young men in heated discussion, though they could not understand them because they spoke English.

When they stepped off the car, Nabashima said, "Ah, but Christians too have conflict, I have heard. They believe one thing and do another."

"How is that?"

"They talk of peace on earth and brotherly love, and make awful wars on each other, and on people who have skin of another color. Does that follow what they call the golden . . . the golden . . . "

"The golden rule?"

"Yes, the golden rule."

Sugawara groped for an answer as they strolled leisurely up the long narrow entrance lane into Asakusa Park. As they entered, they could see the gilded crests of the Asakusa Temple glinting in the sun, and near the end of the lane the gateway to the Kannon Temple. Today the thoroughfare was so thronged with people that the scraping of hundreds of wooden clogs, or *geta,* on its flagstone surface made conversation difficult.

"We Christians are not without sin."

"What did you say?" asked Nabashima.

"Sin . . . we are not without sin," he said in a louder voice.

"Sin," repeated Kojuro, "what is this . . ." but his words emerged in a strange tremolo.

The earth rippled, then jumped. Large slabs of flagstone

leaped into the air. Everyone was knocked off his feet, and some of the red-brick shops that flanked the lane collapsed with a crash. Stones, bricks and tiles flew into the flattened crowd, killing some and gashing many more.

Unscathed, the two friends lay next to each other, their hands clutched at the rippling earth. Then, another terrific shock caused more shops to fall, and another lethal rain of debris. Still, the pair remained unhurt in what had become a pathway of death.

Although he could not look up to see her, a woman lay only two feet to Toshi's left; her head partially severed by a broken tile. She was barely alive, and bleeding horribly.

In a little while, the undulations became slower but more severe. Toshi Sugawara felt a new sensation accompanied by a deep breaking sound, the flagstone slab on which he lay seemed to be inching forward. He raised his head. His friend, who was somewhat behind him and to his right, did so too.

The ground had cracked open in many places. Toshi looked down and recoiled in terror. He stared down into a chasm that appeared bottomless. The slab beneath him was balanced precariously on the edge of this yawning gap, and slowly moving toward it. Quickly, Nabashima rolled over and managed to grab his friends legs.

*   *   *

Sanji Nakamura watched as his son, Toji, started across Ryogokubashi Bridge. *He is a fine son*, he thought, *I'm very proud of him.*

While returning to the police box, he took out his watch and with a slight smile, turned it back a couple of minutes. Unknown to him, his venerable time-piece now showed the exact time, 58 minutes and 46 seconds past 11:00 A.M.

"Jishin," he said when the ground began to vibrate. He grabbed at the shelf-lined wall as a smashing shock moved the police box, and almost knocked it down. Everything on the shelves fell, but Nakamura held on with one hand, while clutching his glasses with the other. He shoved the lenses forcefully against his head. If they broke, he'd be almost blind.

There were shouts and shrieks in the distance, and a terrified scream from the bridge. A muffled explosion erupted nearby.

Nakamura, gathering all his strength, dragged himself to the entrance just as a massive shock tipped the police box over on its front, blocking the doorway. Unhurt, he fought the wild motion, managing to pull his body upward, partially out of the window, which was now on top of the toppled police box.

Facing away from the bridge he could see fallen houses, gateways demolished, and tumbling walls. Ryogokubashi creaked and groaned. He turned and watched as it writhed and jerked, convulsing like the back of a skewered dragon, tossing people in the air.

For some reason, Nakamura couldn't get all the way out of the opening. *I must help those people.* He beat his hands on the window sash, yelling in frustration, then realized it was his sword wedged across the outlet, that prevented his escape. He dropped back through the window, pressed the scabbard against his body and popped out again and onto the bridge.

The tremors, though still powerful, had lessened. No matter where he looked he saw chaos and destruction. Buildings were nothing but heaps of rubble covering unseen victims who he could hear moaning pitifully. There was so much for him to do he stood momentarily stunned not knowing where to begin.

Ryogokubashi seemed relatively undamaged. *It must have rolled with the shocks,* he surmised. He wondered if Toji had gotten across the bridge before the earthquake hit.

A burning boat floating unattended on the river caught

his eye. He adjusted his glasses, to make sure he could see as clearly as possible.

In the water, beyond the burning boat, he could make out a body that appeared to be dressed in the dark uniform of a university student.

*   *   *

Yes, Riordan was sure of it, the sparrows in the garden had stopped chirping. The unexpected silence was eerie, and he felt a damp flush on his face. When the quiet was broken by the wild cry of a pheasant, he grabbed Heise's arm and yelled, "Come on!"

The German Professor had no time to think as Hugh pulled him out the door. The stairs were already buckling as they dove off them and into the garden, rolling away from the house. Both of them came to a stop, face down, near the Mulberry bushes. Even as their bodies bounced on the rippling carpet of grass, they could hear a massive roar from downtown Tokyo.

"Lieb Gott," yelled Heise gasping, "das jishin!"

Hugh struggled to get up so he could see into the city.

"Another shock like that and there won't be . . ." he paused as the distant pheasant cried again "much left of . . ." Suddenly, he was thrown onto his back. He tried to turn toward his friend. Near his face and throughout the garden, he could see groups of sparrows lying in strange positions, where they had fallen after being knocked out of the bushes.

An ominous crash caused both men to cover their heads with their arms. They could hear the house ripping apart. The shaking and cracking ground was accompanied by shock reverberations, that sounded as distinct and menacing as boom guns.

Hugh thought of Tatiana. Where was she? *Oh Lord, I hope she's safe.* Shock followed shock. The awful roar of the huge city tumbling down became louder by the second. A sickening fear gripped his guts. She was somewhere inside that terrible chaos.

September 1, Noon

Hugh managed to roll toward Heise, who winked, and gave him a slight reassuring wave of his hand. The American rose up, trying to check the condition of their house. Once more the pheasant cried, this time with a special wildness. Again they were smashed to earth by a dreadful concussion; Riordan pinning a couple of the unfortunate sparrows under his chest. He was unable to move as the shocks continued.

Suddenly, the second floor master-bedroom and study, directly over the front porch, seemed to explode with a thunderous crack. Some of it dropped away from the rest of the house and landed in the garden. Luckily, the jagged pieces missed the prone figures on the ground.

Hugh got to his knees when he felt the tremors lessening. He scarcely noticed the mess on his white shirt from the birds. Unsteadily, he stood up, then gave a hand to his German friend. Neither of them spoke for a few moments.

Most of the house remained standing, but the front was badly damaged. They could hardly see down into the city. Though it was some four miles away, usually a clear view of midtown Tokyo could be had from their vantage point. But now, even the glaring sun couldn't penetrate the grayish-yellow cloud overlaying the city. Some of the houses that had so gracefully terraced the hill had been severely damaged.

"Ach," Heise grunted, throwing up his hands and calling out for the maid. Both turned and ran to their stricken dwelling.

"Goko-san! Goko-san!" Riordan called as they approached the back of the house which appeared intact.

"She should be back here," said Heise.

They burst through the screen-door into the kitchen. "Goko-san, Goko-san!" yelled Heise. But, they heard no answer. The lunch which she had prepared for them lay scattered across the floor.

The two men rushed through the first floor rooms, but she wasn't there. "Goko-san, Goko-san!"

Then a soft, muffled voice called, "Herr Heise, Herr . . . "

They stood before a barrier of what seemed to be the porch roof covered with bits of cracked plaster and splintered wood. Underneath this lay Goko-san, now beginning to sob in fear.

"Are you hurt?" Heise called to her.

"No," she replied," I do not think so."

Hugh dropped to his knees and tried to peer beneath the wreckage. The roof section rested about two feet from the floor. "Where are you, can you see me?"

"Under the table, under the table."

"Can you move at all?"

"Hai, a little."

"Ach, good," grunted Heise, "the table must protect her."

"Don't worry," Riordan reassured her, "we're going to get you out." He stood up and grasped Heise's arm. "Come on, we have to get around to the front."

As they reached the collapsed porch outside, a substantial aftershock rattled the ground causing the German professor to stumble and fall. "Bitte, please, no more," he gasped. When it had subsided, they began clearing the smaller debris off the fallen roof section.

"Goko-san, are you still O.K.?" called Riordan.

"Hai, O.K."

"Can you see any light?"

"Hai, but much dust."

The American turned to Heise, "We may have to raise it up, but we need to know her position exactly."

"Yah, maybe from her voice," the German suggested. "We need to keep her talking constantly."

"Yes," agreed Riordan, then he brightened—"Goko-san, sing Kimigayo," he said, referring to the Japanese national anthem. There was a slight pause, then a tremulous melody.

"A thousand years of happy reign be there; rule on, my lord, till what are pebbles now, by age united to mighty rocks shall grow, whose venerable sides the moss doth line," sang Goko-san.

"Ach, good Goko-san. Again, sing it again," encouraged Heise.

Riordan, now laying with his head nearly under the roof edge, exclaimed, "I can see you!" He squirmed back out and told Heise, "we'll have to raise it up to get her out." He thought for a moment. "Do you think we can lift it?"

"No—we need a lever," responded Heise.

A strong section of planking from the fallen second story was found. Using the porch deck as a fulcrum they carefully raised the corner of the roof. "Goko-san, can you make it now?" gasped Hugh, straining with effort.

They heard a bit of scraping and suddenly she was out scampering to her feet.

The men released their hold on the makeshift lever and the roof settled back again with a whump!

"Arigato, arigato," she bowed deeply. Both professors resisted the impulse to touch her reassuringly, and bowed deeply in return.

Suddenly a man's voice interrupted their celebration. Yelling in Japanese, it came from the nearby street, the one that went in a straight line all the way to the Imperial Palace. He sounded as though he were in great difficulty. They all spotted him at the same time.

He was pulling a low two-wheeled cart filled with slosh-

ing night-soil toward the stricken city. Although he ran quite
rapidly, his vehicle must have been overloaded, and the pitch
of the hill made it roll faster than he could run. With an
anguished shout, he lost control, his burden tipping forward
as he fell to the street. He still gripped the handrails, but as
they struck the pavement the cart jolted to a halt spilling its
contents over him.

Apparently uninjured, he sat in the middle of the thoroughfare covered with human excrement, spitting vigorously.

Maybe it was a nervous reaction to their close brush with
death; or perhaps they realized they had experienced one of
natures most awesome cataclysms—whatever the reason, they
couldn't stop laughing at this unlucky man trying to regain
his feet in a pool of slippery dung.

Finally, just when he'd managed to stand, a policeman ran
toward him, stepping warily, and began to reprimand him
severely. He backed away, but the officer kept after him, yelling and gesturing at the overturned cart and the attendant
mess. They could not hear what was said, but the policeman
made his points forcefully apparent by his frantic movements.

They gasped when he drew his sword, and surveyed his
hapless victim. Had he lost his head? Would he kill the poor
man? No, he only began whacking the pitiful figure on the
seat with the flat of his blade. The cart-puller ran down the
street, the officer close behind repeatedly batting him across
the buttocks.

"They're mad," said Hugh, "the whole area has blown up
and they're worried about one spilled cart."

"Yah," agreed Heise, "and we may go crazy with them."

They shaded their eyes, straining to see deep into Tokyo,
or where Tokyo should have been. Hugh thought again of
Tatiana. *Oh, God, I hope she's safe.*

Thick smoke rose ominously above the land obscuring the
city with a murky pall. While they watched, the veil of smoke
turned from yellow to brown to black.

Under their feet, the earth still trembled. Now, an ever increasing number of well-defined smoke columns swirled upward to join the filthy clouds hanging over the doomed city. The wind rose and they could see tiny flames flickering, and beginning to spread.

"Gotter Dammerung," whispered Heise.

"Yes," observed Riordan with tears in his eyes, "and it's only the beginning." He touched the German professor's shoulder, "I must go and find her."

Heise looked at his friend pensively, but only for a moment. He knew it would be useless to point out that he could very well be killed while searching for the Russian girl. "Yah, Fraulein Tanya! Yah, of course you must go."

About fifteen minutes later, Riordan was striding down the road leading in to Tokyo. He wore a straw hat, a knapsack over his white shirt, two canteens of water with lemon juice added, comfortable trousers, stout shoes topped with leather gaiters reaching almost to the knee and a walking stick in his gloved hands.

He recalled utilizing many of these same items last July when he ascended Mount Fuji. He had witnessed one of the most beautiful sights on earth, sunrise from the top of Mount Fuji.

A brief, smoky blast of wind jarred him into reality, as he tapped along with his stick. Through the smoke he could tell the fires had spread. And, she must be somewhere in that ever widening cauldron.

From the summit of Mount Fuji he had felt close to heaven. Today, he realized, he'd be much closer to hell.

*   *   *

As he and his bathtub were propelled from the third floor toward the Bay, Frederick Keefe's toes relaxed their grip on the top of the tub and he partially sat up. The bright sunlight dazzled him. His eyes were almost closed when the tub crashed through the roof of a parked limousine and settled into the back seat.

The entire Belmont Hotel had been smashed down only a split second before.

*   *   *

Klavdia Davidovna Appfelbaum sat on the ground with her arms clasped around her knees, crying, and rocking back and forth. Her mother had rocked her when she was a child. She needed to be comforted now too.

When the vagaries of life and her pregnancy had become too much for her, she had made up her mind to commit suicide. Now, as her present circumstances became a fiery holocaust, destroying her home and friends, she became numbed. Her eyes saw, but her brain did not fully realize.

Klavdia did not hear the shouts and screams, the snap of flames nor the crash of buildings coming down. She did not object even when a fireman picked her up and carried her further away from the fires. She simply kept rocking, in his arms, and then on the ground. He said something kindly, but she did not acknowledge his words. Her rocking however, became less pronounced, then stopped altogether. She rose to her feet and began to walk, now with a purpose. *I must get to the bridge. Midori recommended the bridge over the train line at Shinjuku.*

Klavdia knew there were both streetcar and train stations at Ueno Park, Tokyo's largest and most beautiful. It was close and she loved it there. Today, there seemed to be vast throngs of people going through the entrance, some carrying or pulling carts with household goods, which surprised her, as did the fact that her knees and her chin hurt, and that her hands were lacerated.

Never mind, there was Shinobazu Pond, with many lotus blossoms still to be seen, even if it were a bit late in the season. Surprisingly, hardly anyone else sat down to admire the lotus blossoms, and the crowd, though larger than she'd ever remembered it, did not exude its usual joyousness.

A light breeze smelled of smoke, which she found curious. *I must visit the zoo. I love to watch the monkeys.*

The booming of the Time Bell brought her to her senses. Although she did not have one, she saw people checking their watches to make sure they registered one o'clock. *One o'clock. I must get to the bridge at Shinjuku, as Midori has advised. She is such a dear friend.*

The Ueno railroad station at the southeastern end of the park was only a short walk from her bench near the pond. She expected large crowds, but there was hardly anyone, and the station was closed. A few deserted streetcars and one train stood upright, but obviously off the tracks. Many of the rails were twisted into grotesque, random patterns and sprung off their ties. A frantic Klavdia quickly realized there would be no ride to Shinjuku today.

Immediately, she felt lost. Despair gradually took control of her and her body shook with sobs. Taking her life by jumping from the railroad bridge seemed quite simple. She even had a strong sash around her waist to tie her legs together as Midori had recommended. She must find another way.

Ueno Park was located in one of the highest parts of the city. Klavdia looked in a generally southern direction toward the location of Ryogokubashi, the large bridge over the Sumidagawa River that Midori had recommended as an alternative site for taking one's own life. It wasn't very far, and she had been there twice with Tanya to enjoy colorful displays of fireworks. It was downtown, adjoining Asakusa Ward, the lively ward with its large amusement park, and Honjo Ward.

The original city of Tokyo was divided informally by the wide and swift Sumidagawa River, which flowed from north to south, into Tokyo Bay. The land rises to a couple of hundred feet above sea level on the western side, often called

Professor Hugh Riordan (1922). *(left)*
Tatiana in the Nabashima family ceremonial kimono. *(right)*

Professor Hugh Riordan *(far left)* with faculty members of the Tokyo
Imperial University. Seated at the table are Dr. and Mrs. Albert Einstein.

Victims caught in a tidal pool near the Yoshiwara district—killed by the heat of the water that they entered in hopes of surviving the fires.

The Kannon Temple in Asakusa—untouched by fires though everything surrounding it was consumed in the flames.

Refugees at the site of the former Honjo Army Clothing Depot.

The Clothing Depot after the tornado of fire had hit—35,000 died.

Mitsukoshi Department Store, Nihonbashi—this structure held during the quake, but succumbed to fire later.

The Maruzen bookstore, which withstood the earthquake but not the subsequent fires.

Ryogoku Sumo arena.

The Nagai Building, Marunouchi—more than two hundred people were buried alive here when what was a four-story structure suddenly became a two-story one.

Refugees trying to escape Tokyo by train; many of the people on top of the cars were swept off and killed.

A train burned at Shimbashi Station.

The Yokohama Specie Bank, where bank officers were found dead from the heat in the bank vault where they had unwisely taken refuge to avoid the fires.

Smoke rising from the fires of central Tokyo as seen from Riordan's home in Shinjuku.

Prince Regent Hirohito along with the Chief of Metropolitan Police, Governor of Tokyo, Minister of House Affairs, Baron Goto, and General Fukuda.

The prince regent surveying the damage on horseback.

Yamate, or uptown. The other, eastern side of the river, a wide, rather unkempt area, contained the Honjo and Fukagawa Wards, called *Shitamachi*, or downtown. Asakusa was considered downtown, also.

Klavdia could see Asakusa Park blanketed in flames. A little further on many individual fires were spreading through the Yoshiwara district also. Nihonbashi Ward, near the foot of *her* bridge was covered with dense smoke, fires winking within. *Is the Imperial Hotel burning?* Buildings near it were. Where were Midori, Tanya, the Morozovs? *Oh, God, I know. It cannot be.* Smoke stung her eyes even as her tears flowed. Several embers carried on the breeze landed on her arm. They hurt only briefly. Downtown had eruptions of flame on both sides of the river.

She felt faint and unbelieving at what she saw toward downtown and the extensive business and administration centers. The smoke and sheer number of fires overcame her sensibilities, again. She grasped the rough surface of a telephone pole to keep from swooning. It supported her.

What can I do? From her upland point of observation she could see that the Imperial Palace and its spacious environs were in good condition—no fires and smoke emanating only from other, less fortunate, areas.

A Japanese friend had told Klavdia that if one looks at a full map of the city, it appears rather like an overblown peony, with the Imperial Palace and its enclosing moat as its still center. It was the true center, both spiritual and patriotic, of Tokyo and Japan. But, now, many petals of the peony were burning. And, although her body felt weak, her resolve returned. She'd go to the Ryogokubashi Bridge.

Klavdia, of course, knew the general direction she must travel, through Asakusa Ward to the river.

Wreckage seemed to be everywhere. She tried not to notice, and averted her eyes from the few corpses. The flames were still separate, but beginning to spread. Yet, the people are not hysterical she thought. There is excitement but no panic in the narrow side streets, nor the broad avenues. But, these people are going in many different directions. There are regular flows moving in opposite ways, often confused, colliding with each other.

In Okachimachi Klavdia saw firemen trying to save a shop with living quarters above. The men were extraordinarily brave. Using what little water they had, they literally tried to beat the fire out with their gloved hands and tarpaulins. It was remarkably courageous and heroic, but their efforts proved to be futile.

The flimsy two-story building, so typical of Japan, with half-inch floors under straw mats, walls of bamboo laths, and exterior sides covered by wide, unpainted clapboard—appeared to explode in a burst of flame, searing even distant onlookers.

The people moving in the direction of her destination quickened their pace, and she had to keep up with them. Fortunately, stepping over debris was not a big problem due to the generous width of the street. Empty streetcars could be seen in the middle of the road, mostly upright, but a couple on their sides laying over broken or twisted rails. On the other side of the street, thick crowds of people tramped in the opposite direction. A few pulled or pushed carts. There were some carts in Klavdia's stream of agitated people, too.

Where are they all going? she wondered. I know my objective, but do they? Are they simply fleeing the many fires in Asakusa Ward? She tried to move a bit faster, but found the effort useless. The general pace was not too quick for her condition. Many were pressing against her when their footing became unsure on irregular surfaces, or pieces and sometime piles of rubble. She must not fall down. It would be so easy to be trampled.

The crowd was forced to stop when it reached Asakusa-bashi Bridge, traversing a canal. It ballooned in size as the people waited in more or less orderly fashion to cross. Klavdia, feeling somewhat faint again, brightened when she found herself surrounded by women wearing the usual white and blue cotton summer kimono. She had always thought them charming, wanting one for herself. Suddenly a deluge of embers descended on the crowd, turning it quickly into a mob. She and the women near her held onto each other for support. The men pushed and shoved, and began yelling. The crush of bodies got worse.

Near her a cart of household goods tipped over. The owners tried to retrieve a few things but were trampled and crushed. Their blood reminded Klavdia that her ultimate objective was death. She knelt to help them. Instantly she was knocked flat. *Yes, kill me. I want to die!* An excruciating pain shot from her left hand. She screamed. It seemed impossible that anyone heard her in the mass of sound, but even so someone grabbed her right hand and, coupled with other strong arms, lifted her erect.

She sensed rather than saw the white and blue kimonos and then stumbled with the continually shouting mob onto the bridge. A boat with sails afire stood in the water. Then she was off the short bridge, approaching her ultimate destination, Ryogokubashi Bridge.

There she would take her own life simply, quickly, and with dignity. She had heard Americans say that Ryogokubashi was "Japan's Brooklyn Bridge" which she knew must be in America, and must also be long, and wide, and very high in order to have sea-going ships pass easily beneath it. She intended to wait for one of these huge sea-going ships, or if one did not come along, to leap into the Sumidagawa River with her legs tied together. Would her painfully throbbing left wrist make the tying of her sash difficult?

But the young woman had become part of thousands trying to gain access to the huge bridge. The many fires on this, the Asakusa side, added to their determination. They felt if they could cross into the Honjo Ward they would be safe. The bridge however, was already jammed with people. The Honjo side had many fires too, so refugees from that ward poured onto the bridge to cross into what they thought would be a safer haven.

Both terror-stricken mobs clashed savagely somewhere near the middle of the bridge. Their struggles became more savage by the second. There was no possibility of retreat because more panicked men, and women, and children were pushing from behind. Klavdia was not even on the bridge, but caught up in the mass hysteria and in a hysteria of her own. She hadn't counted on anything like this. She was simply part of the huge mass trying to get on the bridge.

Neither terrified mob would retreat. Members of both were convinced that safety lay on the other side. A wall of bodies quickly piled up near the middle, but the pressure from both sides continued to increase.

The bridge was bursting, far above any capacity the builders had planned. People were crushed against the railings, many dying slowly, clinging to this barrier. Some climbed over it and jumped or were pushed off the bridge into the water over a hundred feet below. A few retained their senses and began to swim. Most drowned rather rapidly. The lucky ones were pulled into boats or clung to debris.

The fires on both sides of the bridge were multiplying. Embers, sparks, and a few firebrands descended on the helpless crowds. A half dozen carts with clothing or household articles flared up amidst the frenzied people who were wedged together, unable to move in any direction. Some struck out blindly in an attempt to escape by climbing on and over their neighbors. Desperate, terrified people pushed from both sides, trying in a maddened frenzy to get on the bridge.

Gradually, although she was able to inch her way a little closer to her objective every ten or fifteen minutes, Klavdia realized the crushing mob of thousands would keep her off the bridge. Even though waves of nausea swept over her, she turned completely around and pushed in the opposite direction. Her left wrist hurt dreadfully. She used her right arm as a wedge, slowly clawing her way out of the mass. A few of the usually polite Japanese cursed her, or shouted at her. She found if she approached them at an angle rather than head on she could make some progress. Often, the aching left hand stabbed her with excruciating pain. She moaned in agony.

She noticed that when she shrieked in pain the packed mob almost imperceptibly shrank back and gave her a tiny bit more room. If they hadn't, she might have been trampled on the spot. Yet, they were not moving, but rather wedged together. *I must shout so they'll let me squeeze past them.* Waves of nausea poured over her. She felt about to faint. A word popped into her darkening mind and gave her a glimmer of hope.

"*Benjo,*" she shouted, using a word for toilet. "Benjo! Benjo!" People she wriggled by stared in shocked surprise. "Benjo!" Everyone understood an urgent call of nature. Packed by the thousands, they gave her oblique cracks of room. "Benjo!" There were looks of amazement. "Benjo!"

"Benjo!"

"Benjo!"

"Benjo!"

She stumbled and fell blindly on a paved street.

"Benjo!"

She expected to be trampled by the terrified throng. There were, however, relatively few people around her, as she painfully got to her feet.

The street was wide. It must lead into Nihonbashi Ward, in the general direction of where Midori lived. *Midori, how very much I need Midori. This street must be Yokoyamacho.* Her body throbbing with pain from so many sources, weak from exertion and hunger, Klavdia walked slowly into Nihonbashi Ward, away from Ryogokubashi Bridge.

There were plenty of people, as she had seen before, all apparently confused and rushing in many directions. This street was wide enough to accommodate them. She looked ahead and saw buildings burning furiously. On both sides of the street houses exploded violently into flame, creating waves of flame that engulfed many passing near them. Their screams were overpowering. *I must be insane*, she thought as parts of the crowd ahead were incinerated. Yes, she had planned to take her own life, but she did not want to burn. It was too horrible.

Quickly, searching for another route, she recalled a street that ran parallel to this one, fairly close by. *Or,* she wondered, *am I confused? The pain. The awful heat.*

Klavdia took the first opening to her right, a very narrow street, hardly more than a path for one person, between nearly touching tiny houses. She had to be careful not to bump her throbbing wrist.

The path ended at an alley that ran in the same direction as the wide street from which she had just escaped. She usually avoided these alleys, which passed for streets all over Tokyo, but now she had no choice. There were some fires, and when she looked to the right she thought she could see huge conflagrations in Asakusa. Embers pushed along by a strong breeze stung her flesh.

Until she got into the alley proper, after turning left, she hadn't realized the strength of the wind behind her. Its force ruffled her skirt and streamed her hair forward over her face. The few people moving toward her had difficulty making headway against it.

At crossings, the wind seemed to come from all directions, fire brands and flame whirling in tight little circles. A man was caught in one of these whirlwinds only a few yards from Klavdia, and she turned from the sight of his merciless incineration. Her body shuddered at the sound of his screams, and she tried to run.

Near the next intersection, an incredible scene pierced her with terror and tore at the very soul of the Jewish girl. A woman was on her knees, dead, with a baby swaddled to her back. One of the fiery whirlwinds must have caught her. Her charred hands were extended as if she had tried to push it away. The clothes at the front part of her body were burned. So too were her contorted facial features. Klavdia vomited dryly, but she pulled the baby off the woman's back, and stumbled further down the alley toward the more substantial buildings in western Nihonbashi Ward.

Was the baby dead? Probably, thought Klavdia as she carefully held it tightly against her right breast. But the fire had not touched its mother's back, nor had it touched the infant.

It was only one baby. There was so much chaos, so much destruction and death around her, but she could not bear to think of this baby as being dead. As she walked, uncertainly, along the narrow alley, she began to sob. *How many times have I cried, today?* But, this was different. She cried for the bundle she held gently, yet tightly. Tears streaked her dusty face.

A tiny temple appeared on her right, between long lengths of bamboo fence. She saw the quiet, gilded, empty Buddhist enclosure as a haven where they could be completely alone. She considered a moment, then moved quickly inside.

Klavdia had to kneel because the sloping tile roof would not permit her to stand. She and her precious bundle were completely alone. Bushes made up the walls, shutting them off from the horrors outside.

The diminutive shrine's gold and black interior gave her a feeling of comfortable isolation. It had beauty and tranquillity. She knew Buddhist gods were kind, and had the reputation for giving comfort. There was the candle stick. There was the incense pot. There was the flower vase, with a fresh bloom in it. And there was a small, golden Buddha—like the huge one in Kamakura.

Klavdia recognized all this in wonderment—when the baby moved. Again, it moved. Startled, and terrified that she might drop it—she reached to further support the infant with her damaged left hand. If it hurt, she did not notice.

She held the bundle in front of her with both hands. The baby whimpered, and cried out. It opened its eyes and let out a shriek. It wrinkled its tiny face and continued crying. Klavdia's tears washed her dusty cheeks and mingled with those of the tiny person.

"My baby, my baby, *this* is my baby!" she said aloud as she rocked it, back and forth.

Miss Tatiana Lunskaya Walks to the West

The rumbling became a deafening roar. Tanya's ceiling ripped even further and she crawled quickly under her futon for protection, cutting her hands on the shards of porcelain from her lamp.

She sank her face into her pillow, her body spread prone on the tatami, cowering under the futon. Everything shook constantly.

Without warning the floor dropped beneath, then came up like a fist knocking the breath out of her. Tanya fought for breath, tearing off the futon with a gasp. *I must be dying.* The entire world trembled as she sat up gulping in air and plaster dust. *I must get out.* Shortly, the shocks seemed less intense, and the deafening roar had diminished.

In its place were shouts from outside, mixed with painful yells and screams. From somewhere came mournful sobs. *I must get out of here.* Without looking back at her collapsed wall or torn ceiling, she grabbed her white purse, stuffed a small icon of St. Sergei and two bananas into it, and stepped carefully into the hallway.

It was slanted inward at an acute angle, but seemed to be intact. She used her hands to brace herself against the inner walls, many of which were damaged, until she made the stairs. These were no longer straight up and down, but twisted into a curve, with some of the risers broken or missing. Falling to her knees a few times, ripping her stockings on splinters, Tanya descended to the bottom step which was now two or three feet above the floor. She jumped. The walls of the lobby were cracked and broken, and no one was around.

She put on her shoes which, amazingly, were right where she'd left them, and squeezed through the damaged entrance. She gasped at what she saw. The catastrophic sights and sounds almost overcame her. A dead woman gaping skyward with part of her blood-soaked head missing. A group of bloody children being ministered to by parents. A shower of roof tiles must have killed the woman. The air was filled with dust, and a smoky odor. There a man lay under his crushed cart. Houses of varying size lay in the alley—she used to call it her lane—and there, past the outlet to Hongodori Avenue, a house was burning.

Perhaps, they were cooking lunch and the coals were knocked to the floor, thought Tanya. *My God, almost everyone must have been cooking lunch!* She picked her way toward the alley exit and saw Mr. Fuji's car partially buried under wreckage.

Mr. Fuji was not under the wreckage. His body lay on its back cradled in a huge dent that ran across the hood of his car, the telephone pole resting on his chest.

Tanya ran ahead with some wild hope of helping him. Gripping the front fender she recoiled at the pretty doll's face and the black hair of the young girl hanging down between it and the wheel. Anguish contorted the little girl's features. Obviously she was dead. Tanya had seen the gaze of death before, during the Russian Revolution.

She tried to reach Mr. Fuji, bracing herself on the telephone pole and leaning over the hood. Why, she did not know. His chest seemed a bloody mess and his eyes were closed. His ever present glasses weren't there. She could do nothing for Mr. Fuji. As she inched her way back, she spied the pool of blood in the dent under his body, and the little girl's arm. Tanya gagged, she could not keep the gorge down. Out came the bananas, crackers, and green tea she had lunched on in her room only a few minutes ago. None of it got on her white dress. Even with all the chaos around her, she noticed that fact.

Tatiana moved quickly into the alley that would take her to the nearby main street. It should be safer there because she could walk in it and avoid the potentially lethal overhangs of the two-storied buildings. She thought of poor Monsieur Fuji, her pupil, who would never be able to drive her to Yokohama, or drive anywhere at all. *Perhaps, it is a tiny bit of providence that he is unaware of the condition of his beloved motorcar.* She crossed herself.

Hongodori Avenue was the main north-south street located behind Tanya's lodging. It was quite wide, some fifty yards across, and held two streetcar tracks that bisected its middle. Tanya had ridden the trams regularly, because the service could be counted on to be cheap and efficient.

Not so today. The shocks had lifted the imbedded rails into wildly twisted shapes, some snaking and clawing into the air. Four crippled street cars stood upright but at strange angles and devoid of passengers. One lay on it's side with many people crawling over it. She could see three or four uniformed conductors directing efforts to help the poor souls trapped inside.

Cracks and fissures crisscrossed the pavement, fortunately none of them very wide. But Tanya wondered when the next smashing jolt would come. The ground constantly trembled as if in fear.

A few yards to the south lay the overturned cart of Atsui-san, the street vendor who had sold tasty warm snacks to the Russian girl for many months. He did a thriving business, being located right across from the Imperial University, and she bought from him so often that she considered him a friend. She called him "Gaspodin Atsui," *gaspodin* meaning Mister in Russian.

He always seemed proud of his food: rice, buckwheat noodles, fish, boiled eggs, and sweet potato, Tanya's favorite. He sat on the ground near his stricken two-wheeled tiny caféteria, close to the smoldering coals that covered a mixed pile of food. "Atsui-san," she called from behind him.

He seemed to hesitate, but got up and bowed, a stunned smile on his lips. His arms swept over the scene. "Jishin," he announced.

"Hai, jishin!"

"Kemuri," he said, indicating smoke, and pointing in the general direction of the Imperial University buildings across the street.

She had noted the two pillars of smoke rising straight up in the choking, steamy air. These pillars were immediately joined by two more, and she could see flame at the bases of the original two, which had widened considerably.

A fire engine came from the south, picking its way gingerly through, around, and over the bits of wreckage in the street. The university side, since most of the buildings were set back, appeared reasonably clear. The fire engine went into the extensive grounds, apparently ignoring the two leveled houses burning on the other side.

"Hiru gohan," said Atsui-san using the word for lunch as he handed her three warm white eggs wrapped in thin paper.

She accepted them gratefully and reached into her purse. He smiled but shook his head, and then helped others to find edible pieces among the hot coals. Tatiana thanked the vendor. As she cracked one salt-encrusted shell, she realized she felt famished. She ate another, remembering that one could eat anything near the vendor, but walking down a street while eating was considered ill bred. She put the third egg in her purse.

The street under her kept an almost constant vibration, punctuated intermittently with what felt like a powerful blow deep beneath the surface. You could almost hear it, or was that her imagination?

She braced her feet, standing away from cracks and fissures, looking toward downtown Tokyo. The brown dust pall had become gray, with increasing areas of black smudge. There were many fires she judged, probably like the two piles of wreckage that were burning so savagely down the street. Rescuers were still working in the rubble. As she watched, they were finally successful in pulling out two survivors.

Where can I go? The thought came suddenly, and engulfed her mind with the practicality of its concerns. *Back to the Matsunami?* No, it appeared to be in bad shape, and certainly without water and food. She had seen the rampant destruction in the alley, and the bodies. Of course, Yokohama and the Peacocks, her original destination, were eighteen miles away, and pretty certain to be unreachable. The Morozovs and Klavdia? She sensed their building would not have fared well against the awful shocks. But since they were so close, she must find out their condition.

What about Professor Riordan? She knew he lived on higher ground near the outskirts of Tokyo with his friend Professor Heise. Having been there once for dinner, she recalled they had gotten off the train at Shinjuku Station. Judging from the wildly twisted streetcar rails she assumed the train would not be in operation either. She remembered standing on the front porch of Heise-san's house with Hugh before dinner some time ago, admiring the view and his saying it was about four miles to downtown Tokyo.

She did not know where Shinjuku was in reference to her

current location, but she began by walking south on Hongodori Avenue, to find her American professor. Because, she now knew she loved him.

This street was one of the few really wide thoroughfares that cut through Tokyo's usual teeming congestion of wooden buildings. Most were one or two stories of flimsy construction, usually with a tile roof. As Tanya moved carefully through the obstacles in the street, she recalled reading the history of large fires throughout Japan, dating back many years. The average Japanese house, while invariably clean, was designed to burn or fall down. They had no foundations and were two or three feet off the ground, resting on cornerstones. Their floors were quite thin, usually about an inch or less, the entire floor plan determined by the tatami, always six feet by three feet, laid in multiples abutting each other on the floor. Rooms were identified as being of four-tatami size, or six, or more or, sometimes, fewer. Whatever the figure for the number of tatami, the average wooden building was twenty yards by twenty yards. Great effort was made to keep them at least three feet apart, but in many areas they literally touched, especially at the overhangs of their tile roofs.

Tanya made her way, noting that the fires were spreading. If one of the super-combustible buildings caught, soon the one next to it was alight, and then the one beside it. The individual blazes, were quickly becoming ever-widening conflagrations, now aided by the sudden appearance of a light breeze.

By the time she arrived in the general area of the Morozovs residence, the piles of wreckage were burning so furiously she could not separate the individual structures. Where were her friends? As she searched the bystanders for a familiar face she prayed they hadn't been home. If they survived they almost certainly would be seeking a safer location.

Ashes and embers floating on the wind began to alarm the Russian girl, as did the knots of people, some pulling carts full of personal belongings moving quickly, but often in different directions. She thought of the spacious grounds near the Imperial Palace. She felt pretty certain of the general direction, remembering having dinner with Professor Riordan at a restaurant on Kudan Hill that stood near a corner of the Palace grounds. If she could make it there, she should be relatively safe from fires and probably be able to get her bearings and survey the situation in many areas of the city.

The bridge. I must cross the canal at the bridge. There it was directly ahead, Suidobashi, a stream of people hurrying over it in orderly fashion. Tanya joined them, staying close to the railing on her right.

As always, the stench from the canal revolted her. Today, she almost vomited. It stunk worse than ever. A number of houses which came to the water's edge on both sides were burning, some of the fiery wreckage having fallen into the canal. A smoldering boat seemed to have grounded.

What really amazed the Russian girl while she walked were the many people moving about in or simply standing in the water. It came up only a little above their knees. Something was very wrong. The canal water should be much deeper.

While she traveled as fast as the crowds, fires, and scattered debris would allow, she felt in danger of losing her mind. Everything became confused and overwhelmed her usually orderly brain—cracks in a ground that constantly trembled, steadily increasing fires and smoke, screams of trapped or maimed people, the few dead to step over, or because of the crush of men, women and children, forced to step upon. She felt light-headed—it was difficult to breath—would she faint?

Then, shortly after crossing a narrow canal, she realized she had reached Kudan Hill. A huge gate she did not recall from her previous visits stood wide open. She went through with streams of others who were heading toward the roughly two-square miles of open Palace ground. A few grim-faced soldiers with fixed bayonets hurried them along, and helped the few citizens who fell or had difficulty pulling two-wheeled carts, many with small children perched atop their household belongings.

She recalled that the hill had statues, monuments, shrines, assorted buildings and even a stone light-house. Much of Japan's proud history was commemorated here. Professor Riordan had explained most of Kudan Hill when he took her to dinner at the Fujimiken restaurant, with its foreign-style cooking. There, she spotted it—burning furiously.

Tatiana broke out of the streams of people to look around and try to assess her situation. Nearby in the temple yard stood the colossal bronze *torii* gate, that inspired her to pray whenever she had seen it. She paused a moment and prayed for direction. Her view to the north was blocked, but she had come from that way so it didn't matter. Every other area, particularly south and east, both sides of the Sumidagawa River, seemed engulfed in flame. The west, and particularly the higher ground in the northwest, had many fewer fires, even though there were plenty with which to contend.

Once again, she joined the throng heading for the palace grounds. She could see many fire engines parked in front of the palace moat. She checked her lapel-watch. Almost one o'clock. There were already many people in the relatively safe, open space of two square miles. It appeared to her that the area could shelter perhaps three or four times as many.

She decided to leave this haven and seek Professor Riordan, who should be at Professor Heise's house. But which way to go?

She had come to have great faith and trust in the police. One in his white uniform, sword, and pith helmet stood nearby. She approached him and when he noticed her she bowed and asked which direction Shinjuku was in.

The policeman smiled, "Shinjuku?" A look of puzzlement came over his face, then he seemed to comprehend what she was asking, and reported that Shinjuku lay to the northwest.

Now, she must have appeared puzzled, because he pointed to the northwest and announced decisively, *"Asoko,"* or over there. Tatiana bowed and thanked him. The policeman smiled again, then bowed, acknowledging her heartfelt thanks.

Tatiana set out to follow his direction, but before leaving the palace grounds, she sought a place outside the stream of refugees where she hoped to be relatively unnoticed. She sat down on the ground and opened her purse. Tanya knew the grass would stain her white dress, but she was so filthy already, it wouldn't matter. She felt concerned the two bananas inside her purse probably would spoil in the steamy weather. She was rather an expert on bananas, since a steady diet of them had saved her from starving to death during her first year in Japan.

Yes, they were both rather brown inside their skins, but she leisurely ate them, one after the other, and folded the skins back into her purse. She recalled eating the skins, when there had been little else. Who knew what lay ahead during this disaster. From what she had seen in the city panorama from Kudan Hill, she knew conditions were steadily worsening.

She felt quite thirsty. There might be drinking water near the palace. But now it would be too far a distance to go back. As she contemplated her journey she suffered a moment of panic, but forced her mind to compose itself. When she was on the hill, she had seen many fingers of smoke toward the northwest, and this was the direction in which she had to go. It had appeared to be the least engulfed area at the time, but with the steady breeze aiding their spread, there could be hundreds of blazes by now.

Tanya crossed the canal at Yotsuya Station, and immediately found herself in Yotsuya Ward. There were no printed signs telling her that fact, but Professor Riordan had described it as a ward of many contrasts with a section of ridges and valleys, and yet also including uniformly flat areas that rose only a little. Here were many impressive residences in among some of the city's shabbiest areas.

After only a short walk, there on her left stood the magnificent marble and stone palace of the crown prince. It stood far back from the street, but she could see its regal three stories and stone walls. In front a forbidding yet beautiful iron gate stood closed, guarded at each side by a golden Phoenix. It took her breath away as did the smoke and intermittent fires ahead.

The Russian girl remembered the direction the policeman had pointed and entered a narrow street which went roughly that way. It was residential, with high bamboo fences on both sides. There were no people and thankfully no fires. She could, however, see much smoke ahead, and flames leaping above adjoining streets. When the bamboo fencing ran out, so did the narrow street. She must go either right or left to find a path heading in the desired direction.

She quickly examined both, and found them to be alleys, each with burning houses. *Can I make it through?* She chose the one on her right. Its surface was slippery with mud. A few houses on both sides burned even as their owners ran in and out pulling household goods into the thin lane while people shouted and children cried. Tanya pushed on through, swatting ashes and embers from her clothing.

Quite a distance ahead, she thought she saw houses burning in the middle of the alley. What would she do? She couldn't retrace her steps, yet when she got to this fire, she knew she must. She was in an alley with no exit. Could she go back? She had to, but found she couldn't face the ordeal. She could not mentally prepare for it. She felt suddenly terrified.

The heat was overpowering. Her hands were wet, her entire body an exhausted, sweating mess. There was no other choice, she must head back the way she had come. As she began to retrace her path she noticed many new fires. They were impossible to pinpoint, but there were definitely more.

She was surprised that a breeze from behind pushed her along. The flames pulled drafts down the narrow alley, just as though it were a chimney. There was no panic, no mass hysteria, but the people who were burning screamed. A few ran down the alley alight, as neighbors tried to beat out the flames. As she pushed through the people, slipping now and again on the muddy surface, Tatiana wondered, *will I burn?*

Exhausted, Tatiana approached the intersection where she had entered the alley that had led to a dead end. There had been so many choices. Which one now? Perhaps, they were all blind alleys. *No, they couldn't be.*

A handful of people, including a woman with a baby, stood at the crossing, trying to decide which direction to go. A whirlwind of fire appeared and danced around them, enfolding them in its embrace. Some screamed briefly before they crumbled in a flaming heap. Tanya's eyes instantly searched for the baby, but it too had disappeared in the fiery swirl.

The breezes were strong where the alleys came together. They came from many directions and spun the fire into these searing whirlwinds. From the ground they rotated upward carrying burning material, sparks, fire-flakes, and gouts of flame.

As she watched horrified, group after group was incinerated. *Get out of the intersection!* Tanya dove into another alley, one with many flaming houses, but headed roughly in the direction she wanted to go. Would this turn out to be another dead end? Was this another fiery trap?

Here many people, far enough away from the crossroads, seemed to be standing in small groups watching their homes and those of their neighbors be consumed. They stood in shocked silence, uneasy, not sure what to do. If no one were trapped inside, what could they do? No water was available to stem blazes of this magnitude.

Tanya pushed through as politely as possible. Hardly anyone appeared to notice her. They seemed to be stunned. Now and then a charred corpse sprawled at the side of the alley, doubtlessly pulled from an adjacent burning dwelling. Usually a small group kneeled beside it. The torrid breeze swooping down the lane scorched her face. She was walking into it. In the former alley the breeze had been behind her. What did this mean, if anything? Was she moving in the right direction? She thought she was, but how to be sure? *How can I ask these suffering people for directions?*

A cloud of embers swirled around her. She slapped at those that landed on her clothing. Were some burning her hair? She beat her head in anguish, but there wasn't any pain. Oh Lord, the strap on her formerly white purse had broken. She'd have to carry it like a sack or hug it to her chest. She certainly wasn't dressed for this kind of trip. She wished she had on her trousers instead of this silly dress.

Another house collapsed, exploding in flames. Tanya continued, but now more people were running—running in the opposite direction. They bumped into her, or did she simply get in their way, impeding their progress? She grappled with a lady, asking about the way to Shinjuku. The lady wrestled past. A man confronted her, trying to get by. She tried asking him for directions, he smiled wanly and shook his head.

The crowd was past her. There were few people ahead, but many fires. Shinjuku, she knew as a train station. Was it a ward? She didn't think so. Should these people know of it? She had no idea. The sizzling breeze continued in her face, accompanied by many sparks and a few firebrands. Would she catch fire?

As in the previous alley a cluster of people stood facing the burning houses, almost absently beating out the firebrands that landed on them. They didn't appear to notice her when she paused beside them. They too had that now familiar stunned look. Should she ask for directions? She thought not. She did not fear them in the slightest sense. She had never felt afraid of the Japanese, but, it seemed an inappropriate time to interrupt their thoughts. They stood so silently watching the conflagration consume their individual worlds.

The Russian girl, stumbling now and then, continued on, her steps mechanical. She felt beyond pain, so miserable she hardly noticed her singed skin, her parched throat. Her legs and feet began to ache even more as the ground started to rise. Again, the alley had bamboo fences on either side, but intermittent flames erupted behind the barriers.

People's terror-filled voices echoed from beyond the fences. Hardly anyone was in the alley, which widened and continued to rise. Suddenly to her right a gate opened and an elderly man tottered out, stumbled and fell to his hands and knees. He tried to raise himself but the effort was too much and he collapsed on his side. With a quick glance up the alley Tanya crouched near him and grabbed his hand.

"No, no" he cried hoarsely, "no," he pushed her hand away. It seemed she could only help herself.

She moved on into the hot wind still torturing her face and hands. Carefully approaching the next crossroads, which she knew could be deadly, she kept to the left side. Why the left? She did not know.

As she edged closer to it, a cyclonic gust of savage wind swooped around the corner, and caromed down the opposite side of the alley exploding entire sections of bamboo fence and doors with its horrific blast.

Tanya thought briefly of the old man on the alley's right side. She did not look back. Calling on a small reserve of strength, she dashed, praying, across the intersection into another alley, which led off to the right. She seemed to have lost her senses. She did not feel, she did not see in any way that made an impression, yet she knew she traveled again up a slight incline which made walking harder. She beat constantly at her clothing, even if there were no reason.

Suddenly, the gusty breeze became a gale. Once more she stopped her desperate walk as a twisting mass of fire boiled toward her from further down the alley where a group of burning buildings had collapsed. She screamed in terror and leaped into a cross-lane, barely wide enough for two or three people.

She could see light at the end of this lane, and no flames, but there were broken wooden beams blocking the way. She squeezed her way through the barriers. Splinters cut her arms and legs. A few became imbedded, but she hardly felt it when she pulled them out. A broken corner post blocked her way. She pushed at it, but it felt tightly wedged in. It was too high to climb over. On her hands and knees, in the middle of the lane, she began to crawl under the obstruction, cutting her hands and legs cruelly on the wreckage. *Thank God the Japanese don't use glass in their houses.*

Another cracked beam blocked her way a bit further on. She crawled, again. When she came out of the narrow alley, she found herself upon a wide street, strewn with considerable wreckage but only one fire. A line of people stood in front of her, and a policeman motioned her to join it.

Some of the Japanese smiled at her and bowed their heads slightly as she went to the end of the line. She bowed to them in passing. Others got into line behind her. The line was long, but it moved quickly. At its front another policeman carefully ladled some water out of a water-cart, always returning some back before pouring it into the next eager mouth. Some held out cupped hands to catch any drop that might fall. Nothing had ever tasted so good to the Russian girl.

"Thank you," she said, after letting the hot stinking liquid travel around her mouth and cracked lips.

The policeman jerked his head, indicating she should move along. She stepped away, stared at the street momentarily, and croaked in a questioning tone, "Maitomachi?"

"Hai, Maitomachi," a woman acknowledged with a hoarse voice, as Tatiana bowed deeply in thanks.

It might be a long way, but she knew Maitomachi Road

went past the Shinjuku train station. Eventually it would lead between Professor Heise's Japanese and foreign houses. Professor Riordan would be there! He must be there.

With a burst of renewed hope, she moved along the side of the street. *What time is it?* Her watch was smashed. No matter, if she could just keep on this street. Oh Lord, she had just enjoyed some water. The air was cooler and devoid of smoke. What would Professor Riordan say? She stumbled less and walked more erect. He would be glad to see her.

Tatiana did not know how long it took. She roughly estimated an hour or so. She recognized the Japanese house on her side of the street, and the European house across from it. When she came closer Professor Heise trotted to her side.

"Fraulein Tanya!"

She almost laughed with happiness.

He reached forward as though to embrace her, then obviously thought better of it, because she might be burned or hurt. "Leibchen, come inside. We will take good care of you." He gently took her hand.

They walked a few yards, then Heise stopped and looked down the street into Tokyo. A large cloud hung above the city. Under it was thick gray smoke supported by flickering waves of flame.

He cleared his throat and looked directly at her. "Hugh . . . Hugh is not here—he went into the city to look for you."

Major Phillip Faymonville and the Imperial Hotel

Damn, thought Major Faymonville as he ran along the bucking hallway, careening from wall to wall, *if this had come when I was in my office—I'd be out the window.*

The incredible bucking diminished as he reached the stairs. He took them two at a time down to the ground floor, where a large crowd of men, some in uniform, swarmed about, many dashing toward the front exits. A few stared warily at the roof span above them that joined the Imperial's five hundred foot wings.

With some of his staff around him, Hotel Manager Inumaru encouraged the guests to go outside to the courtyard around the reflecting pool. *A very wise idea,* thought Faymonville. *It should be the safest location, just in case the hotel comes down like a house of cards as Yoshida predicted.*

While the ground continued to shake, he moved to an exit only to literally run into one of his friends from the American Embassy. As the man pushed past, he shouted, "Phil, the kitchen's on fire!" The Major turned to look after him. Now he too could see the smoke billowing. *The staff should be able to handle this,* he thought. But, perhaps because he had an office here and lived within its substantial (he hoped) walls, he felt a sense of responsibility for the American-designed structure. The decision took only a second, then he too ran toward the smoky kitchen.

When he got to the large banquet hall, he noticed people sheltering under the heavy tables. *Not a bad move,* he thought. Then a huge shock hit again. It was a terrific blow that dropped the floor beneath Faymonville's feet and threw him to his knees. Was the roar a result of the hotel beginning to collapse? *No, it's from outside,* realized the major. *It's not the hotel, it's the sound of Tokyo coming down.*

As the roar of overpowering destruction diminished a bit, he got to his feet and continued on his mission. *Well even if the floor dropped* (he had to step up from the banquet room) *our hotel still stands.*

When he reached the kitchen area he spied Manager Inumaru directing scurrying staff members in the smoke. "Ah Major, thank you for your concern. Our fire is out. An electric range toppled and some fat burned. But, the electricity has been shut off and all fire extinguished."

"That is good news Mr. Inumaru. Thank you. I'll go to the courtyard now."

"Yes, yes, that's a good idea. My staff and I will join you, shortly.

Faymonville knew there was no gas utilized in the hotel, and with the electric power off, there shouldn't be much danger of fire. Still, there could be faulty wiring.

There appeared to be at least a few hundred men in the courtyard around the large, blossom-filled reflecting pool. Faymonville appreciated even more the foresight of Wright who'd included the pool in his design to serve as a handy reservoir in case of fire.

The American looked toward the nearby Imperial Palace and its spacious grounds. It seemed unaffected by the Earthquake. Hibiya Park, across the street, began to fill with refugees. A food store close by spewed a pillar of smoke into the clear hot air.

"Hello Phil," said a British colonel touching his cap with his swagger-stick. "It looks as though tiffin will be somewhat delayed, today."

"Hello Roger," he brushed his cap with an informal salute "You'll be glad to know I've got a box of chocolates in my room."

"Please," replied the Englishman with mock seriousness, "let's keep that our secret. We might need your chocolates to keep body and soul together."

They both nodded to people they knew, but for the most part, members of the crowd seemed transfixed, as though waiting for developments.

Roger gestured toward the east, using his swagger stick like a pointer. "Well, Asakusa is really brewing up." The smoke and flame were visible to all. The stick moved toward the south. "And, all those tawdry areas across the Sumidagawa.

There's some real smoke for you—turning into a bloody bonfire."

They both noted that the ornamental Hibiya Park water fountain across the plaza had stopped functioning. Lazy smoke climbed into the sky above the distinctive and luxurious Peers Club. It was obvious it had been damaged structurally.

"You know Phil," said the Englishman offering a cigarette from his case, then taking one for himself and lighting both with a match. "I've made quite a study of Japanese history, and after one of these really smashing shakes, there's always a bloody huge fire. All those flimsy paper houses in the neighborhoods burn like kindling."

Faymonville dragged on his cigarette. "Yes, I've studied too, and learned the same."

"Well, I better be damned careful where I put this match stick," chuckled Roger. "This earthquake coming at tiffin time! Good God, can we even imagine how many tens of thousands of people were cooking on those charcoal grills they use?"

"There must be tons of glowing coals spilled all over Tokyo, waiting to flare up," agreed the Major. Deliberately he stomped out his cigarette, looked at it carefully, then covering it with his handkerchief, put it in his pocket.

"The flowers of Edo," observed the Colonel, as he made a sweeping gesture with his swagger stick. "They're beginning to bloom all over." As though to punctuate his observations, a brick and masonry building close by collapsed with a jarring roar. They both stared at the cloud of debris and dust which hung over the pile of rubble.

Someone next to them cleared his throat. It was Captain Yoshida, in blue uniform with choker collar fastened and wearing white gloves. He saluted the British Colonel, then Major Faymonville. He extended his hand and shook the American's. "Thank you for you hospitality, Major." Then he glanced at the white letters, designating Imperial Hotel over the entrance. "I see the Imperial Hotel sign is still with us," he said bowing slightly.

The American thought of making some remark referring to Yoshida's earlier jibe about falling "like a house of cards." But, he knew the earthquake and the mounting dangers must have saddened his friend.

"Captain, you are most welcome to share my room for as long as you see fit."

Yoshida bowed slightly, again. "Once more, I thank you for your kindness, but, I must rejoin my unit." He saluted the colonel, then the American.

A smile appeared on his face, "It can't be helped." Then he spun on his heel and marched into the street and the increasing destruction.

As Major Philip Faymonville watched the Japanese officer disappear from sight, he thought, *I'll never see Captain Yoshida again.*

Raita Kanoh in the Yoshiwara

When Raita Kanoh hurriedly left the split apart house of pleasure behind him, he did so with the thought that he might avoid paying his huge bill. Oh, the proprietor quite certainly knew who he was, but with the earthquake and all the confusion, who could tell about future payment? It might be forgotten.

As he picked his way with considerable difficulty toward the main street, Nakanocho, over shattered tiles, bricks, splintered wood and glass, he could hear many women shrieking and crying. The crossing was quite narrow, but as he stepped carefully, he found a section of broken masonry large enough to perch on. He put his socks, and thick soled English dress shoes on his aching feet. Above him protruded a large but sagging balcony festooned with brilliantly colored feminine sleeping garments intended to dry and air out in the sun. The sight brought a smile to the customs official. Indeed, he knew he appreciated women.

His smile instantly left him when he reached the central street and looked toward the main gate. The destruction was appalling! He judged that at least half the buildings were down, and most of these were emitting towers of smoke. Many structures still erect were burning too. From the rubble piles along the way bursts of flame erupted and multiplied. And, in among all these horrors were hundreds of gaily attired women, some with bright parasols, who had been crushed to death, mutilated, or grievously wounded.

He could not see those directly under the wreckage. Some were partially trapped, a few struggled to free themselves, and were aided by their sisters who could move about. Shrieks and screams came from every direction, punctuated intermittently by the crash of another building. Crying women, a few with attendants close behind, ran about in confusion.

Kanoh could see a fire engine accompanied by a few police arrive at the main gate. Because of all the wreckage and fires in the way, he assumed he wouldn't be able to reach the wide entrance gate. So he turned around and carefully made his way, still carrying his suit, in the opposite direction, toward the Medical Inspection Bureau, which was at the end of Nakanocho.

Branching off at right angles were short side streets, which were terminated by locked gates during the night, but opened as exits in the day time. Some of these side streets ran between very ornate, expensive, European-style houses, many featuring decorative balconies that almost touched a similar structure across the narrow street. Kanoh had spent the night in one of this design, but he carefully searched for an unfamiliar street.

He had almost reached the Medical Bureau when he made his sharp right turn. In a short time he found himself out of the confines of the Yoshiwara. The chaos out here was almost as awful as that within. There were fewer buildings to crumble, but the extensive fires were worse. Kanoh had almost become used to the shrieks of those who were trapped while eager flames consumed the wreckage around them.

The customs officer sat on a wooden beam that had broken off a nearby house. He removed the paper money from his suit and divided the bills into two piles, inserting one inside each of his wing-tip shoes. There was little discomfort when he arose and took a few steps, after lacing them up. The few coins he would keep in his suit. *My suit.* He wondered what to do with his shirt, tie, and expensive English suit, still on its hanger. *Quite inconvenient to carry it.*

As he moved in the direction of the Sumidagawa River, there appeared to be more bodies, and more fires. A light but steady breeze came from the same direction, pushing the flames ahead of it.

A street vendor's cart stood at a crazy angle, one wheel lodged in a pavement crack. The vendor himself lay close by, one eye remaining to stare skyward through a bloody mess. A number of cracked roof tiles lay only a few feet away.

Suddenly Kanoh realized how hungry he was. He hung his suit on a nearby bush. Then his pudgy hands began stuffing his eager mouth with rice-dumplings, and boiled red beans. He felt lucky to be wearing his thick leather soled shoes because there were many hot coals scattered about, spilled from the food cart. To more comfortably reach the food, Kanoh pulled the dead vendor's stool closer. He surveyed the area around him as he gorged himself.

There were many bodies, most he judged, struck by the heavy tiles which came raining down from the collapsing houses. Fires were everywhere, and, he noticed, spreading rapidly. An alley he could see along for a considerable distance appeared to be totally engulfed. Few houses in the area had so far escaped burning.

His hunger assuaged, Kanoh arose from the stool and took a couple of startled steps as the entire area was deluged with embers. They stung his exposed skin and caused him to beat out those in his hair. He swept them away and felt surprised to see some small chunks of plaster that had come down from the ceiling of his oiran's room. He smiled quickly as he recalled the pleasure house.

The embers disappeared and he quickly decided to find a safer location. He moved toward the bushes where he had hung his suit. A good portion of it was ablaze, already half consumed. Could he save the trousers? He singed his hands in the attempt, and disgustedly threw everything into a heap, back atop the flaming bushes.

A group of brightly dressed Yoshiwara girls, there must have been about sixty or seventy, made their way carefully but rapidly along the littered thoroughfare. Their seemingly unconcerned chatter and occasional laughter cheered Kanoh and roused him out of his deep concern for his own survival. He decided to follow them. Where could they be going, especially in such good spirits? Some had flowery, bamboo-ribbed parasols. They must have some secret refuge to be in such happy, joking moods as they passed between two lines of blazing houses and flaming wreckage.

The group continued their rapid travel with Kanoh in pursuit, but a discreet distance behind. While he exulted in the idea of following such a large number of desirable ladies, he did not want them to realize his presence. Though there were plenty of other people moving in various directions, he felt these women must be going to some shelter perhaps known only to them. But, how could that be?

After a hundred yards or so, they turned directly left along an alley with ramshackle houses on both sides. Many were burning, while their former occupants looked on helplessly.

The girls pushed through, with the Customs Official now following closely. He shoved a whimpering elderly man out of his way. He knew he mustn't lose them.

Finally, successfully scrambling through tightly packed mobs of terrified people in the scorching alley, their objective came into sight, a considerable area of water. He understood immediately—a tidal pool.

A rickety wooden bridge bisected the water. The women on it appeared to be from the Yoshiwara, and were reluctant to jump into the water. Some six feet below them and less than two feet deep, it was too shallow to adequately break their fall. *The tide must be out*, thought Raita Kanoh. The group of women he had been following didn't hesitate, but plunged right in from the shore still laughing and joking. They sobered almost immediately, when they realized how shallow the water was.

He assumed the water would deepen when the tide came in. He studied the shoreline around this pool that would probably save his life, and those of its female occupants. Where he stood were shabby dwellings that came almost to the edge of the water. About two thirds of the pond was surrounded by these structures, which were divided by many narrow alleys that ran directly away from it—like strands from the center of a spider's web. The rest of the shore had thick shrubbery and a regular forest of massive trees. Kanoh did not know what kind they were. Interspersed among the dense growth were small huts made of stone. Directly below them, he could see the marks of the high water line, when the tide was in. But, try as he would, he could not find the inlet for the water. It must be well over to his right, where the ramshackle buildings ended and the wall of hedges and verdant trees began.

He splashed down off the flat stones that served as a retaining wall, into the water. Some of the brightly clad girls who were already in laughed tolerantly at him, but moved further away rather quickly.

His hangover now waning, Kanoh found this so amusing and charming that when he took a few steps in their direction he slipped on the uneven bottom of the pool and fell on his backside. The women moved even further away, but the customs official did not lose face, instead he roared with laughter. As far as he could tell, he was the only male in the water.

It felt quite warm, but not as hot as the air. He splashed himself all over with water until he became completely soaked. Being damp all over was pleasant, especially with the shifting breezes. However, his clothing quickly dried in the torrid air, and it became necessary to wet the yukata more and more frequently.

Sometime later, he didn't know how much later because his wristwatch had stopped, he was aware of the water deepening until it reached three-and-a-half or four feet. He still could not find its source, but he noticed a spreading oily sheen on the surface. The water was very warm, but at least he could completely immerse himself. The fires now surrounded the pool, and this immersion could be life saving. In fact, Kanoh realized, this could very well be his only escape.

Many more people, mostly women, had taken refuge in this pond during the last hour or so. The heat of the encircling flames became steadily more unbearable, forcing the occupants to duck their heads under water at shorter and shorter intervals.

Where flimsy, wood and bamboo houses ringed the water, the fire leapt with explosive force from wall to wall, from structure to structure. When Kanoh looked down the alleys that once divided the lines of buildings, he saw nothing but a fiery hell. Where some semblance of alley still existed, it acted like a chimney, causing a searing draft. In one alley the draft might go away from the water, in the one next to it, the scorching breeze would go the opposite way. When these winds of fire joined they danced together into a whirling cyclone of flame. They spun in various directions, but many moved over the water, instantly cremating upper torsos and faces of those unfortunate enough to be touched by their dance.

Most of those luckless ones had been closer to shore than Raita Kanoh who had reasoned that midpool would be the safest location.

Opposite the fiery buildings, and covering about one third of the tidal pool's shoreline were the thick hedges backed by a solid mass of leafy trees. To Kanoh the spread of flame there seemed like a huge forest fire blazing in dry timber. It did not simply burn as it moved along. Rather it exploded.

People screamed around him. The water upon which they now depended for their survival was itself becoming hot, terribly hot. He recalled being goaded by other boys, when he was young, to perform an experiment with a tiny frog. He put the frog into a dish with water and food and lit a fire under it. The water began to boil but the frog would not jump out, and died. When he dropped similar frogs into hot water, they jumped out immediately. He fervently wished he could jump out of the tidal pool. But, there was no place to jump.

The hundreds of souls in the pool were completely surrounded by an extended wall of fire. Much of the burning shoreline of bushes and trees now crashed into the water. Some people pushed up to get a breath of air, but the superheated water vapor was so hot it choked some of them into unconsciousness, or killed them after a few gasps. Whether you lived or died while taking a breath depended on the varying location of the superheated air.

A man wearing a wet shirt and trousers climbed onto a rock next to the shoreline. He almost slipped but regained his balance and began to rise up. But before he could stand up, his hair, shirt, then entire body became a pillar of flame. As the water became too hot to bear, a few more people scrambled out. Some leapt upward, ran crazily for a few steps, then crumpled like dry corn stalks. All were struck down whether they stood or ran. They found no place for safety, no place to hide, no shelter of any kind. They lay where they had fallen, smoldering briefly, becoming only a new place for flames to dance.

From the tidal pool Kanoh could see into a hut beneath the blazing trees where a mother clasped her child. Both became fiery torches—hair, clothes, skin, in a split second all was afire. He could not hear above the roar of the flames, but he saw shrieks from flaming throats, and then body fluids burst into steam. The remains began to twist as they fell to ground. Kanoh watched them as they writhed.

But, he gave them only fleeting moments. The temperature of the pond, ever climbing toward boiling, reached that point. Bubbles rose in flurries, some from the lucky ones who had drowned, and those who were in the throes of death. Kanoh ducked his head under the water. He was afraid to touch his puffy face because his hands, even though submerged, were beginning to blister.

Each time he moved he was seized by a spasm of coughing that brought blood up from his lungs. He vomited into the bubbling water, and slipped beneath the surface. He fought his way up again through the bloody haze. When he could see, he cried out in anguish.

Yet, he did not yet contemplate dying. His heavy shoes enabled him to grip solidly the bottom of the pool. The oily film atop the water was not burning . . . the safe in his office held one of the largest diamonds in Tokyo . . .

The heat beat down upon him like unending physical blows. His lungs were tortured and his throat raw. All his strength had left him. He locked his fingers on a smoldering piece of wood. It may have been a part of the bridge. Both his eyes felt like blazing coals. The pain—constant, intense, mounting—engulfed him. Now, with the skin peeled away, the very bone structure of his hands was exposed.

Shimaku Suzuki at Mitsukoshi

Shimaku tightened her grip on her mother's right hand, and her mother increased her hold on the maid's, bringing her close. One of Mitsukoshi's main stairways, toward which they and many others had been rushing, went crashing down just before they reached it.

Amid the frightened screams and shouts for help, Shimaku pulled her mother to her, and yelled, "This way!" Still joined hand in hand, they turned and headed back, pushing through the crowd until Shimaku could lead them to the left, close to an outer wall.

Mother Suzuki knew they must get out, and they might have a chance on the elevator where her daughter seemed to be heading. But no, Shimaku had some other idea. The older woman felt amazed at her daughter's independence of action.

She led them to the door of an inconspicuous narrow staircase, intended, according to a small sign, only for employees. Instead of going down—there were sounds of a few people below—Shimaku headed up followed by her Mother and the maid. It was difficult climbing in kimonos, but a number of pulls on the handy railing helped. They encountered only two white-gloved store employees before they reached a door that opened onto the roof. The beautiful, canopied roof garden was nearby. Once again hand in hand, the trio surveyed Tokyo from this superb vantage point.

"Oh look," exclaimed Shimaku, "Asakusa is burning! Oh, there are so many fires!"

Her mother could see this was true, and that most of the dense pillars of smoke were coming from the Yoshiwara section that was close to Asakusa Park. Of course, Shimaku knew nothing of that particular area.

The large building jumped, then jumped again, like a giant stamping his foot. Once more the three women huddled together under a table, even though there was nothing directly above them but an attractive cloth canopy. Down below, from near and far came the roar of structures falling. As they emerged from their impromptu shelter Mrs. Suzuki said, "We must get to the ground." As she looked around, however, she realized their more immediate danger could come from above. The renowned and impressive Mitsukoshi Tower and ornamental cupola still perched atop the right side of the building. It rose over them more than four stories to the tip of its distinctive pole, and could be seen from most everywhere in the city. Would it fall on them? No, it seemed solidly in place, even as the building trembled.

Not so fortunate was the tallest structure in Tokyo, the twelve-story tower in Asakusa Park. Once again looking toward Asakusa, Shimaku brought her hand to her pretty mouth and exclaimed, "Oh, the top of Asakusa Tower has broken off! And Honjo is burning."

Still holding hands, all three of them could see more than a dozen fingers of smoke pointing to the sky. "We must leave this roof," proclaimed Mrs. Suzuki, "the fires will be spreading." Indeed there were fingers of smoke emanating from much closer locations, even Nihonbashi itself. "The Imperial Palace area seems undamaged," she observed. They dipped their heads a tiny bit in sincere gratitude.

"Come, let us move to the other side so we can see Mount Atago." They moved to this better vantage point. Mount Atago was a little mountain with a viewing tower. This was west in one of the upland areas, close to Shiba Park and their home. There were a few small fires in the area, but it generally seemed pretty clear.

The roof garden had emptied rather quickly. "Should we risk the elevator?" queried her mother.

"That was my intention all along in coming up here." Shimaku answered respectfully.

A smiling store executive standing by in the ubiquitous foreign suit, tie, and French cuffs, bowed and said, "Please do not be concerned ladies. Mitsukoshi is built like a fortress and has plenty of electric power."

They entered the elevator, still linked hand in hand. The pretty white-gloved elevator operator smiled at them. Shimaku returned her smile.

By the third floor, their car was completely filled. But, the main floor seemed almost deserted, enabling them to continue holding hands as a trio. There were, of course, the ever conscientious, ever polite Mitsukoshi employees and managers bowing and smiling. There wasn't the slightest hint of panic.

They left, no longer gripping each other, via what was often referred to as the "wide, imposing entrance," between the tall columns and the stone lions that crouched on either side. The maid and Shimaku grabbed Mrs. Suzuki's hands again. Here on the street there was panic.

Tram cars had come off the double tracks that ran down the main street of the Ginza area. A fire engine's crew tried to douse fires that had broken out in some of the smaller shops. There were a few shrieks and screams from people who were burning. Nihonbashi Bridge and the approach on this side was completely jammed with frightened people who appeared to be trying to go in different directions. A squad of police in their usual summer pith helmets tried to achieve some order, but were losing the fight.

Mrs. Suzuki, Shimaku, and the maid went down a street that ran on the store's right side. The absence of smoke was encouraging. Mitsukoshi still stood proudly, but it showed battle scars. The earthquake had shaken off most of the con-crete that covered the strong brick inner core.

In front of the next building, the Specie Bank, stood the newly acquired Suzuki family ricksha with its faithful driver dressed in navy blue. Banker Suzuki who was presently out of town thought a personal ricksha would add prestige to his name, and be a great convenience. Mrs. Suzuki, although not consulted about its acquisition, loved the vehicle, with its rubber tires and nickel-plated wheels. She knew that the driver who was now bowing deeply, would be able to avoid wreckage and trouble spots and get them home. He helped Mrs. Suzuki and then Shimaku up to the seat. Because there was only room for two, the maid was provided a similar but less pretentious vehicle.

The drivers swung into motion, both carefully avoiding the dead body of a young man in a business suit, who must have been hit by a roof tile or some piece of masonry. Blood soaked his chest, obliterating the striped design of his tie.

Mrs. Suzuki averted her eyes and, wanting to avoid the awful congestion on the Nihonbashi Bridge, called the name of a much smaller, less traveled bridge over the canal, "Gofukubashi!"

Shimaku stared at the dead man as they passed. Was he a younger version of her father, a banker? Would he have been chosen to be her husband or rather she as his wife? She loved her father. Oh, how Tanya would love to ride in their rick-sha. Where was Tanya? Safe! She must be safe. When could she pick up all her kimonos at Mitsukoshi? She could see many fires. She took her mother's hand and squeezed it. Her mother squeezed in return but did not look at her.

Shimaku glanced behind and waved to the maid, who waved back. She recalled the significance of the ancient phrase about fires being the flowers of Edo. Would these flow-ers of fire blossom into much larger bouquets?

Yoshinari Yamamoto and His Family

When Yoshinari Yamamoto, after a long and harrowing trip, finally turned into the bamboo-fenced alley on which he lived, he momentarily felt relief that there was only one fire. It seemed small, and on the opposite side from his home. He reached out to steady himself on a corner post. His coat and tie were gone. Black soot smeared his shirt and parts of his face. Blood streaked his torn trousers marking an ugly wound. But still, he carried the presents for his wife and children. The wrappings were ruined but he had taken pains to preserve the gifts.

A burst of anticipation and concern sent him running down the alley. His house, about a hundred yards from where he entered, was similar to others on both sides, but longer. It had an extra room that served as a somewhat Westernized kitchen with round copper pots resting on brick fireplaces. Next to the kitchen came the dinette with a table and foreign chairs where they all sat and ate together.

The rest of the rooms were typically Japanese. Nothing distinguished them except the different woods used in the framing of their walls and their ceilings which indicated more expense only to the most experienced eye. Each room, its floor completely covered with golden tatami edged with black braid, was clean and entirely bare. Nothing broke the similarity of these rooms but the double alcove or tokonoma.

Yamamoto had been grateful for the extra room, especially because directly behind his and the other houses on the alley, was a neighborhood business district. Its mostly small two story shops of brick, cement, or wood fronted on a busy street.

He also had been grateful for the tiny yard between his house and the bamboo fence, and the fact that his elderly uncle lived alone, right next door.

Uncle Toda, in his mid-seventies, was a man of independent thought, but only Japanese independent thought. He thoroughly disapproved of Yoshinari's American education, his foreign ways, and specifically the dinette set where he never ate, though often invited.

When his wife died he stoically accepted and gave no voice to his loneliness, but as time passed he decided it did not diminish his dignity to be closer to his remaining family. And so, he moved into the small house next to his interesting nephew, Yoshinari, for whom he had developed considerable affection and even referred to as "Yoshi." This was, for him rather undignified, but he recognized the obvious charm of the beautiful family who lived next door.

As Yamamoto got closer to his house, he quickly realized something was terribly wrong. He tore open the bamboo gate, calling the names of his wife and children. He stared in shock momentarily, then dashed forward. The tailor shop next door had crumbled, its second floor cascading bricks, tiles and chunks of masonry down upon the middle of his home. The flimsy walls had burst open. Dropping his parcels, he tore at the bricks with his hands. He threw some out of the way, and was about to climb the pile of debris when a strong hand grabbed and held him back. It was his Uncle.

"Uncle?" It was less a greeting than a question.

His uncle, who was considerably shorter than Yamamoto stood silently looking up at him. His hands and arms were covered with bloody lacerations. His grimy face and dusty bald head leaked blood in several places. He shook his head—then coughed—and, shook his head again.

Yamamoto had reached his home, impervious to any other emotion other than his desire to find his family. Even knowing how close to death he had come, he'd felt sure they would be alive, especially when he first saw the favorable conditions of the alley.

"Hana?" he asked his uncle.

Uncle Toda shook his head.

"Kiku?" he asked.

Toda shook his head.

"Tsubaki?"

Toda shook his head.

"Yoshi? Koshiro?"

Uncle Toda shook his head repeatedly from side to side. Then he climbed, barefoot, to the top of the pile of rubble. His nephew followed him. There, deep inside the deadly mountain of bricks, mortar, and tiles—inside this crater of death Yamamoto could catch glimpses of his wife and children, who must have been close together when destruction came raining down upon them. Probably Hana had been shielding the children. How terribly hard Toda must have worked to save them, or at least to expose their bodies enough to see there was no hope.

For a couple of hours Yamamoto worked insanely, throwing bricks, carrying cement sections, lifting, sometimes pushing chunks of walls, always with his uncle close by, helping. He knew his uncle had done the most important work before he'd arrived.

While he couldn't pull them out of the debris-filled crater they'd excavated, he knew they were all dead. He could see enough of each one of them to witness their grievous wounds, and sadly admit they could not have been breathing. Hana wore a foreign dress, and the children their new school clothing. He couldn't bear the thought that they had wanted to come shopping with him. Exhausted now, his uncle beside him, Yoshinari Yamamoto sat numbly on the ground, not knowing what to do, where to go, drowning in his grief. He imagined he heard the children chattering in high voices. They were laughing, happy. He began crying gently.

Uncle Toda fiercely grabbed Yamamoto's arm with one of his battered hands. He proclaimed loudly. "The eyelids of a samurai know not moisture!" It was an old and well known saying. He kneeled and clapped his hands together three times, repeating a basic chant of the Nichiren Sect of Buddhists. He ordered Yoshinari to clap his hands in the same way and repeat the words in unison with him. The younger man did as his uncle asked.

Toda explained, "We believe that the spirits of the dead are here, and we must be very good to them. They have our respect, and are very precious to us." They repeated the clapping and the words together, a number of times.

Then, for a short period they were silent until Yamamoto stood up and said, "Uncle Toda, bring the swords!" His uncle sucked in his breath as though he had been struck sharply in the chest. He stood up quickly, bowed, and went off to fetch the family's pair of samurai swords.

During his younger days Yoshinari had been trained to suppress his emotions. He remembered occasions in past years when some friend would tell him about the lingering death of a loved one, while remaining stoic throughout the entire narrative. He felt glad that among many modern Japanese, emotions were allowed to show. This terrible jishin would evoke horrendous grief.

Although he had been educated in a foreign land, and even sent his family abroad to avoid the earthquake, he was supremely and everlastingly Japanese. A number of minutes later, Yamamoto and his Uncle Toda were in an immaculate, completely undamaged room of the house. The paper doors at both ends were closed. All the tatami mats except one had been removed. The futon was folded in a neat pile set away in a far corner.

The one remaining tatami had been placed in the middle of the room. The surrounding naked floor served as a frame for the dramatic events on the tatami. On it knelt Yamamoto clad in a gray kimono. His back was bowed, with his head down as if he were in prayer. A brief shaft of outside light gleamed on his thick, black, shiny hair.

At his right side knelt Uncle Toda, settled at an angle so that he could see his nephew's profile. He too was dressed formally in an black silk kimono lined in scarlet.

The absolute stillness of the room came from the depths of the ceremony, in which they both had become completely immersed.

Then, as sharp and clear as the first clap of thunder from and unexpected storm came a sound that froze their souls.

It was the slither of forged steel against the sheath.

Yamamoto's right arm moved with unbelievable speed and for the briefest part of a second he saw his family surrounded by impossibly pink cherry blossoms, a picture as lasting as his movement was irrevocable.

Even in the dull light the blade flashed blinding silver, as brilliant as the sun, instantly snuffed out when the blow reached its consummation, into the left side of the abdomen.

A slight cry emerged from his throat but no fear showed on his face. His body remained upright and still. A small movement, the perfect folds of the gray silk kimono disturbed for the blink of an eye just before the wild pull with both hands on the hilt, left to right, horizontally across the stomach cavity. Only now the shoulders trembled a tiny bit, and the abdomen sucked at the new found air. Beads of sweat burst out on his forehead, dribbling into a pool on the tatami.

Now, he saw the verdant green surrounding his family, beyond the impossibly pink cherry blossoms that could not hide their loving smiles. Incredible tension steadied his elbows as he brought the blade upward toward his rib-cage. *Who but he could possess such strength and force of will?*

With infinite slowness, as if settling by degrees, his fists still locked around the hilt, Yamamoto's body began to crumple forward still in complete control—a living monu-

ment. His forehead touched the floor, beyond the edge of the
tatami.

As if this were a signal, Uncle Toda moved. His right hand
flew to his side. With a silken whoosh the sword, up until
now hidden within the folds of his kimono, appeared naked
in his grasp. Standing now, he raised it over his head. It remained there, for a couple of seconds as he planted his feet
and took careful aim. When the blade began its downward
plunge it made a hot hissing sound that increased in volume,
and then fell silent.

Yamamoto's head was cleanly severed from his neck. Only
then did the body lose its control and completely collapse.
Blood spotted darkly nearby, in small droplets as if from a
tiny broken tea cup.

Toda knelt next to Yoshinari's head and touched it. There
were tears in his eyes.

At the Temple
of the Goddess of Mercy

Nabashima slowly pulled Sugawara, who helped by pushing
himself carefully away from the chasm—inch by inch. It was
terribly hard work because the flagstones continued to undu-
late. Finally, away from immediate peril, they both lay prone,
covering their heads with their arms. All sorts of debris continued to rain down. Bricks and tiles flew in amongst the
slivers of wood.

When the earth's movements diminished the young men
got shakily to their feet. Others in the vicinity did so, too.

"Are you all right?" asked Nabashima.

"Yes, I think so," answered Sugawara, "thanks to you. If it
weren't for you I might now be somewhere in the bowels of

the earth." He moved his arms around, rolled his head and did a few deep knee bends.

Nabashima twisted his body and swung his arms. "Our jishin has arrived. I hope the worst shocks are over."

Suddenly, before either one could survey the area's damage, or their situation, a thunderous shock struck and the stones seemed to push up from beneath them. There was not even time to yell out. The stones lifted again, as if a giant hammer was striking from below. While the two men struggled to keep their footing, something heavy flew by, grazing Sugawara's cheek. Whether it were a tile or a piece of zinc roofing, he could not tell.

As Nabashima grabbed his companion's shoulder to examine the cut, a hideous splintering crack, clearly heard above the constant background roar of destruction, pierced the dusty air. Now, abruptly, the shouts and cries of people in terror increased in volume. Somewhere amid the scorched smoky stench a voice shouted. "The tower has broken in half!"

The violent shocks slowly became a tremble. Their tennis rackets lay forgotten near a large broken cement lantern as they ran into the main Asakusa Amusement Park toward the twelve-story Asakusa Tower. It was the tallest structure in Tokyo. There were winding stairs inside, all the way up to the twelfth floor balcony, where the view was breathtaking. There was always a lengthy wait before the long climb. Everyone seeing Tokyo for the first time, especially those from other parts of the country, *had* to visit it.

The large number of fires they had to avoid along the way surprised them. Many of the lunch counters and food stands dispersed throughout the amusement park had caught fire with the first shocks. The hot coals that were cooking noon meals scattered and spilled in every direction. When the proprietors and workers at these eating establishments found they couldn't put these rapidly spreading fires out, they deserted their counters in an effort to save themselves.

Toshi and Kojuro saw only one fire engine. But, there were many police at the tower, which had been sheared off at the eighth floor. By a lucky happenstance the top four floors had dropped on an empty patch of ground rather than on the large crowd awaiting admittance below. It seemed everyone who had been in the building had died, or suffered almost certainly fatal injuries.

Presently, fires were the greatest danger to the crowds of screaming people. Rather than spreading they exploded from shop to shop. Even the trees began to burn. Pillars of smoke multiplied at an awesome rate. Both men remarked on at least a dozen blazes only a quarter of a mile away, in the Yoshiwara section.

Dodging flames, wild-eyed people, and some cracks in the ground, the two returned to the park entrance. A crowd milled around twisted street car tracks.

"I guess we won't be taking a tram as our means of escape," observed Sugawara.

"Ah, but Toshi," said Nabashima in a tone of reassurance, "do not be concerned. We shall be perfectly safe. We are only a few steps from the Temple of the Goddess of Mercy."

"My dear Kojuro," smiled Sugawara. "I have been in this temple many times." He indicated the main building with a polite sweep of his hand. "It is beautiful, magnificent. But, we should not be inside *any* building if another great shock occurs. Nothing will fall on us if we are outside."

"Well, we've been outside and your cheek is bleeding."

"It's merely a scratch," assured Sugawara touching his wound with fingers that came away with some blood. "I'm more afraid of the entire building coming down on us."

"As you see the temple and its gate remain standing. The fires are spreading. Come, let's go inside while there's still room. I promise you, Toshi, we'll be safe."

"But, isn't there some side entrance?" asked Toshi. "All the shops along the way are blazing."

"Not quite all of them," pointed out Kojuro. "If we're careful we'll make it through. Then we'll be safe."

Toshi shook his head doubtfully, but followed his friend.

At first the fires were confined to the small food shops and restaurants on this main entrance side of the temple. There were, of course, many of these. Now, however, the adjoining one-story, brick curio stores were afire as well. Like the owners and proprietors of the food shops, the managers of these shops had fled too. This was not an act of irresponsibility or cowardice, they simply had no means of fighting back. The quickly-spreading flames now merged and stormed higher and higher above the multitude.

Nabashima and Sugawara encountered numerous fires and were forced to backtrack many times, but eventually arrived at the main gate, where a number of police were shouting "Move along now," and directing people through the courtyard of the temple.

"We've made it!" exclaimed Toshi. "I had my doubts a couple of times."

"Don't worry my friend," said Kojuro assuringly, affectionately squeezing his cohort's arm. "We're now about to enter the Temple of the Goddess of Mercy. We're under Her protection."

Almost entirely surrounded by fires, and soon to be beneath a beautiful, large, heavy roof, Sugawara had some nagging doubts.

Once through the gate, they slowly progressed along the flagstone walk, along with scores of other people, flanked by stone and bronze lanterns. There was much to observe as they made their way to the main temple.

Just inside the main gate stood a magnificent and elaborate gold statue of Kannon, the Goddess of Mercy. Its beauty moved Nabashima visibly, and Toshi felt his friend became even calmer than before. Toshi too felt quite moved.

"Let us pray to Jizo," said Nabashima as they approached

the massive prayer wheel. He appeared to be almost in a reverent trance. "I know you are an avowed Christian, but Jizo will not mind."

"Why don't you pray for both of us," suggested Toshi.

"Why yes, of course I will," answered his companion with a smile and a slight bow, "thank you."

He took a paper off one of the piles provided, wrote a goodly amount of kanji characters, then awaited his turn to affix it to the large wheel. After he attached the petition, he gave the wheel a half turn.

When he stood near Sugawara again, his friend commented, "Most people use the wheel to pray for a better life the next time around."

"Yes, that's true," agreed Nabashima.

"Did you pray for a better life or that you would survive, today?" He swung his arm indicating the blazes in every direction.

"Oh, no," smiled Nabashima. "I'm not at all worried about us, for today; and, I'm quite content with my present life." He bowed slightly to his friend. "I prayed for you. I prayed that you would see the light."

They looked at the big bell which was presently silent. Nearby were two tall, bronze figures of Kannon on individual lotus blossoms. To their left stood what untold number of Buddhists came uncountable miles to gaze upon: the revolving library, which contained the magnificently vast literature of Buddhism, all of the main sutras were within this structure, and it was said that rotating it once was equivalent to having read all of them.

"I've always loved the library and been fascinated by it." said Sugawara.

"As have I, Toshi. But, for the present, you are a Christian."

"Yes."

Neither of the good friends wanted to offend the other, especially when they discussed the delicate subject of religion. Still, Kojuro felt it his duty to bring Sugawara back into the fold.

Suddenly, many people were pointing to the west and re-marking that the inside of the broken Asakusa Tower was aflame. "I'm surprised it took so long. Now we have fires all round us."

"Well," said Sugawara, as they continued slowly toward the main Temple, "at least those filthy pigeons have gone. So have the cockerels. Perhaps, they are smarter that we."

"The pigeons are part of the temple, too."

"I know. I know. I only don't like the mess they make."

"Toshi, have you prayed since we've been here—your Christian prayer?"

Nabashima detoured them for a moment to stand before a number of ginkgo trees. He looked up at them. "Aren't these beautiful? They're so golden later in the autumn."

"Yes, I've admired them too. And yes, I have prayed—to our heavenly Father that His will be done."

"Please, my old friend, I don't wish to offend you in any way—but, I did not know you had prayed. Of course you were with me at the library."

"Yes, I was."

"Are you afraid, Toshi?"

"Well, since we're encircled by ever mounting fires with-out any obvious routes for escape, yes I am."

"Happily, you need not be." said Nabashima. "I'm not at all afraid. Come," he cupped his partner's elbow. "Let us go inside under the shelter of the Goddess of Mercy."

Back in the stream of people, on the flagstone entrance walk, Kojuro mused, so Toshi would hear, "Buddhism is ap-proximately five hundred years older than Christianity."

"Approximately, if you go by the birth dates of Christ and Buddha."

"And, you have the 'Sermon on the Mount.' And, we have the 'Sermon on the Ganges.'"

"Yes, I believe that is correct. The Sermon on the Mount, however . . ."

Kojuro put his finger to his lips as a large statue of the Buddha looked benignly down upon them, and then they were at the foot of the great temple.

Four immense red-lacquered pillars set in huge bronze sockets supported a splendid tile-covered roof of exquisite shaping and proportions. Bronze-sheathed steps led upward into the building—108 feet square and circled round the outside by a beautiful, wide gallery. The two men joined a huge crowd milling about inside.

There were hanging and standing displays of every kind. Even these two worldly gentlemen felt some confusion. As they examined them, many items became more and more inexplicable. Banners hung everywhere. There was a shop in which gold Buddhas shone and brass lamps for temple use were available, along with queer utensils and mysterious little bits of stone whose secret was hidden in the cabalistic signs of Chinese script.

There was such a quantity on display, most of it for sale, it was almost too much to comprehend. Many Buddhist deities were in evidence, but Kannon was everywhere. She stood as a relatively simple golden figure, and also, if rarely, as a forty-handed, forty-footed, all-feeling, but certainly kind, dispenser of mercy. She appeared amidst bottles of scents, lanterns, bronzes, emblems, furniture, banners, pictures, and cards of her likeness, a few of portrait size, and thousands more similar to a postcard, but certainly not for mailing. If a devout pilgrim had visited all 188 notable Buddhist temples throughout the country and had understandably saved the Temple of the Goddess of Mercy in Asakusa for last—there was a pennant announcing this 189th visit, one of pure adoration.

Sugawara had noticed this pennant in particular. "Please let the pilgrim reach your heaven, Holy Father."

"What did you say, my friend?" asked Nabashima. It was difficult to carry on a conversation with so many people clapping hands to attract the deity's attention.

"The pine trees in the rear are an inferno." said Toshi loudly.

"Yes," answered Kojuro, "and the breeze has really picked up. It's almost a gale."

"Are you becoming concerned?"

"Not for us," said Kojuro, "only for those outside."

They moved toward the front through masses of people who called on the merciful goddess. Many, especially those grievously ill, called on Kannon to help them.

Near the front of the temple, Nabashima announced, "The ginkgo trees are burning. We will not have their beauty this autumn."

Toshi had not heard him because of the wind. He put his hand to his ear. "What?"

"The ginkgo trees are burning!" he shouted. "It's getting too dark for this time." He indicated his wristwatch. He put his head closer to his friend's. "Let's go to the inner shrine."

The inner shrine displayed cards saying there would be no admittance, but some lucky souls were entering, accompanied by a priest.

"I have never been to the inner shrine," admitted Sugawara.

"Oh, then you must go in. The goddess will be pleased."

"Have you been allowed to enter only because you belong to such a distinctive family?"

"Oh no," said Nabashima. "That had nothing to do with it. But, you know our Japanese saying: It is better to be born without hands or feet than to be born without family."

Sugawara nodded. He followed Kojuro, feeling amazed that all these people were not in a huge panic. Embers from the surrounding blazes were blown everywhere by the gusty wind. *In reality the temple should be burning, out of control.*

After checking their shoes for ten sen per pair, and depositing twenty-five sen each for admission, they and a large group of people were led inside by a priest. He was their official guide and handled the crowd with an ease born of experience.

The floor consisted of a fine matting. Just about all the statues and figurines of Kannon appeared to be of gold, and the overall impression was of gold, gold, and more gold. Besides the goddess, there were a few statues portraying various devils and divinities that were also made of gold but peered out of dusky niches.

Arrayed overhead were fishing nets which, according to the priest, were from the seventh century, and had been pulled up at the mouth of the Sumidagawa River with a one-and-three-quarter-inch pure gold figurine of Kannon inside. He said the nets were merely symbolic and while the figurine was here in the inner shrine, it was never shown.

"I've had some difficulty with that story since I reached the age of reason," observed Kojuro.

"But, why?" asked Sugawara. "I thought you were a true believer."

"I am. I've simply never understood why that particular likeness is never displayed. I want to see it." He smiled.

The priest pointed out a row of thirty-three manifestations of Kannon. He referred to them as "terrestrial." Nearby were brass and bronze incense burners accenting paintings depicting twenty-eight volumes of Buddhist scriptures.

Their guide said Shōgun Tokugawa Ieyasu had built the temple, and then a later Tokugawa shogun added the large gold statue of the Goddess. The priest seemed particularly proud to point out the ornate case that ran along one entire wall of the inner shrine containing one thousand seated images of Kannon.

"Oh, this always takes my breath away." said Kojuro.

"Mine too," agreed Toshi.

Then the entire group stood in front of a huge plate glass mirror. Each individual stared at the rare full-size likeness of himself or herself in the perfect mirror, some in amazement. For many, it was a brand new experience, and they registered their disbelief.

"We look horrible," commented Nabashima, "not at all fit to be in the Temple of the Goddess Kannon."

"Yes," agreed Sugawara. "We look as if we have been playing in soot, and smoke. Of course, we have!"

Suddenly, a huge crowd of people came pouring into the inner shrine, bringing with them almost unbearable heat. Soon Toshi and Kojuro perspired freely and breathed rapidly, but if one were to faint there simply wasn't any room to keel over.

"Are we going to die, my friend?" gasped Sugawara.

"Of course not," answered Nabashima somewhat cheerily. "We are in the Temple of Kannon, the Goddess of Mercy. We will all be saved."

The brass and bronze incense burners were out. Prayers from the crowd multiplied. Cries to Amida Buddha. Entreaties to the goddess.

Both men were pressed into a corner facing a tall wooden, statuesque Kannon — quite slender with her right hand extended palm up seemingly asking to help. The date on her base was 593.

"She's beautiful." commented Sugawara, in awe.

"Yes, she certainly is exquisite," agreed Nabashima. He took up a length of paper that was on a tiny pile nearby. Hastily he wrote some kanji characters, rolled the paper into a ball and placed it in her outstretched hand.

Others, close enough to reach the outstretched arm did the same. The two friends had so little room they were forced to extend their arms to keep the statue from toppling from its stand. They inched forward a little, pouring sweat, taking small, panting breaths in the oven-like air. "We are surrounded by fire!" some poor soul shouted. The chanting of prayers continued. Most of the lanterns had gradually gone out. Bodies sagged in the descending darkness, and life itself seemed tenuous in the mounting heat.

"Have you any final thoughts?" whispered Sugawara.

Nabashima coughed drily, then touched his friend's arm. He realized this had become an affectionate habit. "Yes, I have. Within two months, I'll be beating you regularly in tennis."

They both tried to laugh, but it came out more as a croak, followed by their coughing. How many coughs sounded in the inner shrine? What staggering number of whispered prayers wafted among the sweating, compressed multitude? It was impossible to know. How long were they there? That too was impossible to know.

And then, just outside this beautiful Temple dedicated to Kannon the Goddess of Mercy, the huge bell began to ring. Could this be? It had been silent since the earthquake.

Cooler air swept into the inner shrine like a breath of life. People began to move. The two friends were the last to leave, besides the priest who constantly muttered incantations while following them out. Priests were helping many people, particularly the sick and elderly. A strong, gusty breeze swept the gallery, and the sky was dark with smoke.

Everything around the shrine, for a substantial distance, had been destroyed. To the west the hulk of the broken park tower and a couple of gutted concrete buildings only accented the bleakness of the burned-out landscape. Toward the east, the view reminded one of a smoking scrap heap. Across the river, Honjo Ward seemed to be a huge bonfire.

Even the trees outside the temple were burned to blackened stumps. The Kannon Shrine alone appeared to be intact, with only a few superficial scars.

"It is a true miracle!" marveled Sugawara. "How do you explain it, Kojuro?"

They had left the temple environs and were sitting on the base of the broken, soot-covered lantern where Sugawara examined what was left of their tennis rackets. The strings were gone, and only the lower part of one handle had not been consumed. Nabashima smiled. "I believe we would call it *faith*. I never doubted we'd be safe. Toshi," he paused, "I believe my prayer for you has been answered"

Sugawara gazed for a few seconds, seriously at his friend. "Yes Kojuro, I have seen the light."

Sanji Nakamura and the Honjo Horror

Sanji Nakamura pushed up his glasses. Had that been the body of his beloved son in the river? The burning boat blazed furiously and there were other bodies, but only one that had looked to be in a student's uniform.

He must help those injured people on the Ryogokubashi Bridge. With the assistance of two other policemen who had arrived suddenly, the police box had been set upright again, in its proper place. Sanji grabbed a first-aid kit and raced onto the bridge, his fellow officers close behind. It continued to sway.

About the middle, he reached an elderly woman propped on an elbow with a bloody head. He wiped away the blood with gauze, while she continuously smiled and nodded, then yelled when he applied disinfectant. Just after he bandaged her head, the bridge bucked mightily and he was thrown off his feet.

When he felt he could stand, he ignored the elderly lady's concerns about him. The police were supposed to be impervious to emotion. A cart nearby had lost its two bundles, but when its handler had picked himself and the bundles up, Nakamura placed the lady on the cart, indicating where she should hold on. The "puller" smiled and bowed, the lady called something, but it was lost in the background roar that had begun with the first shock and still continued. The cart moved on toward the Honjo side. He appreciated the fact that the people respected and never questioned the police. Quickly, he covered his side of the bridge, to help those in need. There were fewer than he had expected, and he did his best for all of them. So did his comrades.

The three of them paused for a moment as they stood roughly at the middle of the long bridge, and spoke briefly with two of their counterparts who had come from the station on the other, or Asakusa, side. These two pointed out the deluge of fires on their side of the river, evidenced by merging fingers of smoke that even as they watched became a solid pall over the amusement park and Yoshiwara. They took off at a trot toward their posts, as did Nakamura and his compatriots. Back at the police box, they were surprised to realize that Honjo, too, had many fires. They were spreading rapidly even with two fire engines working to contain them, one pumping water from the Sumidagawa River. Nakamura knew there were just four fire brigades covering the Honjo and Fukagawa Wards and that they wouldn't have a chance to work effectively in such circumstances.

For the most part, the houses were closely packed together and terribly flammable. Many doubled as small family machine shops, so the occupants could eke out a living. Cans of lubricating oils and grease could be found in abundance. The separate fires merged and hundreds of terrified people headed for the Ryogokubashi Bridge, many carrying household goods or food. Not only did the bridge seem to offer some sort of haven away from the fire, but conditions on the other side were probably better.

Sanji, along with his two comrades, had anticipated this,

and now saw them approaching by the hundreds. Three more policemen arrived to help. There had been a general plan to keep people off the bridge in an emergency, but nothing on this scale had been foreseen.

When the refugees from Honjo got to Ryogokubashi Bridge they could see there was even more fire on the other north, or Asakusa, side. They could not turn back however because by now a huge throng was pouring in behind them. Everyone—families, children, people pulling carts of belongings—was pushed from the rear onto the bridge. The few police, including Nakamura, tried briefly to stop them, but not even an army of police could have stopped this panic-driven tide.

The situation on the other side of the river mirrored the Honjo chaos. Might there be less danger at the middle of the bridge? From the flames—for the moment, yes. But, the bridge was now completely packed.

The two huge, desperate mobs met and battled savagely in an insane struggle somewhere near the middle of the span. There was not time, or room, to be polite. No quarter was asked, nor any given. Bodies piled up. Some were smashed against the railings. People were crushed. Some jumped off the bridge to the water over a hundred feet below. Some were pushed.

Those from the Asakusa side appeared to be making more headway as the crazed throngs did deadly battle. Perhaps, they had more impetus because their ward had taken fire first, and these had so far been the deadliest conflagrations. Thus, they had more thousands behind them than the battlers from Honjo. There were thousands on the bridge, and still its approaches became more and more jammed with fighting and pushing people. The fires on both sides of the river had merged and become even larger conflagrations.

A breeze sprung up, and the people on or in the vicinity of the bridge were deluged with burning embers, bits of burning wood and sparks. Many screamed in pain, surprised by these fiery objects that went out quickly if they found nothing to feed on. Unfortunately, some found the carts piled with belongings and household goods that had been pulled onto Ryogokubashi Bridge. Now, there were fires on the bridge itself.

Police reinforcements arrived, about two dozen including a sergeant, whom Sanji had known for years. He informed the men that the Metropolitan Police Headquarters had issued orders to direct the residents of the Honjo and Fukagawa Wards to the former Army Clothing Depot, whose buildings had been torn down recently. It now provided the only open field in the area—and it adjoined the Yasuda Residence Gardens on the river which were walled and not ordinarily open to the public; but these were unusual circumstances. The two areas provided about thirty acres of open territory. All the people on the eastern side of the Sumidagawa River were to be directed to the clothing depot area. It was suggested that directions be given forcefully. This must be a result of the chaos that reigned on and around the bridge, and no doubt in many other areas of this woefully stricken city, thought Nakamura. The people usually respected his wishes and obeyed police orders. The earthquake, and ever multiplying blazes, had changed their world, and his, in a few minutes. He worried about his modest home, only about a mile away, where surely his wife and sons were doing their best. He felt some guilt that Toji was his favorite son. Though his family was somewhere in the bowels of this flaming ward, his official police post was here at the foot of Ryogokubashi Bridge. Sanji Nakamura would, of course, carry out his assignment.

He dutifully directed people to the former Army Clothing Depot. The residents of Honjo knew immediately where he wanted them to go. "Yes, the open field. It should be a safe place." Thick smoke filled the air, but even those on the bridge thought it a practical alternative. Some exhausted firemen momentarily stopped their truck to tell Sanji and his sergeant that the field had a fair number of refugees already, but there was plenty of room. They also suggested that the policemen discourage those who were pulling carts of belongings. Those that had caught fire on the bridge had caused grievous burns and just added to the panic.

According to Sanji Nakamura's watch, it was now half-past one, and even with fires all about, the people he directed were excited, and fearful, but now in less of a panic. Most of them knew of the large open space at the clothing depot, and it promised to be a safe haven.

The bridge was still jammed with a terrified mob, but the Honjo side had thinned out as word of the depot site spread. Sanji and his comrades were able to direct groups of people away from Ryogokubashi Bridge. Underneath he could see boats picking bodies out of the water. He fought back thoughts of his young son. Many boats were burning, including some that were usually available for a trip on the foul smelling river. This had been the festive bridge, from whence came glorious fireworks displays, as well as being a structure from whose heights Sanji had stopped disconsolate lovers from leaping to their deaths.

Some of the people Sanji was directing toward the depot pointed to a single, large, wonderfully puffy white cloud which had formed over the city. "Perhaps there will be rain to quench the fires." Sanji though, was educated enough to realize this cloud must be from the intense heat below reaching into the much cooler air high above. There must be a huge upward draft. He didn't discuss the hope for rain. He hurried people toward the clothing depot.

One of his sons appeared suddenly with a bag containing some rice balls. He told his father that there were many blazes around the house, but so far it had not taken fire.

"Are you all together?" the older man asked. His son nodded and held his hands out in an empty gesture, "except for Toji."

Nakamura nodded slightly in acknowledgment. Then his son said they were all going to take refuge in the clothing depot.

"Yes, yes," agreed Sanji as both a policeman and a father. "That is the safest place. Better go there immediately, all of you."

His son smiled and moved quickly away down the crowded street. Nakamura wondered if he would ever see him again. He returned to moving people along. He knew he should not eat the rice cakes in front of civilians, but he felt famished and they went down rapidly. Carefully, he folded the bag and put it in his trouser pocket.

Some frightened people from the western side had made it all the way across the bridge. They said the entire downtown area appeared to them to be overwhelmed by fire. They had originally expected to avoid flames on this side of the water. After all it was approximately 250 yards wide. They also remarked that a strong westerly breeze had developed.

Sanji pointed out the general direction of the depot. The narrow streets and alleys were becoming clogged with frightened citizens heading that way and piles of burning wreckage made the trip even more difficult. Fortunately, it wasn't far.

His sergeant, having seen the situation at the refuge returned again with reinforcements, and once more urged Sanji to discourage people from pulling carts of furniture and household goods, or carrying anything along. When the first people had arrived at the depot there was so much empty space some returned home, loaded a cart and pulled it back to the site. This, of course, took up extra room—the depot was pretty well filled now—and the added flammable materials would flare up easily, as they had seen on the bridge.

The Sergeant had said the depot was close to capacity. That would mean thousands of people, hopefully safe. But, the strong, gusty west winds were now actually blowing the flames from the Nihonbashi commercial district all the way across the Sumidagawa River. They had lighted two piles of empty boxes nearby. Sanji worried about his family. These winds. These flames. They were bad signs.

Another policeman told him the awful blazes from Asakusa were also being blown across the wide river. And, Honjo itself continued burning. How would these conditions affect the depot and the thousands there? Unless the winds changed, or lessened, it could turn into a terrible catastrophe. During his years as a policeman, Nakamura had been forced to deal with many blazes. After all Tokyo was certainly the most flammable city in the world. He knew a great deal about how fires behaved—nothing that approached this size, of course—but, he remembered fires were attracted to each other because the air above them created a strong wind that sucked them together.

Was any of this significant now? He really wasn't certain. What was certain, and he could observe the awful scene even through his dirty glasses, was that many on the bridge had been incinerated. Some were covered with flames. Many dead continued to smolder. There were hundreds of bodies in the water, a few small boats among them. The wind-borne stench sickened him.

Was there anything viable he or his fellow policeman could do in this general location? After a quick meeting outside the police box, they decided there wasn't. Even without their sergeant's orders, they decided they'd leave one man here and the rest would go help at the depot. The police certainly would be short-handed there. Here, most of the people whom they might have aided were beyond the help of anyone.

Sanji and his men—he did have seniority and they respected him—set out for the refuge. They found it hard going from alley to alley, trying to avoid flames and debris. Under his instruction, the men quickly learned to dash across alley intersections that often held whirlwinds of fire. They had to change directions, double back, and sometimes help those confused or injured. Their first-aid kits were now virtually empty. "There, this salve and bandages should help. Please, take your mother and wife to the depot directly. You'll be safe there."

"No, no, please do not take household things, or even small pieces of furniture. There won't be enough room."

"Yes, one futon should be all right, and yes, I do think we will be there overnight."

More and more residents of Honjo filled the alleys, and paths, and the few streets. *Where have they been up to now?* wondered Sanji. *Go to where it is safe. Hurry!*

"No, I do not think the clouds above will bring a rain-storm on us."

He and his fellows keep moving the crowd along. There were many in front, but few behind them. They no longer took notice of the dead bodies along the way. How was all this possible? *Has the world gone completely mad?* Nakamura knew he must not lose control of himself.

When Sanji arrived at the depot entrance, he could not believe it was so packed with people. Neither could his companions, most of whom could see better than he. "Even the Yasuda Gardens are almost filled."

Sanji looked at his watch—it was quarter-to four. *Is this the correct time,* he wondered, recalling his affectionate spat with his beloved Toji this morning. The wind was still quite strong, mainly from the west, but it changed direction—from the north, the east, and sometimes the dense smoke appeared to be twisting in the air. He remembered that there had been construction going on, in its beginning stages, in a corner of the depot area. There were sheets of zinc; stacked piles of lumber, and . . . Sanji lost his train of thought as he hurried to assist nurses and other medical staff as they brought patients from a nearby hospital and transported them into the crowded Yasuda Gardens.

Sanji took the front handles of a very sick-looking man's

stretcher. His fellow policemen helped too. This was not really a police duty, but the medical people were very short-handed. Nakamura led, steering the way with the first stretcher. Patients on crutches followed closely, many aided by the medics, and then many more stretchers. Sanji assumed his uniform and those of his few colleagues would aid in finding a place in the garden for these sick ones and their attendants.

He found the size of this huge crowd difficult to believe. Dense black smoke spun over the thousands of refugees. No, there must have been tens of thousands, jammed closely together, along with carts full of clothing, futons, small items of furniture, children, food, even pets in cages.

Parts of the huge throng began to scream and cry for aid from their neighbors, the gods, anyone. In many areas the swirling smoke had become twisting cyclones of fire hovering overhead. *Will they touch down, and burn us? No, it's impossible, too horrible. Like the smoke, they must stay above us.* But, the horror did descend—spinning around, relentlessly cutting paths through the humanity who wilted like ancient flowers. Carts of prized possessions turned into blazing torches—a funeral pyre for those perched atop them.

Sanji could hear the terrified screams and the crackle of flame. More fire whirlwinds cut into the crowd toward which they seem to be inexorably drawn. They appeared to come from all different directions, as the wind continually shifted.

The garden was jammed. The police tried to find any opening for the hospital patients, nurses, and other faithful staff. Sanji was still in the forefront, desperately gripping the handles of his stretcher. "Move aside," he shouted, "we have hospital patients here!" Those in front actually tried to make a little room by squeezing together a tiny bit. Sanji thanked them and led the group a bit farther.

But, he did not see the mud. No one expected the mud. The garden had been watered quite heavily earlier in the morning. Sanji lost his balance in the slippery earth. He felt

his ankle twist then slipped to his knees. The heavy tide behind continued. The stretcher and its body and rear bearer
propelled him forward. Then a deluge of bodies forced his
hands and face down into the mud. His helmet was lost, but
more importantly his glasses were dislodged. He tried to escape, attempting first to roll one way, then the other. But, he
was completely pinned down and felt the increasing weight
as more bodies piled upon him, driving even his face full down
into the three-or-four-inch deep mud. Only his hands were
relatively free. He barely noticed his aching ankle.

The screams were such a constant presence that he only
noticed them when they increased in volume or pitch. He
assumed that they were orchestrated by the whirlwinds of
fire. He recognized the sweet odor of burning flesh. Yes, the
air was getting hotter, and he found it more and more difficult to breathe. He fervently hoped his wife and family were
doing better than he.

How many bodies, or to be more accurate, layers of bodies
were above him? He could not tell, but he could feel movement and hear the crying and weeping and intermittent
screams from atop him. Somewhere nearby a voice noted the
"black sky." Strong winds spun around him and felt insufferably hot. Was this super-heated air, or was this fire? He pushed
his face as deeply as possible into the mud. More than once
he inhaled bits of sodden dirt.

Sanji now heard the ever mounting roar of what sounded
like a low flying airplane. A blast of flame driven by a super
wind reached down to him, touching his exposed skin.
Though he experienced it, he could not then realize the exact
details of what was to become known as the Honjo Horror—
a tornado of fire, approximately three hundred yards wide at
its base. It came from the direction of the river and swept
through the forty thousand souls at the clothing depot.

Police Officer Nakamura knew just when it was happen-
ing—the doomed thousands above and around him gave a

hideous groaning sigh that could be heard even above the roar of the tornado of fire.

Children, carts, bicycles, and even adults of small stature were picked up and transported by the tornado, sometimes hundreds of feet, even as they were incinerated.

More, but smaller, fire tornadoes developed. A blazing boat was tossed onto the Honjo shoreline, as were a number of other small boats, their occupants all dead. Firebrands flared in the darkened sky. Clouds of embers descended on the bodies. Sanji became aware that most of the unfortunate people crammed on top of him were dead. Their hot body fluids began to drip down onto him.

Now, as the sky became even darker with the approach of evening, it was more evident to him that some bodies above were still burning. He could hear the flames snapping and spitting. The air was a bit cooler now—he could breathe less painfully. He knew he was burned, but he didn't feel any localized pain except for his head, and the backs of his hands. He was totally exhausted. He could not believe it, but he was actually falling asleep.

Had he really fallen asleep? Or had he lost consciousness? He could not tell, but he realized it didn't make any difference.

However, some conditions had changed. The shallow mud underneath him had dried to dirt. He could see that night had come, and while there were few large fires nearby, whole sections of the sky seemed to be burning. He heard a few yells and an intermittent soulful scream, but they sounded rather distant. What tortured Sanji the most and made him aware he was fully awake was the pain, in parts of his body. The top of his head felt afire, although he knew it wasn't when he touched it with his few fingers that could still move. The backs of his hands were so burned even this effort was excruciating, and his ears seemed incandescent. He could not see details without his glasses, but he could move his body onto its side, and that encouraged him. The weight that had been crushing him felt much lighter now. The sweet pervading smell that continually gagged him was very much worse.

Among his fellow policemen Nakamura had a reputation for being experienced, wise, and strong. First he called out— he did not recognize his own voice because it sounded more like a croak coming from his scorched lungs and throat. He tried to rouse someone above him or close by. His voice improved but there was not a single reply.

He found he could roll left, and then right. Bones and cooked flesh tumbled over him. He ignored this and struggled to his hands and knees. The effort was immense. More human debris fell on him. If only he had his glasses. He shifted to his right, trying to stand up. The pain almost caused him to faint. "I must!" he muttered. His right ankle must be severely sprained as fierce pain shot through it with every stumble out and over the burned bodies.

The dead were all around him. He did not dwell on what had happened. Every action now was blind instinct. *Flee this horrible place! Get out!* Sanji stomped and shuffled through bodies whose flesh had been completely burned away. Bones snapped and cracked underfoot like dry branches.

Sometime, a little while later, his senses informed him that he had arrived in the Honjo Ward, near where his house once was. Everything had been burned to the ground.

There were only small, widely separated fires here, but there were several thousand corpses in the vicinity. Faces were unrecognizable. While there were few fires here, the sky itself seemed to be aflame. The great city of Tokyo was burning to oblivion, destroyed by a fiery, ravenous beast.

The clouds and thick smoke continually changed colors in their dance above this disappearing metropolis. Nakamura saw orange, yellow, pink, and all shades of red. A huge, thundering explosion hurled brilliant white-yellow into the flaming; sky. "The Naval Arsenal," mumbled Sanji.

Even though he had not come across a single living person, as he limped close to where his house had once stood, he was proud that he still had his sword. He had always considered this his official badge of authority. He wished he had his helmet, but he knew it had been lost.

When Nakamura touched the top of his head where his helmet should have been, he surmised that his fingers were touching his bare, uncovered skull. He also discovered that the skin on his right hand had been burned away, and that his right ear was gone.

The world is a terrifying nightmare. The sky threw eerie shadows, then lit them up. He felt a moment of joy—*there is the drain!* It was the drain he and his sons had dug, many years ago, and had fought to keep open since to keep puddles from forming around the house. It was low-lying ground, but the drain had usually worked pretty well. There was the heavy grating they had installed over it only a few months ago. He tried to bend over to get closer, to touch it, but the pain was too great.

As he straightened up, he was aware that someone was standing next to him. He should have been startled, instead he felt only a sense of relief. He cleared his throat.

The other figure spoke first, "Father!"

Sanji Nakamura tried to lift his burned hands, but instead could only acknowledge with his croaking voice, "Toji!"

Professor Hugh Riordan Walks to the East

As he strode away from his Tokyo home, one of his friend Heise's two houses, Professor Hugh Riordan planned his route to Hongo. He must find and rescue Tanya. He loved this beautiful and feisty Russian woman. He hoped and prayed he'd find her safe at her lodgings, the Matsunami Hotel. He imagined she wouldn't be as feisty today, what with the earthquake and the fires that continued to spread and merge throughout the city. It was a terrifying sight, and he felt certain thousands of people had already died beneath the ever-expanding smoke.

He used his stout walking stick to make better time on his way along the road into central Tokyo. Fortunately such a fine, wide street was available to him, and only a few house fires were to be seen in this area. He noticed some policemen dispensing drinks from a water wagon to people along the side of the road. Riordan admired the Japanese police. They were polite, efficient, and effective. He had his canteens. He hoped they'd be a sufficient water supply, both for himself and Mademoiselle Tanya.

He knew that Tatiana lived almost directly west of the Imperial University, and her hotel, really an inn, faced an alley just across Hongodori Avenue. Hugh had never actually been in the Russian girl's residence. She had strict rules. But, being a professor, he knew the way to the university quite well, though usually he went by streetcar. Today, without any trams or trains, he must avoid the dangerous residential areas, and get there as quickly as possible. His first objective would be the spacious Imperial Palace plaza.

This, he estimated, contained at least two square miles of rather open area and should be pretty safe from the constantly increasing numbers of fires. A substantial crowd of people crossed the canal with him at Yotsuya Station. He remembered there were 477 bridges in Tokyo. If it weren't so spread out, the city would have some likeness to Venice. Tokyo was huge however, a fact that would not be of help today, with so many people suffering from the effects of the quake and fires that followed. Today Tokyo's many bridges linked areas of smoke and fire. He and the people who had entered the grounds of the Imperial Palace seemed to be relatively secure from danger.

The plaza appeared to be about half full, but refugees were streaming in from every access route. A few carried household items, or pulled carts filled with personal treasures, and small children. Most everyone tried to get as close as possible to the Imperial Palace.

As Hugh climbed atop Kudan Hill he was deluged with breeze-driven embers. He quickly slapped at them but a few stung his exposed skin. They seemed to be swirling on a breeze that came from the direction of downtown. Asakusa, Honjo, Fukagawa and Nihonbashi wards looked to be almost totally engulfed by flame. There were spots without fire, but these were few. He caught a glimpse of the Imperial Hotel, remembering he should have been there, but the dense smoke quickly obscured the view. The fewest blazes were evident to the west. He tried to look in each direction to get his bearings.

Below, a group of fire engines guarded the front of the palace grounds. Near him on the hill were monuments and tributes to the glorious history of Japan. He rapidly surveyed the bronze torii gate, the lighthouse, the small temples and statues, and the now-gutted restaurant, where he had once dined with Tatiana—*I must find her!* Much smoke rose from her area in Hongo, near the university.

Riordan came down the sacred hill that so fascinated him and headed for Suidobashi, the bridge that would get him over the canal. Crowds of people made the going difficult. Almost all of them were hurrying in a direction directly opposite from the one in which he wanted to go.

A closely packed stream of people came over the bridge, probably heading for the palace grounds. Hugh wanted to cross in the other direction. He had made up his mind to try when two soldiers with bayonets affixed to their rifles barred his path shouting, "No entry", and waved their weapons to the side, indicating he should bypass the bridge.

While this initially irritated him, he of course realized they were right. How could he expect to get across going in the opposite direction to these compacted mobs of terrified people?

Clouds of smoke were leisurely emanating from the canal. What he saw looking into it was hardly encouraging. Many houses on both sides were blazing fiercely. A few had already been totally destroyed, their wreckage smoldering in the water. The smoke stung his eyes. How could there be so many dead bodies in the water? Maybe they'd sought safety there, but the fire had still engulfed them.

He scrambled down the embankment, grasping a fence and using his stick to keep his balance. There was no other alternative, he simply must cross the canal. When he reached the bottom, he encountered a partially beached boat, burning quietly with no one on board. Now, he almost felt thankful for the smoke because it muted some of the canal's usual stench.

Disconsolate people were wading in the water, which, surprisingly, only came up to their knees. The water should be much deeper. What had happened? Even at low tide the water was never this shallow. Even so, Hugh tested with his stick. It confirmed the lack of depth. Avoiding the wreckage and floating debris, he strode out—almost falling many times because the bottom was very slippery. Barefoot people experienced little difficulty; still, he was grateful for his boots. The thought of his bare feet on the canal bottom repulsed him. He was surprised that even through his boots, the water felt quite warm.

Riordan made it to the opposite side without incident. The few others he encountered as he climbed the bank seemed in a state of shock. Most ignored his greetings, solemn as they were, or briefly nodded as he grasped wreckage to pull himself up, or dug in his walking stick as a lever. At last he reached the top.

His feeling of accomplishment faded instantly at the fiery destruction that lay before him. Not a single structure remained standing between him and Hongodori Avenue, the wide street he sought. The single-story, flimsy private homes had been attacked by a ravenous beast, a maddened creature that devoured everything. The rows of alleys that had contained so many houses were simply burning piles, with a blackened body here and there to break the terrifying sameness. Riordan had fought in a few, large, horrible battles in Europe during World War I, but he'd never experienced such utter devastation.

The sight momentarily transfixed him. Clouds of smoke began to swirl as the breeze strengthened. From the south? It kept shifting. A small whirlwind of smoke from the debris flamed up, then suddenly went out. He plunged through the ruins, carefully avoiding bodies, moving toward Hongodori Avenue.

When he reached this wide street, he felt appalled. Nearly all the structures on its west side, both one-and two-story, were collapsed and still in flames. The better part of them had been consumed already. The glowing remnants burned even brighter when the breeze stoked them. Luckily the street was wide enough so he could make headway, if he were careful. Most of the corpses appeared to have been victims of the fires on the west side. Three trams had gone off the twisted rails, and one lay on its side, a dead body, apparently caught in the act of climbing out, was wedged in a window. A conductor studied it.

The American had taken these trams almost daily to meet his classes at the Imperial University directly ahead on the eastern side of the street. The buildings were set back from the thoroughfare. A few were engulfed in flame, and what really concerned him; the University Hospital emitted considerable smoke. Two fire engines were on hand at the front and a third in the rear. The firefighters worked efficiently.

His worry and nervousness took hold of him as he approached Tatiana's lane. Although she had never allowed him to visit, he had secretly strolled by to see where she lived. She had once told him she only allowed Japanese men to take their French and Russian lessons in her residence. The Japanese men were always perfect gentlemen. She said she could never count on this considerate behavior from any other nationality. Hugh had promised to be a perfect gentleman, but to no avail. He remembered asking her how could she have any concern about him, "a farm-boy from Wisconsin," but she remained adamant.

Now, of course, he was hoping and praying that she was still alive.

Atsui-san, the popular street vendor, was not at his usual spot. His generous cart was overturned there, a mountain of cooking coals glowing in the breeze. But, he was not there, and his tumbled food appeared pretty sparse. Hugh was suddenly aware of the many cracks in the pavement around him.

With a renewed sense of urgency, Riordan plunged into the opening that led to what Tatiana called "her lane." The alley, along with the Matsunami Hotel had taken a terrible beating. Many fires raged on both sides. A pitiful woman with a head gash must have been killed by a deluge of roof-tiles which were strewn everywhere. Near the front of the Matsunami, a young Japanese man had been crushed on the hood of his car by a telephone pole. *He must have been foolish to have driven into the alley.* A little girl was jammed between the right fender and wheel of the car, with her head hanging upside down. The American Professor gagged, then bent over her, gently shutting her eyes.

While there was plenty of wreckage, a number of bodies, and many fires in the neighborhood, the Matsunami Hotel looked to be in no immediate danger, at least from where he stood, Actually, it should have been classified as a rooming house. Its two-story structure was somewhat askew, and its inconspicuous entrance had been squeezed together, making it even smaller.

Riordan wriggled through it with considerable effort. He was both too tall and too wide, but he got in to the lobby. The staircase had been twisted out of shape, but not broken. The first step was about two and a half feet above the lobby floor. There remained only one pair of dirty battered sandals in sight, so the inhabitants must have fled. Tatiana would have been wearing shoes. The absence of footwear was reassuring. He thought of his own muddy boots, but quickly dismissed this concern.

No one stood behind the small desk, and it seemed strangely quiet. Hugh noted the contrast of being inside as opposed to the cacophony of evil sounds outside, especially the rather constant roar of things falling down.

He clapped his hands and called out, "Is anyone home?"

No response came immediately, but after a minute or so a middle-aged man wearing a plain kimono appeared, and bowed.

"Saito-san?" questioned Hugh, recalling the owners name.

"Hai."

Hugh bowed also, and introduced himself. Then he asked for Miss Lunskaya, explaining that she was his teacher. He felt somewhat awkward, though this seemed foolish, because she would never have allowed him to call on her.

Saito-san said he had seen her leave hastily after the initial shocks, and that all the guests had fled the building. Riordan bowed, thanked the innkeeper profusely and wished him good fortune. Saito-san bowed and returned the wish sincerely.

Outside, the alley fires had continued to spread slowly. Luckily they were rather shielded from the stiff breeze, and a number of intrepid people had formed a bucket brigade which seemed to be somewhat effective. Hugh wondered where the water came from, but the brigade worked feverishly. Further up the alley, the fires were much worse. He turned the corner and walked rapidly back to Hongodori Avenue.

Thank goodness she survived the initial shocks in her hotel, he thought, she was out there, somewhere in this modified hell. *Where would she go?* he asked himself while taking a sip from one of his canteens. (The lemon juice had been a good idea). *Perhaps, across the street to the university? No, probably not.* He knew she loved the library, but it was crumpled in many places, and a number of other buildings were burning wildly now, including the hospital. Swarms of people attempted to help the firemen who were trying valiantly to douse the flames.

Would she have tried to reach the Morozovs and Klavdia Davidovna? Almost certainly. They lived only a short way to the south.

When he arrived in their area, after making his way over and around piles of flaming debris and a few unfortunate dead, he stared at something like a moonscape. Everything had been burned to the ground. Under the blowing smoke there was nothing but utter devastation, a huge space so flat that Hugh had a horrifying thought. *It's so flat you could almost lay pavement on it.* All this must have crashed down with the first shocks. If Tanya had come here, she had almost certainly found nothing. But, where would she have gone? He did not even let himself think that she might be dead.

Again, he asked himself—after searching briefly for Klavdia and the Morozovs—*where might she have gone?* The safest, closest potential haven. The destination of hundreds of people who were streaming by him at this very moment. Ueno Park, of course, the largest and handsomest of the metropolitan parks. Tanya and he had spent many hours in this beautiful park, admiring the lotus blossoms in Shinobazu Pond, the Benten Shrine, the beautiful Mausolea of the Shogun, the zoo, and walking the shaded avenues, many heading to dainty shrines and sequestered retreats. He recalled the joyousness that pervaded the place at all times of the year.

But, not this particular day. The tolling of the bronze time bell brought him back to reality. *It rings even on this horren-*

dous day. The bell was close to the Tsukiji-Seiyoken Hotel and restaurant in the park. Hugh and Tanya had enjoyed dinner a number of times at the restaurant, but now he could see the swirl of heavy smoke above it. The breezes had strengthened, often shifting direction, but now seemed mainly from the west.

Where would she have gone? The causeway across Shinobazu Pond was crowded with people entering the park. Even now he could overhear some commenting on the beauty of the lotus blossoms that were slightly beyond their prime. The Benten Shrine on the small island in the middle of the pond was jammed, but he wedged inside. He and Tanya had loved the place, and all prayers were important. Finally, he was across the pond and still among a throng of people.

They did not seem to be particularly afraid, as though they had reached a safe haven. *Perhaps, we have*, thought the American. A few smiled at him, and he returned the bows and smiles. Did they think him a crazy foreigner, dressed as he was to climb Mount Fuji? The absence of dead bodies certainly helped his spirits, as it must have those around him. At the bluff overlooking the railway station had been a small group of rather simple restaurants and tea houses. These had all burned down and were throwing clouds of smoke towards the southeast. No doubt dead bodies could be found there, but he was determined to avoid that area.

Ueno Park was located in one of the city's highest sections. Within the park the highest point was called Suribachiyama because of the similarity of its shape to a *suribachi*—an earthenware vessel in which bean soup was prepared. Tanya thought this concept quite humorous, but when Hugh arrived on the small hill, he could not find her in the multitude.

Close by stood the impressive Fine Arts Building. No tensen admission was being charged today, but while it still was magnificent, many pieces of hanging art had fallen to the floor. Riordan though, was mainly concerned with Tatiana, and she could not be found there. Outside, he saw a tipped-over train car, the closed station, and the usual superb view of the city that lay to the south, and to the east of the Sumidagawa River. These sights, taken as a whole, or individually, horrified him.

Asakusa Ward appeared totally burned out, as did the amusement park, with the exception of the Temple of the Goddess of Mercy. The Yoshiwara was on its way to a fiery extinction. The Nihonbashi commercial area burned savagely, its sheets of massive flame being blown intermittently across the three hundred foot wide river by a merciless wind into Honjo and Fukagawa, two wards already badly stricken.

Most of the dense smoke blew east and south away from Ueno Park. But, in the areas of most damage, particularly over Asakusa and Honjo, it was as dark as night.

Was this the smoke? Yes, even with the strong breeze from the west, other winds were generated by the awesome heat that gusted in every direction, setting up whirlwinds that spun in ever changing patterns.

Although the American possessed excellent vision and was on elevated ground only a mile, or a little more, from the worst conflagrations, he decided to turn to his knapsack for help. Inside were the mother-of-pearl opera glasses Tatiana had lent him for his recent climb up Mount Fuji. He had forgotten to return them. They had come in handy during the sold-out performance of Pavlova, the world renowned Russian dancer. The Tokyo audience had loved her.

And he loved Tatiana. How he wished he could peer through the glasses and find her. The ornate handle and the mother-of pearl finish seemed incongruous in these awful circumstances; they were meant to be beautiful and to look upon lovely objects.

Hugh could see around and through the smoke much more efficiently with the glasses. Yes, Asakusa, virtually the entire ward, had become a smoldering wasteland. The huge Nihonbashi Fish Market, where he had bought superb fish, was a bonfire, as was most of Nihonbashi. There were fires just about everywhere in the Ginza area. The very street burned; his glasses were strong enough to confirm that fact. The American felt proud when he focused on the Imperial Hotel, still solid and unscathed. Could Tanya have gone there?

Then his glasses pointed across the Sumidagawa River, into Honjo. He did not raise them to check Fukagawa. Honjo was so engulfed in flame that it riveted his attention. He adjusted the glasses for an optimum view. A little way east of the Ryogokubashi Bridge, adjoining the river, was an enormous crowd of people jammed closely together into what must have been a huge open field. For some reason he thought of the family farm that had been given to his father by a grateful State, after the brave Irish immigrant had served in America's Civil War of the 1860's. Hugh had seen it from the air, and he recalled the farm was forty acres. In between dark swirls of blowing smoke, Riordan estimated this crowd of people covered something close to forty acres.

He studied these poor packed-together souls, surrounded on three sides by Honjo, in flames. There must be thousands. No, no, there must be tens of thousands, many with carts of belongings and household items, even some tables.

As he watched, whirlwinds of smoke containing cores of pure flame danced over and through the assembled throng, leaving smoldering bodies in their wakes. He felt a sudden strong gust of wind directly in his face. He also heard it when it whipped past his ears. The strengthening winds were changing directions with great suddenness. What had been a strong wind from the west, now gusted from the south, then east, then seemingly from all directions at the same time.

Waves kicked up on the Sumidagawa River, causing consternation among the hundreds of small boats that were now being tossed about by white caps. Many were overturned; the turbulence was unbelievable on a river only a bit more than three hundred yards wide.

The wind! Now and then Riordan and the thousands in Ueno Park were deluged with embers and streams of sparks that rode the changing, swirling winds. Were these from across the river? It seemed impossible. Then these sparks rode a different, stronger breeze that changed direction in a split second, then came from all sides at once.

People had remarked on the pretty cumulus clouds that hung over Tokyo. The spinning, rapidly changing winds generated ever stronger updrafts. The burning areas looked out of control, especially across the river—but Riordan noted nearly the same condition on this side too.

He felt relatively safe on the edge of the park, but there were so many factors involved in the worsening disaster—the surging, unpredictable winds, and the periodic swirling rains of fiery particles to name but two. He remembered the fireplace on the family farm, the draft becoming stronger as the fire became hotter.

A partial vacuum was created near the ground, causing the winds to rush in from every direction to fill it. The flames wanted to move leeward, or with the wind. The air pushing from almost every direction meant that there was no one direction for the wind to move in. Instead, the mass of fire was spun like a propeller by the strongest gusts, and climbed, spinning around a core of oxygen.

Soon, a pillar of pure flame became visible, swirling, rotating, twisting high above the blazing rooftops, reaching for the clouds. Before the tower of flame reached the clouds, the air itself started to burn. Driven by the ever-increasing gale coming from all sides the top of the thick pillar erupted like an exploding volcano. Its edges rolled over and descended to the ground, where the oxygen was more plentiful. Temperatures reached unimaginable levels. Even non-combustible items simply vanished. People one or two hundred yards away became instant skeletons. This was the world's first firestorm. Mercifully the exact conditions mandatory for its creation didn't last very long. Tokyo continued to burn fiercely, but the firestorm and its volcanic fury were quickly spent.

The people in Ueno Park survived. Riordan could only hope that Tanya was here somewhere. Oh yes, he could see the whirlwinds of fire going up and down the alleys on the other side of Hongodori Avenue. So far though, the park remained a haven. Fortunately, the spinning cones of fire that danced to the south, mostly near the river or across it, had not been pushed in this direction. They were small but deadly when they dipped into the huge crowd packed together in Honjo Ward.

Hugh studied the area around the Sumidagawa River with his opera glasses. He could see quite well without them, but they picked up more detail in the spots where he aimed them. Some of the "whirlwinds" were probably tornadoes. He had seen many "dust whirlwinds" on the farm during his boyhood, and four full-sized tornadoes. These were usually much bigger and spun counter-clockwise, because of the earth's rotation. Proud of his rapidly growing knowledge of the Japanese language, he wondered if *tatsumaki* (dragon twist) was the appropriate word.

He tried to keep his glasses on the tens of thousands in the field near the river in Honjo. Billows of gray smoke got in the way, and it was getting darker. The time bell had just boomed four times, indicating that it was four o'clock. Riordan resisted the urge to check his watch. Somehow, he felt that would be disrespectful. When it came to duty, the Japanese had no peers. Even in the midst of this cataclysm, he felt sure the man who attended the bell would have to die rather than miss striking the exact hour.

Suddenly, he was intensely aware of a deep, deafening thunder close by. It pained his ears and head so much he shouted to relieve the pressure. The Japanese near him were also looking south. The excruciating roar continued. The sound was horrible. The sight, much worse.

A huge tornado of fire moved slowly up the west bank of the Sumidagawa River. For the most part it roared above the shoreline, touching down only briefly. It was at least two hundred yards wide, growing as he watched, and twisting more violently as the velocity of its turbulence gained speed. Around him, the gusty, multidirectional winds grew to nearly gale force.

The huge mass moved slowly up the Asakusa side sucking up flames from buildings and increasing its energy. Whenever it came close to the river it picked up debris, small craft, and people. These were lifted into the air, and some of the lighter objects were drawn in when it swirled down onto the water. Hugh could see unfortunate souls in the river writhing while they were incinerated down to the level of the waterline. There was a small tree being consumed in the torrid spin—and part of a house; a bicycle. And always the deep roaring thunder of the deafening, ever widening twisting furnace.

When it reached the expansive torch that had been the Polytechnic School, it seemed to gorge itself on the school's smoke and fire. Now strengthened, it grew larger and even more ferocious.

Had the winds changed? Riordan couldn't tell. But, he gaped in disbelief; slowly, the massive tornado of fire began to spin toward the opposite side of the Sumidagawa River. It was surely wider and taller than before. The Japanese on both sides of him gasped at this sight. Of course, the few things in its path on the river were instantly consumed, the water turning to steam in its wake. *Good God, it's almost as wide as the river itself!*

Hugh used the glasses again. How tall was it? *Oh God!* A hundred yards, no, no, at least two hundred yards. No, it certainly was taller than its width. There was so much smoke;

clouds of steam that erupted counter-clockwise. Then, as though steered by a demoniacal hand that must be the epitome of all evil—the huge mass of pure, spinning flame engulfed the tens of thousands cramped together in the area of the clothing depot.

Continuing to roar, it leisurely spread over this ideally confined, combustible mass. He expected to hear screams. Instead, above every other sound, came a terrified drawn out moan from tens of thousands of lungs being scorched.

The underlying thunder of the tornado persisted. Its turbulent radiance of oranges, reds, and yellows made it difficult to look at. It spun so many objects aloft, and with such speed, that Riordan could hardly distinguish them. Certainly there were people, though they had the aspect of flaming dolls; small carts, futons, baskets, pillows, bicycles, zinc sheeting, tables, thousands of pieces of cloth, a tree, and even a smattering of umbrellas. The scenes were too horrible when he concentrated his gaze on the ground. He lowered the glasses and shook his head. The man next to him shook his as well.

How long did the ravenous tornado feed on the contents of the field upon which once stood the clothing depot? To Riordan's horror-stricken mind it seemed forever, an eternity. It was still there spinning, devouring everything within the depot and its environs. *At least ten minutes.* His usually precise mind had become somewhat fuzzy this awful day. *At least twelve minutes. No, more like fifteen.* It seemed an awfully long time. Then dark smoke billowed toward his vantage point, obscuring his view of the carnage.

Gusts of searing wind from that area stung his face. He and those near him were showered with large embers and burning fragments of wood. He joined those around him in beating at the ones that landed, smoldering, on himself and his neighbors. The man next to him extinguished a persistent burn on Hugh's back, and the professor returned the favor by brushing away glowing particles in two places on the man's kimono. Throughout the park people continued to slap at the more tenacious cinders.

The southerly wind now became a strong, steady breeze; and, using his glasses again, Hugh felt a sense of relief as he discovered that the fire tornado had partially entered the Sumidagawa River. No doubt the change in wind had been a factor, and now huge columns of steam mixed with the smoke and towered above the flames. More and more of the tornado went into the water. Was it losing some of its punch? He hoped so—there could hardly be anything left to burn in the clothing depot and the surrounding area. The horrifying twister became a comparatively slender pillar of flame slowly making its way across the river from south to north. Around him the hail of embers lessened to only a few.

While vast sections were totally leveled, there were still plenty of spots where fire still raged. Riordan felt more assured that he and the thousands in Ueno Park were safe, baring something unforeseen. But, he knew he must find his dear Russian, Tatiana. That was his mission.

He recalled their conversation about the grand opening luncheon at the Imperial Hotel. He was supposed to attend, but had decided not to because he wanted to be with Tatiana. She had refused his invitation because one of her Japanese pupils was going to drive her to Yokohama in his new motorcar. Well, she usually spent her weekends with the Peacocks in Yokohama so she could sing services in the Russian Church.

She must have seen his disappointment when she'd refused him, so there was probably a strong chance she thought he had decided to attend the reception after all. The odds were good she would look for him there. And, with the aid of her opera glasses, he could see the Imperial Hotel was still in very fine shape. Yes, she might be waiting for him at Frank Lloyd Wright's solid fortress.

Before he left his point of observation at Ueno, Riordan viewed the city in wide arc, from west to south to east. Yes, the tornado of fire had disappeared into the Sumidagawa River. Below his vantage point though, incredible agony stalked the narrow blazing streets. Thousands of people were dying, being roasted alive. He felt almost guilty at being in a relatively safe location. The winds still whipped around him. A Japanese professor had once told him, "Winds are to Tokyo what fog is to London." Today's winds were, of course, generated by many unusual causes, such as the fires spreading and trying to merge, the differences in temperature, the varying density of oxygen, and the generation of partial vacuums.

To the north, just a little way away, was Hugh's beloved university. He had just thought of going there on the way to the Imperial Hotel, even if it were a bit out of the way. Now, however, he could see most of it furiously ablaze. No place was completely safe. Ueno was still the most promising haven. Still, the most beloved woman in his small, but genuinely romantic world, was likely inquiring about him at the Imperial Hotel. Yes, it would be dangerous, but he must find Mademoiselle Tatiana.

As the American professor left the confines of Ueno Park, he wondered about the best route. There certainly was plenty of smoke and flame between him and his objective. He stood in the middle of the streetcar and train tracks at Ueno Station, gazing in the desired direction, toward the Imperial Hotel, through Tanya's binoculars.

He knew the trams ran to the Central Station, and then on, to a point directly behind the Imperial Hotel. Plenty of twisted rails and upset streetcars complicated the right-of-way, and a short distance further were piles of wreckage and burning rubble. It was a start, however. He returned the glasses to his knapsack, drank from his canteen, and set off walking next to the tracks.

Initially the tracks crossed streets wide enough for him to make his way, even if they were strewn with debris and an occasional body. There were few people, and these moved slowly and aimlessly, looking stunned and incredulous. They didn't seem to notice him, even though he was a somewhat strangely-dressed foreigner.

He tried to move as fast as possible over the area of wide streets, but noticed a little extra exertion made his lungs ache from the large quantities of smoke he inhaled. He coughed, almost choking when billows of it thickened in his path.

Hugh realized he was now in a residential section which had become a burning field. Some of the few brick or stone buildings stood mostly upright, their interiors gutted. What remained continued to burn, but the narrow streets and alleys, so typical of Tokyo, could hardly be defined anymore.

He had come to an area where the trams had proceeded on an elevated embankment. A gutted car lay on its side at the bottom to the right. Tracks were either missing or twisted into serpentine shapes. Overhead wires were non-existent. The material forming the embankment was crumbled and cracked ahead, and in some places swallowed up by the earth beneath. On the left was a jagged tear, a massive, gaping fissure in the earth itself. It sparked and spewed flame like a creature alive.

Riordan knew he must avoid this "creature," and wondered if there were more of them ahead. Probably. He picked his way down the slope after deciding to leave the right-of-way and change his route.

There were a considerable number of bodies here. It tore at his heart to see an unrecognizable body wrapped around a much smaller body, also damaged beyond recognition, generating in his imagination a devoted mother trying desperately to save her child.

Grateful for the sturdy boots that kept the small fires from his feet, he angled a bit to the right. After climbing over wreckage, and numerous small fires, he felt relieved to find Gokencho Street. It contained plenty of rubble that had fallen into it from both sides, but it was wide enough to be passable.

He recalled passing through this street once, after speaking to the ladies of the Women's Higher Normal School. He remembered their pretty, shiny, straight, black hair. Of course, all Japanese had straight black hair, but these ladies had been unusually attractive. After all, he'd never spoken to a large number of young women before. He had been treated royally too, because he was a man, a foreigner, and a professor at the Imperial University

Hair was particularly important to him, because all his fifteen brothers and sisters had curly black hair, but he, the youngest, born when his mother was fifty-four, had pure white hair until he was about twelve. The boys in his parochial school taunted him about it, so he learned to use his fists when quite young.

It felt good to let his thoughts briefly wander from the horrors around him. He had loved to travel around Tokyo on foot during happier days, so he felt a familiarity with Gokencho Street knowing it led to Manseibashi Bridge, where he should be able to cross the nearby canal. The houses on Gokencho had been undistinguished, and of the plainest variety. Now, they were piles of rubble that merged on both sides of the street, here and there pouring forth pockets of guttering flame. Certain of the shops had catered to foreigners. He pictured some of the advertising signs he could remember. Barber Shot; Advertising Agent and Undertaker; Trunks and Bugs. This was also the street where Umbrella and Company was located, and Nobody Medicine—oral contraceptives—was offered for sale. Sadly, the amusing signs had met the fate of the buildings to which they were attached.

Somewhere in the fires ahead should be the bridge. A number of others seemed to be heading that way too, probably to seek refuge within the Imperial Palace grounds.

Hugh felt quiet anticipation during his labored approach to Manseibashi, one of those old humpbacked bridges of considerable charm. On both sides of the canal near the bridge were steps of quaint, doll-like houses that climbed up from the bank and squeezed tightly against each other. Quite a few were built on wooden piles and featured overhanging rear balconies. These usually displayed colorful flowers and some had cages with songbirds in them.

When Riordan came upon the crossing though, he realized its picturesqueness would only live on in his memory. The bridge itself was no longer identifiable. On either side, as far as he could see, were heaps of smoking wreckage and not a sign of a songbird or any flowers. He sat on his haunches surveying the awful sights and all at once felt overcome with sadness. *All those poor, unfortunate people, they had tried so hard to make it beautiful.*

Many near him began to make their way down the embankment toward the water. It was far from easy. Hugh picked his way carefully, again glad he had brought the stout walking stick to help him gain a solid footing as he descended. As he clambered over the piles of ruin strewn along the bottom, he felt grateful that Japanese carpenters seldom used nails. Even with his stout boots, nails could have added greatly to his difficulty as he crossed. As it was, the boots did not keep out the shallow, filthy, overly warm water.

There were many dead bodies, most of them charred. A disconsolate man stood in water that just covered his ankles, pointed at it, and mumbled something about its being hot. Riordan replied that yes, it was hot, and spread his hands to indicate that he didn't understand the cause either. He guessed that the massive fires were heating the water, but its lack of depth perplexed him.

One characteristic of the canals had not changed—the awful odor. How could the Japanese stand it? He proceeded across the slippery bottom and began ascending the still smoldering mess on the opposite side. The Japanese, from the highest to the lowest station in life, loved beauty and adored every kind of fragrant blossom. How could they exist near these narrow waterways that were essentially open sewers? Their sense of smell must be so atrophied that it failed to apprise them of stenches that all but staggered Westerners. Hugh found himself gagging as he staggered up the bank.

Just as he approached the top, a particularly strong gust of this stench overcame him. He gasped and felt his legs giving way beneath him, and, despite his stick, slid to his knees. Sweat poured from him. His breath became labored, and dizziness took hold of him. Gradually the whirring roar in his ears left him, and the frightened shouts of distraught men and women came as if from a distance. He took a number of deep breaths, no longer noticing the frightful smells as his head cleared. As he clambered over the edge, a strong, slightly fresher breeze engulfed him. He uncapped one of his canteens and let the lemon-laced water refresh him. *I must be hungry,* he thought. Then he realized that he could easily skip a few meals, those thousands of suffering Japanese who would survive the flames would certainly miss many meals. *I'd better think of survival myself.*

An explosion from the general direction in which he wanted to travel startled him. Then there was another, and yet another. They sounded like dynamite, but he couldn't be sure, nor could he explain them.

The smoke cleared momentarily and he took stock of his position. Directly to the north was the Russian Cathedral where he and Tanya had attended services a few times. Three hours of standing through mass—now that was devotion. But, she certainly would not be there, though the large stone building stood solidly, even if the huge gold cross over its entrance had disappeared. Many fires burned near the cathedral.

He recognized that he was in Kanda Ward, just a few steps away from Nihonbashi Ward, a large commercial area, containing the massive fish market he knew rather well. But, much of that area was engulfed in flames. Getting through it on his way to the Imperial Hotel might prove impossible. *Damn!* There was another of those strange explosions.

He also wanted to avoid having to cross Nihonbashi Bridge. Because of its importance, he surmised it would be jammed beyond belief. So, Riordan decided to remain in Kanda Ward and work his way to the Imperial Palace grounds. He knew the southwestern corner at Hibiya Park stood across a wide intersection from his goal—Frank Lloyd Wright's hotel.

He crossed twisted railroad tracks nearby, just south of a demolished station. There were people about, but he was nonetheless surprised when an amazingly fresh looking Japanese couple with two children approached him and asked in Japanese, "Excuse me, but have they got the trains going yet?"

Riordan was dumbfounded by the question, since a mere glance around would reveal sights of past and ongoing destruction. "The trains—the tracks are broken, embankments have been swept away—landslides . . . "

He felt grateful when a nearby man who had heard the question shouted loudly, "Fools—all downtown is gone. Shitaya and Asakusa, too. Tokyo Bay is a sea of flames! We'll all be next!"

Hugh began making his way through the devastation, determined to make his next objective, via Sudacho, and some narrower but more direct streets to Kandabashi. It was only a little ways, but as always, difficult. Now, more ruggedly constructed buildings of brick and stone or cement appeared; some or all about four or five stories high. Many still standing had their backs broken at the second floor, as though the entire structure had been twisted by a giant hand.

Riordan plunged toward Kandabashi, and made it across with surprising ease. As planned, he found himself close to what had once been the huge main gate at the southeast corner of the Imperial Palace. Here beneath the trees of an outer garden, hundreds, perhaps thousands, of crazed people demanded to be admitted.

To get them all in would have been virtually impossible. The space was very limited, taken up by the picturesque moats of varying depth and width, and the beautiful but extremely dense trees. Soldiers with fixed bayonets kept the throng at bay outside the massive gate and attached fencing. As politely as possible, policemen directed people to the other side of the castle buildings, where the two square miles of the Imperial Palace Plaza awaited them. Riordan wished them luck, having come from Kanda Ward, he knew much of the plaza was packed already.

Surrounding the palace enclosure were several parks, the chief government buildings, many of the foreign embassies and legations, several schools, churches, shrines, and many other important places. He tried to take note of as many of them as possible while he picked his way the last half mile or so to his final objective. Most of these structures were of solid, fireproof construction. Many had tumbled down and were simply piles of brick or stone, but the Sumitomo Bank stood unscathed, as was the Tokyo Chamber of Commerce. Tragically, the Mitsukoshi Department Store, though standing, had become a furnace inside. The beautiful Imperial Theater, its incomparable decor featuring rows of comfortable seats in the European style, poured thick smoke across the nearby moat. Close by, covered by a gigantic network of collapsed phone and tram lines, Police Headquarters spewed flame from most windows despite the best efforts of the crew of a fire engine parked in front.

The Central Railway Station, featuring solid brick columns holding up its stairways and roof, was surprisingly only lightly damaged. Some of the columns were slightly cracked but bore scorch marks. Fire must have visited it earlier. The handsome Peers Club had become an undistinguished pile of rubble. Even its renowned penthouse had disappeared. The

Hypothec Bank, built in a modern style of home-grown, Japanese architecture had fared a little better.

Just beyond the Peers Club, squatting serene and unscathed, was what some Japanese architects had referred to as a "Sorcerer's Palace," Frank Lloyd Wright's Imperial Hotel. Because of the constant concerns about earthquakes, Wright said he designed his building like "a super dreadnought." The Imperial used double-shelled walls, with outer layers of brick bonded to a core of steel reinforcing bars and poured concrete. The first floor walls were especially rigid. They were thicker and had fewer windows than the upper, more tapering walls. "Roof tiles of Japanese buildings have murdered countless thousands of Japanese in upheavals." Wright had said. Thus, a light, handworked green copper roof had been designed for the hotel. Each of the hotel's myriad pieces of stonework was hollowed out, fitted with copper reinforcement and bonded to the building with poured concrete. The architect had called the overall style "Modern Aztec." Hugh enjoyed the fact that the hotel had stood the one vital test of earthquake design—it had survived.

When he entered near the reflecting pool, a long line of men had formed a bucket brigade and were passing the sloshing containers to their co-workers who were wetting down the roof. Someone told him they'd been at it since shortly after the shocks. They had even saved a nearby burning building, but had lost another one. Now and then a shower of embers deluged them, so this water reservoir Wright had planned came in very handy.

The inside was packed with men, many more than the two hundred who had been invited for the Grand Opening Luncheon. He searched for a familiar face. It seemed as though most of the foreigners in Tokyo were there. Men stared back at him. He knew he must have been quite a sight, muddy and smoke-begrimed, dirty enough to be a chimney-sweep.

Hugh spied a British colonel, complete with swagger stick,

and moved in front of him. "I hope you're doing well in this difficult time, Colonel. May I ask if you've seen any foreign women about."

The colonel paused, looked him over quickly and with a twinkle in his eyes answered, "I must say you Yanks get right down to cases—but, no, the only women I've seen have been the kitchen help and maids. You do look as if you've been through hell trying to find one."

"Yes, I have. May I ask how long you've been here?"

The officer reached for his box of cigarettes. "I've been here since the collapse of our world interrupted the grand opening."

"Yes, I was supposed to attend, also."

"I'm Colonel Roger Blandings," he announced, offering Hugh a cigarette.

"No thank you, I never took up smoking. I'm Professor Hugh Riordan. I teach at the Imperial University."

"Well, good show, Hugh!" he said, lighting up and extending his hand. "Only a smart fellow like a professor would be wise enough to avoid these damn things—can't be good for a fellow." He took a long drag. "Oh, I say, there's a chap you should meet, fellow countryman of yours." He gestured toward a handsome man wearing an American Army uniform, adorned with the gold leaves of a major.

"Phil!" he called. "Phil Faymonville!"

The American, appearing a bit distracted, changed his direction and came over.

"Phil, I'm happy to introduce you to one of your countrymen, Professor Hugh Riordan of the Imperial University. Hugh, Major Philip Faymonville is your Military Attaché."

"I've heard of you Major." said Hugh.

"And I of you, Professor." They shook hands.

"Goodness," remarked Roger. "You've heard of each other? Are you both in films or something?" They all enjoyed a good laugh at this comment.

"Hugh, I'll be leaving you in Phil's care—about time—he loves to care for Americans. He's a good chap, but remember, no more shaking hands. The Japanese are convinced it's a filthy habit, and of course, they're right—simply an exchange of germs and microbes." He bowed slightly, touching his swagger stick to the visor of his peaked cap. "See you later fellows."

Hugh and Faymonville both gave their thanks. "Not at all," commented the colonel, "always glad to help people from the colonies."

People stared as they echoed each other's laughter. "He's quite a character." said Faymonville.

"May I call you, Hugh?" asked Faymonville, grasping the professor's elbow to help steer him through the crowd. "You look done in, may I get you something to eat?"

"Yes, thank you, Phil. I could do with some food."

"Do you know our manager, Inumaru?"

"Well, I've met him on a few occasions."

The Major moved them toward the banquet hall. "He's done a terrific job—facing every emergency—and solving all kinds of problems. He's been magnificent." He swept his arm around indicating the crowd. "As you can see, we're taking care of a lot of folks. Here, we can get a seat in the banquet hall. Careful, it's dropped a couple of feet."

They both sat on opposite sides of a small table. "I believe we're pupils of the same teacher, Mademoiselle Tatiana Alexandrovna," began the army officer. "She's mentioned you to me—as a fellow American."

Hugh would have preferred being known by a more affectionate term than "fellow American," but he knew Tanya was very reluctant to display any private thoughts. "Yes, as a matter of fact she mentioned you to me. I've been looking for Tanya, since the earthquake. I thought she might have come here because I was supposed to attend the opening ceremonies." Hugh deliberately used the much more intimate form of the Russian woman's name than the major's Tatiana Alexandrovna.

"No, I'm sorry, I haven't seen her. She would be a charming guest, though. It seems as if most of Tokyo's foreign community has gathered here since noon. However, not our teacher."

"She gives you Russian lessons?" asked Hugh.

"Da," replied the Major, "and you French."

"Oui, monsieur." answered Hugh. "She's a brilliant lady."

"Well now, let's see what I can find you to eat."

"Thank you. I'd be glad to help."

"Well, why don't you relax and I'll find some nourishment. Right after the jolts, we had a kitchen fire, and electrical complications. Frank designed the building only for electric power—and, with the fire and refrigeration both out, Inumaru decided we should eat the banquet food right away—a very good idea. Since then we've fed lots of people using charcoal, cooking a kind of sweet potato stew."

"Thank you, Major."

"That's Phil, Hugh—and I'll try to rustle something up. I'll be back in a few minutes. Rest room's over there." He pointed and headed for the kitchen.

About ten minutes later, he returned with a large wooden bowl, a pair of chopsticks and two bottles of beer.

"You'd probably like something stronger to drink," said Faymonville, "but, beer is all I could come up with, along with some of what was supposed to be tomorrow's breakfast." He placed the components in front of Hugh.

"Thank you, Phil. I promised my mother I'd never touch alcohol, but under the circumstances I'm sure she'd understand. It'll hit the spot, and I'm supremely grateful to you."

"Not at all. I'm happy to help anyone, particularly a fellow American and fellow student." He took a sip of beer.

Hugh recognized the breakfast as rice covered with raw

egg. He felt hungry enough to enjoy it, and even the beer went down easily. "Tell me, do you know what these explosions are about?"

"Yes, well the story is that the army is blowing down buildings that might crumble, and also to form fire breaks. Of course, fire is our main danger here. Inumaru ordered all the windows shut right from the beginning—one of the reasons it's so ungodly hot in here."

"A wise move," observed Hugh, "but I've been in places a lot hotter than this today."

"By God, I'll bet you have—you must have gone through an awful lot and you've obviously been close to some very smoky fires."

"Yes, I've witnessed terrible scenes and tragedies—the worst was seeing so many people being burned alive—and all of it, as you know, just since noon." He related some of his worst experiences during his search for Tanya.

When he described the tower of flame, Faymonville took a long drink of beer and said, "Yes, I was able to see it too. It gained altitude in spurts—the winds spinning around and around—I don't know how to explain what I saw." He took another drink. "Many others here said the same thing. It defied any but inadequate descriptions."

"Yes," agreed Hugh. "Probably nothing like it before in history."

"I think the air itself was burning."

"Yes."

"Then," sighed the Major, "it opened up and came crashing down like a giant tidal wave. Good God, it was dreadful—beyond belief."

The raw eggs on Riordan's meal made the rice difficult to handle with his chopsticks. "Darn it Phil, I usually do better with these. The food's fine . . . "

"But, slippery. I know. All you can do is shovel it in. I do, and so do most of my Japanese friends. Well, you know that of course—but I try to sneak a fork and spoon into my uniform pocket."

After a short chuckle at each other's lack of skill with chopsticks, Faymonville asked, "At Ueno Park you could probably see Honjo—the 'Honjo Horror.' "

"What does that term refer to, Phil?"

"Well, those who witnessed it are referring to the fire over the old Army Clothing Depot as the 'Honjo Horror.' "

Hugh set down his bowl and chopsticks. "My God it was a horror! Those poor people. It was a huge tornado—sure I've seen tornadoes on the farm, but . . ." his voice clouded with emotion. "The base was as wide as the Sumidagawa—and pure fire—and it took its time moving across that field." He took a gulp of beer.

The American major did, too. "Yes, we saw much of it from here through binoculars. Some things got in the way, but I'm afraid we saw too much of it."

"Well, I was using Tanya's opera glasses—I forgot to give them back after we saw Pavlova."

"The Russian dancer."

"Yes—I could see carts, construction material, bicycles, and burning people swept into the air." He passed his hands across his eyes. "My God it was horrible—yes, yes, the 'Honjo Horror.' "

"And, you were overseas during the war and must have seen some pretty awful things," observed the Major.

Hugh drank some beer, and reflected momentarily. "Yes, I was at the Belleau Wood. That was an awful battle—but not nearly as horrible as this."

Faymonville surveyed the crowd briefly, then said. "Hugh, you're very welcome to stay the night in my quarters here. We may be a bit crowded—our embassy came down and most of the staff is here—but I know everyone would be glad to see you. And, if we all remain here, we might have a good chance of surviving this catastrophe."

"Thank you, Phil. That's really kind and considerate of you, but I plan to get back to Shinjuku, tonight."

"Well, perhaps most of the fires will have burned themselves out by morning. And, you could start off after some rest, and after another bowl of rice with raw egg topping." An idea to which they both responded with a chuckle.

"Thank you, again, but the last time I looked, there was less fire toward Shinjuku."

"Well, I hope so."

They got up and shouldered their way toward the entrance. The bucket brigade still worked at dampening the roof. A Professor from the Imperial University, an Englishman, recognized Hugh and said, "Good God, you look terrible Hugh—something like a Welsh coal miner."

"As you'd say, Harry—I've had a bit of a go, but I'm all right—and Major Faymonville has kindly allowed me to re-charge my batteries."

Introductions were made all around. When Harry learned that Hugh was going to attempt Shinjuku that evening he was aghast. "Staying here is probably the best chance we have for surviving. Herr Heise can get along without you tonight. My God, there are so many fires—you can read a newspaper by them near the reflecting pool." As he began to move away from them he grinned. "Besides, I don't want you to miss the band concert tomorrow at Hibiya Park."

"Ah," remarked Hugh, "the English sense of humor."

"Yes," added Phil, "but Tatiana Alexandrovna often comments on the American sense of humor."

"Luckily, I'm not very funny."

"But Harry certainly was right," observed the Major, "you could read a newspaper out here."

The entire sky was a livid canopy of red, that pulsed and

vibrated but never revealed an opening or any other color. Wherever you looked upward—it was red.

"Good Lord, the entire Ginza is just about gone," Phil shook his head in disbelief. "It's all so tragically horrible."

Hugh peered through the smoke that was blowing away from them on a westerly wind. Suddenly men on the roof started shouting about fire heading their way. Some on the street yelled warnings, too. A wall of yellow and red flame, likely resulting from the conflagration among the vast forest of Shiba Park—and driven by a gusting west wind—threatened everything in its path. The Imperial Hotel was directly in its path.

Everyone who could, including Hugh and Phil, dove into the protective structure of the hotel. "This could be real bad," observed the American major. "We'd better hunker down."

"And, keep away from the walls," added Hugh.

Somewhere, in the packed multitude, a few men sobbed. Hysterically, one shouted above the prayers being chanted in many languages. "I do not want to burn. God, you can take me, but please don't make me burn." The volume of prayers grew.

"We should be right in it, now," stated Phil calmly.

One of the hotel executives mounted a chair and announced, in English: "The wind has changed to the north. The wave of flames has just missed the Imperial Hotel. Thank you," he said bowing.

There were many clearly audible sighs of relief. Thanks were sent up to God in a number of languages. Hugh particularly noticed a loud, "Mon Dieu, Merci." Tanya had taught him that this meant "My God, thank you," during their first lesson. This thought renewed his sense of urgency in his quest to find Tanya.

"I think we would have survived even if the flames swept over us," conjectured the Major, "just as long as we weren't engulfed for any substantial length of time."

"Yes, I think you're right," agreed Hugh. "It would take a while to cook us."

"So, you agree, this is a pretty safe place," Phil tried to direct his fellow American back toward the stairs, "so let's go to the second floor and see how comfortable we can make you in my office."

"No, thank you, Phil." Said Riordan, shaking Faymonville's hand vigorously. "I sincerely thank you, however I'd better head for Shinjuku, as I planned."

"Are you sure? You just agreed this is a pretty safe spot. You could be burned out there! What if you'd been a bit to the west a few minutes ago?"

Hugh hefted his walking stick. "You're absolutely right. But, I've got to go. I can't thank you enough." He moved toward the entrance.

With arms akimbo, the Major called, "Good luck!"

"I'll be back," called Hugh. Then he was outside.

The wind now blew out of the north. Until it had mercifully blown the advancing wall of fire away from the hotel, Riordan could not recall a constant northerly wind so far this awful day. While it had gusted at times, from every direction, he worried that a steady pressure from a new quarter could force flame into hitherto untouched areas.

A few more brick and stone buildings were emitting smoke than before, but many still seemed relatively unscathed. On his way home, his first decision would be whether to go through Hibiya Park, which he loved, or parallel the moat which ran between it and the palace grounds. The park was full of refugees. Getting through would be terribly hard. There must be thousands sheltered there. Hugging the moat would be slow going, but the crowds there seemed somewhat less dense. Even with the entire sky a bright, livid red, Hugh found the number of people difficult to judge.

As he made his way slowly, he recalled that this general area west of the palace was often called the "Official Quarter," with numerous embassies and legations, shrines, schools, dwellings, and the well known Foreign Office, where international questions were discussed.

A number of the impressive dwellings directly to the west were aflame, but they were better constructed and much less apt to burn quickly. Indeed, it appeared as though their fires were contained inside the sturdy walls.

As he got his bearings, near Parliament, the Naval Department and the Law Courts, he noticed the Italian embassy had burned down. So had the Brazilian legation. He had seen so much fire, and witnessed so much destruction, that he was surprised he still felt shock and sadness. How could he hope to find Tanya? Would he ever find Tanya? Directly between the burned out Italians and the burned out Brazilians, loomed the Russian Embassy. *Would she?* Of course not. These were not *her* Russians. These were the Bolsheviks, the Communists who had killed her entire family—according to conflicting reports. She had escaped from them in a boxcar—thirty-six days across frozen Siberia. She had killed one of their soldiers. She told him of the incident with pride. She wouldn't be here.

Hugh Riordan knocked loudly on the door of the Russian Embassy nonetheless. The building looked undamaged. The brass-hinged door opened to reveal a large, completely bald man with a drooping black beard. He was dressed in a Cossack shirt, and loose trousers tucked into high brown boots.

"Good evening," began Riordan, then, switching to Russian, he added that he was American, and could not speak Russian. Finally, in English he explained that he was looking for a young Russian woman.

"Ah, Amerikanski," said the bald man bowing and opening the door all the way. "Come in. I speak Americanski." He chuckled, "you see, I spent a year in New York city."

"Wonderful!" exclaimed Hugh. "I'm really in luck."

"Please come into the reception room."

They stepped into a large room that held a number of huge sofas and chairs, many occupied by sleeping men. The middle of the room featured a large, wooden carved table with a huge golden samovar surrounded by tea utensils. At the other end were cut glass decanters containing clear liquid and several glasses.

"I am Joseph, a Russian Jew, with a good position here at our embassy," he announced extending his hand.

Riordan took it and replied, "I'm Hugh, an Irish Catholic American."

The Russian laughed heartily, "When I was in New York city, all people were either Irish Catholics or Jews." Hugh laughed.

"How about some vodka, Hugh?" He poured himself a glass.

"No, thank you, but tea would be fine—especially from such a beautiful samovar."

"A glass of tea, of course. We don't have any sugar or lemon." He put a glass inside a silver holder and poured from the samovar. He handed it to Hugh, with a cup of milk. "Tea is good, too."

"Thank you. It's very good."

"Of course." His arm swept the room. "Some of our Italian and Brazilian friends have had a trying day and quite a bit of vodka. As you probably noticed, both their embassies have been destroyed."

"Yes."

"I don't know why we're still here, why we haven't burned up, even though we have watchers on the roof. Perhaps it's God's will that we survive this horror." He looked at Hugh, who may have looked a bit skeptical. "We are Bolsheviks, but we are not all atheists, you know."

Riordan said, "I've seen more stark horror since noon, than any other day of my life." He proceeded to relate some of his terrible experiences, and ghastly sightings.

"This must be one of the greatest disasters in history," observed Joseph. "So," he cupped his hands together, "how may I be of service to you, Hugh?"

"I'm looking for a young Russian woman."

With a mischievous expression Joseph chuckled, "Aren't we all."

They both laughed heartily, disturbing the slumbering men on the sofas.

"She's in her twenties, and her name is Tanya. She's my teacher."

"Ah Tanya—Tatiana, Tanoocha, Tanishock, Tanitchka. No, we've no Tanya's here. Of course, there are many Russians of all varieties in Tokyo." He poured more vodka into his glass, filling it half-way. "Do you suppose she's been killed? Why would she come here?" He took a long swallow.

A somber look crossed Riordan's face. "Well, she likes Russian people."

"As do we. I know of only one Tanya in Tokyo—Mademoiselle La Comtesse, Tatiana Alexandrovna Lunskaya Bachmanoff. But, she wouldn't have anything to do with you, probably has a wealthy boyfriend."

"Yes, no doubt she does," agreed Hugh. "Do you keep watch on these people at church?"

"Oh no," he replied, shaking his head. "We just like to know who the White Russians in town are."

Many of the men on sofas were awake now, smiling sleepily. "You can stay here, Hugh. So far, it's a lucky place and you look as if you could use some rest."

"Thank you," said the American, "but, I'd better push off for Shinjuku."

"Well, I don't know just where that is, but I know it's quite a way." They stepped outside. "My God, the entire sky looks like the color of our flag!"

"Yes," concurred Riordan glancing up, "I hope it changes soon."

"Do you mean the sky, or our flag?" queried Joseph imperiously.

Hugh walked away with a wave of his hand. "Thank you. Good night."

Joseph shouted after him. "I bet your Tanya is a Czarist! I hope you find her!"

The American waved his free arm and his walking stick, and quickened his pace. *Where could she have gone?* He knew he might have missed her by a few yards hundreds of times. Here in the Imperial Palace plaza was as good a place as any. But there were so many people.

The wind continued from the north, blowing in his face as he moved through the crowd past the Belgian, Mexican, and Chinese embassies. He looked closely at his watch for the first time in hours. Its face was smashed and even the hands were disconnected. *Damn, I forgot I had it. I don't even know the time. Maybe I can ask someone.* He knew though, that most Japanese did not wear watches. Now, however, a further complication took on much more importance than the time.

When he'd been at the Imperial Hotel, the wind had switched to steady from the north for the first time. It still came strongly from the north. This meant that the buildings, shops, trees, whatever, that may have so far escaped the wind-driven flames would be at terrible risk. Small forests of leafy trees, hitherto untouched, burned fiercely. The wind, while neither powerful, nor gusty, simply brought the fires from a new direction.

Suddenly, a strong gust dropped sparks, larger embers and firebrands in a grisly shower upon the people bunched together on the plaza's western side. Hugh helped those around him to beat out fires. His arms stung from the fiery flakes. He slapped at them. A woman pressed against him reached up to grab his hat. She beat out a tiny flame and handed it back. He wanted to thank her, but realized that his voice would be lost in the screams. He smiled instead and she got directly behind him. Because he was so much taller he served as a shield from the deluge coming out of the north. Some people were set aflame. Those near them tried to rip off their clothing. But, there was not enough room. It had to be done speedily. However, with a few it was impossible to be quick enough. They dropped like moths engulfed in a candle flame. The radiated heat was suffocating. Everyone gasped for breath, particularly the children, sucking in the superheated air.

Then, as suddenly as it began the flaming shower was over. The living stepped over the dead. Riordan looked behind him for the diminutive woman who had saved his hat, and probably his head, but she was no longer there.

Using his sturdy stick as much for support as propulsion, Hugh passed the Staff Office and Nagatacho. The crowd was much thinner here, and he felt grateful for this. He made good progress to Hoshigaoka Park. The immediate area was considered one of the most select districts in Japan. Tanya and he came to this small, yet superb park often. This month one of the most important annual festivals always took place. Its Shinto shrine received imperial patronage, being dedicated to the imperial ancestors. Could Tanya be here? Likely not, but both of them loved this exquisite shrine, and Hugh had to try. Near the steps leading up to the shrine lay a stone slab commemorating the brave men who died during the Russo-Japanese War. Tanya always averted her eyes from it.

To his left, a large stand of pines and splendid cryptomerias were laced with flickering red, but the stately pines on the hill itself were still intact. During this awful day Riordan had been close to so much fire, and so many flames that, unless he were in imminent danger of burning, he felt a foolish disdain for them. Airborne embers and firebrands were a different matter.

Leading up to the shrine were fifty-two steps on the left. Men usually climbed these steps, known as the *otokozaka*, or men's slope. Women used the easier *onnazaka*, or women's slope, which had fewer steps and was found on the right. A huge torii gate marked the beginning of the incline. Two seated wooden figures sat at the right and left of the great red gateway, representing Imperial Guards. These were covered entirely with little knots of paper with prayers written on them that had been tied or affixed in every possible spot. Hugh searched briefly, found a small scrap of paper, and using a bit of charcoal, thoughtfully added his own prayer. There was plenty to pray for today.

He ascended the right, or women's way, because the left was too close to the burning trees. Generally, a few members of the Imperial Guard were around. Their red-brick barracks stood a little way from the foot of the hill. But not tonight. No doubt they had much to do elsewhere.

Only six people besides the American were in the shrine, which was painted almost entirely in black. Not even the livid red sky clearly lighted the stone monkeys squatting demurely in the background. Nor did it illuminate the many images on the altar, the screens, nor any other fixtures of the shrine. Hugh, however, could see well enough to be certain Tanya was not there, so he whispered a prayer and went outside.

The tea-houses, and the restaurant famous for Japanese cuisine found near the shrine were untouched, and of course closed. One was supposed to feel cool breezes here at the top of the hill and enjoy a magnificent view of the city. The professor pondered these features, but right now all he could see was a huge city in the process of being destroyed.

As he descended the picturesque steps that led down the rear of the hill, he continued watching the city. He felt very sad for all the people caught in this disaster, for Japan, for Tanya, and for himself. Well, he was still alive; and determined to make it to Shinjuku.

There were fewer fires in the hilly northwestern section,

but he must be careful. A short way from the bottom of the steps a blinding pure white light dazzled him. Before his foot reached the next step, a force beyond any he had ever known smashed him left, through the railing, and into the air. *I'm flying, swimming in the air!* He crashed, but before he could feel any pain, the loudest noise he had ever heard assaulted and engulfed his body, then all consciousness left him.

Less than two miles away, the Koishikawa Arsenal had exploded. The smoke that erupted from it looked thick enough to walk on. Not even the wind affected its direction.

One Christmas when he was very young, his parents had given him an Eskimo doll. Because there were so many children, and their farm was only reasonably prosperous, each child received only one present. So, he and his brothers and sisters spent much of the day playing with their individual gifts. Little Hugh would arrange his Eskimo on the floor in a certain way, then attempt to lay next to it in the exact same manner. He created more and more bizarre positions until he got to one with the arms flung around its neck and the legs pointing in opposite directions. As a small child he had not been able to emulate this final pose, and had given up.

As he gradually regained consciousness, face down in an extensive stand of low, verdant bushes, he imagined he were in the unrealized pose of his beloved Eskimo doll. His arms were flung around his jaw and lower neck. His legs were widely spread. The American's entire body lay cradled on the soft greenery, but when he moved, the slender branches cut at his face and hands. His lungs ached, and he could not see.

With considerable and painful effort he untangled his arms and stretched each one. Only the little finger of his right hand felt to be broken. It was almost at a right angle to the adjacent finger. The left side of his thigh and chest throbbed, but his legs grudgingly responded to his wish to move. *If only I could see!*

He tasted blood. It felt as though it came from his nose,

and it had clotted and accumulated on his upper lip. He knew about bloody noses since he had played football during his college days. *I wonder how long I've been out? I wish I could see!* He scrambled around on the thick foliage and was finally able to turn over. There above loomed the blood red sky. *I can see!*

Slowly, he shifted his position until he slipped off the thick bushes and onto his feet. No bones, save his little finger, were broken. He fought to stand up straight. There were many aches and pains. The worst seemed to be his back, but he could bend over and twist from side to side, so his spine should be in pretty good shape.

Happily, he found his walking stick. The canteens and knapsack were still in place, but his hat had blown away with the explosion. *An explosion! That was it!* His thoughts became less scrambled. No wonder his left side and chest ached so much. He had been blown right through the handrail. Looking up the stairs he could see the very spot. Dazed, he sat on the last step trying to sort out what had happened.

It must have been the arsenal! He directed Tanya's opera glasses toward the northeast. The thickness of the smoke emanating from the blazing arsenal was almost beyond belief. It resembled thick, lumpy whipping cream to Hugh, too heavy even to rise into the air. A flash of flame brought his view back inside the plaza. The British embassy poured smoke. Had it been burning before? He couldn't remember. His thoughts came slowly, and in confusion. *It must be a concussion.* He had heard of this during his wartime service, but fortunately had never experienced it.

Never mind, I'd better get moving. Rising to his feet took great effort. His back protested painfully, and each muscle and sprain vied for his attention. At first, he stumbled and walked carefully, afraid he might fall. How thankful he was at finding his walking stick. It had been invaluable today, and now helped him again to keep upright.

The more he moved, the less he ached, but he knew he was approaching total exhaustion. A pleasant looking couple came his way and he asked the time. They both smiled, and moved quickly away.

Even under these catastrophic circumstances, I must look a sight. Oh, well, who cares what time it is. At least it's dark.

Still in the plaza, he arrived at Shimizudani Park, a short way from the much larger and more ornate park where so much had happened to him. He was making progress. He sat for a moment on a bench and drank from a canteen. The warm liquid refreshed him, especially with the tang of the lemon. His mind was still somewhat fuzzy, but he definitely wouldn't enter this park. Tanya and he had never visited this one. He must have sweated buckets today. His clothes clung to him as he continued to perspire in the heat.

The American left the plaza area right near the still intact Austro-Hungarian embassy. This immediately placed him next to the heavily fenced in grounds of the Akasaka Palace, the sometime residence of the crown prince. The elevated grounds were heavily wooded and absolutely superb, but Riordan had seen them a number of times and he certainly had no desire to stop and admire them now. There were some fires beyond, but from what he could see imperial good fortune had left the area unscathed, as it had the Imperial Palace and its grounds.

A soldier inside the tall fence pointed at the sky and in a voice tinged with amazement, shouted, *"Akai!"* referring to the red of the sky.

Surprised though he was at this action, the English professor pointed skyward also, and yelled back, *"Hai, akai!"* He could see the soldier nodding and quickened his pace. The guard's behavior was unusual, but maybe he was merely being friendly, or was lonely. After all, who had ever seen an all red sky before?

Soon Riordan reached Yotsuya Ward, unique because it

contained ridges, valleys, and even a flat area. The shabby areas on the flats—the typical fragile houses, were by now merely wreckage, but some continued to burn. Many of the more substantially built residences, often on the crests of the ridges, were being consumed slowly, and quite a few remained untouched.

Hugh knew a short cut to Maitomachi. Once he stood again on that wide street, he looked northwest to Shinjuku. He could see only a few fires on the way. While he stumbled along the familiar route, his thoughts turned more and more to Tanya.

How long did it take him to reach the garden in front of Heise's house? He didn't know, but the glowing sky had easily lighted his way. Even though it must be deep into the night hours, the plentiful light allowed them to recognize each other. Heise ran to him shouting.

"Hughie, liebe Gott—Hughie!"

They embraced with great affection, *"Mein liebe freund Werner—mein liebe freund."* Tears overflowed from both of them.

"I couldn't find Tanya," said Riordan sadly stepping back, and shaking his head. "I looked . . ."

Heise grabbed his shoulders laughing, "But, Hughie, she is here—completely safe."

She stepped out eagerly from the tall garden foliage and without a word embraced him. They held their embrace for a few moments.

"Thank God!" declared Hugh.

"Mon Dieu, merci," murmured Tanya, slightly increasing the pressure of her arms.

"Ah," said Hugh, "I could do this every day."

"Oh yes," said Tanya in mock seriousness, "The American sense of humor. Besides, you look terrible."

"Oh yes," answered Hugh, "now who has the American sense of humor?"

They both laughed, as did Heise.

Suddenly, Goko-san, appeared and bowed slightly. "Riordan-san, I feel joy that you are safe."

She looked skyward, clapped her hands and said a little prayer of thanks.

"Thank you Goko-san," said Riordan.

Heise took his friend by the arm and guided him toward the house. "Let's get you washed up, disinfected, and some food into you."

"That would be nice. Up until now, this has been the worst day of my life."

"Well, you're home," observed the German professor, "and it's the next day, and we hope this day will be better." They all joined readily with Heise in his wish.

"Say, what time is it?" asked Hugh. "My watch broke."

"Mine too," said the Russian girl.

"It's five-past one in the morning, isn't that the way you say it?" asked the German. To which Hugh responded that, yes, this was how it was said.

Back in the house, Riordan washed up, applied disinfectant where he could, asked Heise to apply it where he couldn't and changed clothes. He had many scratches, bruises, and muscle strains, along with the broken finger, but considered himself most fortunate to be alive.

When he joined everyone in the kitchen, Goko-san produced rice-balls and tea. Tanya and Hugh briefly recounted a couple of their adventures and Heise suggested they all try and get some sleep, or at least some rest. He promised to keep one eye open until morning.

It was decided the women would occupy Heise's Japanese-style house across the street because if a "smasher" came during the night, they'd be much safer there. The house had survived quite well so far, and there weren't any fires in the vicinity. The men would rest as well as possible on the lawn in front of the foreign-style house, keeping watch.

Before the group went to get the ladies settled, they all paused and gazed into Tokyo. The redness of the sky above hadn't diminished. Tanya whispered a Russian prayer. Gokosan clapped her hands and said appropriate words, and then they were all saying prayers, in four different languages, together. Without plan, their hands joined as they watched one of the world's greatest cities in an agony of destruction. Their prayers though, were not for the city, but for its still suffering people.

It took only a few minutes to see that Tanya and Goko-san were comfortable in the pretty house across the street.

Riordan and Heise each carried a futon out on the grass where they planned to spend the night. Hugh also brought his camera. The German professor had his camera also. "You see my dear Hugh, I've been getting some pictures. I avoided it when Fraulein Tanya was around because she might think of this as gauche, taking pictures of our suffering city."

"Oh, I don't think so."

"After all," mused Heise, "she is a noblewoman."

Then they both snapped pictures at random. A solid mass of smoke hovered over the commercial area with flames constantly flickering at its base. Unbelievably thick smoke continued to burble from the Koishikawa Arsenal; and over downtown. Abruptly the ground thundered and dropped beneath them. As they struggled to remain standing, it rebounded and knocked them down. The cameras flew from their hands.

"That's the worst aftershock, yet!" gasped Hugh as he lay next to Heise.

"Yah, it's two o'clock in the morning. Very inconsiderate of the catfish."

"Stay where you are, Werner. I'll arrange the quilts."

Sometime later, both men lay back on their individual futons. They were silent, overwhelmed by the red sky and the anticipation of the next shock.

Sifting Through the Ashes

When the Russian girl awakened early the following morning, she noticed birds singing for the first time since the horrendous earthquake. Perhaps they had sung before, but, watching Tokyo burn for three nights from this comparatively safe, elevated location might have blunted her awareness of the beauty still existing around her.

As she lay staring up at the mosquito net suspended from the ceiling, she considered the fate of those she knew. Klavdia she feared dead, while others she could not be sure of. Today, she decided, she would travel to Yokohama. She felt terrified at what she might find there—the Peacocks, Paula, so many friends. Hugh had promised to go with her if, of course, the trains were running. He had expressed doubt that they would be only the previous evening.

She had been wearing clothes borrowed from Goko-san, but today, again thanks to the wonderful maid, she would wear her newly restored white dress and shoes. Hugh had even repaired her purse. The entire outfit appeared rather worn, but it was clean.

Neither Heise nor Hugh recommended going in to the ruins of the city. They had food and an operating well, and were safe where they were. Although most of the fires seemed to be out, as it had rained heavily the night before, the men said she should wait. But, this morning she was determined to try.

While crossing the wide street on her way to the European-style house, she felt overjoyed to see a policeman coming her way on a bicycle. He slowed, and when he got to her he stopped. She greeted him in Japanese, and bowed.

"Good morning," he responded.

"Excuse me," she then said. "Please, trains today?" Thus she inquired of the policeman in her polite, if somewhat rudimentary Japanese. He answered that yes, there were trains running today. Tatiana then asked what station trains were running from, and if they were going to Yokohama.

"Tabata Station," answered the policeman, pointing in a northeasterly direction. "It's over there, but I don't know if the trains are running all the way to Yokohama."

During breakfast, Tatiana excitedly told her friends about her conversation with the policeman. "He assured me that the trains are running."

Hugh shook his head as he finished his rice cake. "Oh, I doubt that very much. Most of the tracks are destroyed."

Heise agreed. "Oh, leibchen, I don't think it is possible."

"Well, I must get to Yokohama, today. The policeman said trains are running. At least I'm going to try."

"O.K., it's against my better judgment, but I'll go with you," said Hugh. "Who knows what we'll find."

"Well, you don't have to," replied Tanya in a slight pique. "I'll go alone."

"Oh Fraulein Tanya," said Heise shaking his head, "you will see terrible things."

"I've thought of that, but I'm going anyway," she declared.

"I'll get dressed, and be with you in a few minutes." Hugh rose from the table. "Arigato, Goko-san."

With a decorative yet practical parasol borrowed from Goko-san for the occasion, they began their trip down into Tokyo. With the idea that there was a slight possibility they would reach Yokohama, Riordan had put on a blue silk suit, shirt, and tie. He also wore a straw boater hat, had strapped on his knapsack, and had his two canteens hanging from his belt.

"I'm glad you didn't bring your walking stick," commented the Russian girl.

"Mademoiselle Tanya," said Hugh stopping for a moment, "we don't have any idea what we're going to run into. We're not going to a garden party, there may be another earthquake."

She looked down at the pavement because she knew he was right.

"With all due respect to you, I've tried to be somewhat prepared. Water is certain to be an awful problem, food is likely quite scarce, and fires are, after all, the 'flowers of Edo.' "

"Yes, of course, you are right Professor. I'm just so worried about my Yokohama friends. I'm dreaming everything will be all right there."

"Tanya, I hope so," answered Hugh kindly. "Ah look," he exclaimed, trying to cheer her a bit, "we can see Mount Fuji this morning!"

"Oh yes, how beautiful! I am unable to see her from most of the areas in which I travel."

"She appears pensive and silent this morning."

"And you've climbed to the top."

"Yes, the most beautiful mountain in the world. If I were a nature worshiper, she'd be the altar of my adoration."

"My, I have never seen this side of you before Professor. Will you help *me* climb her someday?"

"Of course, I'd be honored."

Hand in hand now, they continued to walk at a leisurely pace. When they were near some of the alleys where Tanya had come close to death, they saw sad groups of people examining acres of wreckage. The entire area was mostly ashes.

"What are they doing?" asked Tanya.

"I'm not sure. Perhaps, they're trying to locate where their houses once stood."

A little further on, they came upon more than a dozen bodies carefully laid next to each other on the side of the street. They were horribly blackened. Some had started to bloat.

"Don't look at them!" admonished Tanya.

"The police probably placed them there," conjectured Hugh.

"What is that?" asked the Russian girl indicating a heap of incinerated forms stuck together.

"Well, I imagine the police decided not to pull the bodies apart."

Tanya looked away and crossed herself, mumbling a prayer.

As they moved further south Hugh felt amazed when he spied the British embassy. "I can't believe it's still there. It was really burning when I passed this way heading home."

"It is quite heavily damaged, though," she pointed out.

"Somehow they must have controlled the fire." he mused.

Hugh showed her where he had been blown through the railing on the steps at Hoshigaoka Park. Being in somewhat of a hurry, they did not climb the stairs to the Shinto shrine atop the hill.

As they passed below the hill they met one of the professor's advanced students, dressed in school uniform. He spoke to his teacher in English. "Good morning, Professor Riordan," he said, bowing.

Hugh bowed slightly, "Good morning Mr. Uchida." Then he introduced Tanya and his young, handsome student.

Uchida said smiling, "I always find it remarkable that the professor remembers the names of his students."

"Well, I really only remember the names of those who do the best work."

The pupil bowed, obviously pleased. Continuing to smile he said, "I'm feeling joy that you have survived our recent cataclysm."

"Yes," agreed Hugh. "I have been very fortunate. I'm happy that you, too have been favored. I hope that your family also survived in good health.

Young Mr. Uchida's smile broke nearly imperceptibly, but only for an instant. "Alas no, my father, mother, brother, and two sisters all perished," he reported.

Tanya gasped.

Riordan wanted to reach out and embrace his pupil in sympathy. He knew, however, that would be a serious breach of custom, so he simply said, "I am much saddened by your news."

"Yes," agreed Uchida without emotion. "It is sad. Professor, do you have any idea when classes will resume at the university? I'm most anxious to return to school."

"No, I've not been informed as yet. The buildings were damaged quite severely. I imagine it will be at least a couple of weeks."

"Yes, I would suppose you are correct. Your class is my favorite. I have been most fortunate in meeting you today." Bowing first to Hugh, and then to Tanya, he turned and walked slowly across the plaza.

Tanya murmured a prayer and crossed herself. "Oh, how awful!" she exclaimed. "He never once stopped smiling even though his family has been completely wiped out. My God, he's all alone, now."

"Yes, I suppose so," agreed Riordan. "He's so polite, he doesn't wish to burden others with his grief."

"Oh these gentle people," remarked Tanya. "They have such quiet courtesy."

"Yes," concurred Hugh. He took Tanya's hand. "And, we're both very lucky to be alive."

As they moved along, they saw more and more bodies. Thousands has been laid out in rows by soldiers—their noses tightly covered by handkerchiefs. The corpses and the smell were equally hideous. Myriad rows of the dead, on their backs; next to each other; contorted faces, where there were faces, pointed toward the sun.

A few people strolled mournfully along the rows, trying to make some identification. It must have been a huge task with so many dead. Now and then a searcher would drop down and kneel at the head of a body. There wasn't room to kneel beside them.

"Oh, it's so horrible—horrible," expressed Tanya. "Some seem to be without any burns. How could that be?"

I don't really know," replied Hugh. "Maybe they were asphyxiated. When the air burned up—they were suffocated by carbon-monoxide."

"That's a gas?" questioned the Russian girl. "Where does it come from?"

"Well, when there is a fire, there must be oxygen. And when that is used up carbon monoxide forms. We can't breathe it."

"Oh," confessed Tanya, "I'm not very smart about such things."

"You don't have to be," comforted Hugh, squeezing her hand, "you know so much about other important subjects."

When they got close to Hibiya Park, they saw it was filled with thousands of refugees. Getting through would be quite difficult. Riordan steered them to the path he had used before, next to the palace moat. As he had found three days ago, the crowds were thinner here, but they still had to step around a few dead bodies.

"Did you know that much of the water in these moats is fresh?" queried Hugh.

"No, I didn't," admitted the Russian girl, "but, what difference does it make?"

"Well, that's why there are so many ducks and geese, herons, and beautiful waterbirds in the center of the city."

"No water flows into them from the canals?"

"Oh no," explained Hugh, "if it did, you wouldn't have the same waterfowl."

"You're so smart," she commented drily.

"Well, water is probably in short supply. We could drink from the moats if we had to."

Finally they arrived at the wide thoroughfare in front of the Imperial Hotel.

"Please remember. I must get to Yokohama.

"Let's see what we can find out here," said Hugh as he smoothed his suit jacket near the reflecting pool. Groups of men, their shirt-sleeves rolled up, tended large cauldrons of rice cooking over small fires in the front driveway and near the parking area. Other members of these "cooking parties" were established with their supplies in the lobby areas.

Downstairs was packed. A large percentage of the foreign community was there. Both Hugh and Tanya nodded to acquaintances. "Hugh, Hugh Riordan!" someone shouted. "Am I glad to see you!"

It was Major Faymonville, dressed in an open-collared shirt, riding breeches and boots. He quickly bowed to Tanya. "Please forgive me, Tatiana Alexandrovna—it's wonderful to see you, alive and well. Hugh, you're just in time to straighten out a problem. Come on!"

He lead Hugh by the arm; who, in turn, took Tanya's hand, and maneuvered them up to the main desk. There in a conspicuous place on an adjoining wall hung a piece of yellow posterboard. Written in bold, black letters across the top was, "Pray for the souls of our departed friends." Underneath this were six names, the fourth one listed was "Hugh L. Riordan, Professor."

"Well, I'll do something about that immediately," announced Hugh. Reaching for the nearby thick black pencil, he obliterated his name, and title. A few of the onlookers applauded, and a couple cheered. One of those who approached the trio clapping vigorously was the impeccably uniformed British Colonel Roger Blandings. "Good show Hugh—at least you're temporarily off the list," he chuckled.

"That's the British sense of humor," explained Riordan to a shocked-looking Tanya.

"What a terrible thing to say," she declared.

Roger touched his visor with his swagger stick. "You're absolutely right, mademoiselle. Please forgive me."

Phil introduced them.

"Major Faymonville," Tanya addressed him directly. "I must get to Yokohama, as quickly as possible."

"Oh dear," commented the Englishman, "I'm sorry, but that's impossible."

Faymonville explained. "All the tracks are wrecked and the roads completely impassable. Some here at the Imperial have tried, but they've all returned quickly."

Hugh took her hand gently. "I'm so sorry Tanya."

"But," she insisted, "isn't there anything running, even from Shinagawa? A policeman said some trains were running."

"No, I'm afraid not," said Phil. "He probably meant trains going to the north, up from Ueno. As a matter of fact, we're getting our food and some water from the north. I've gone on one of the trips myself. Inumaru rounded up an old Ford and Wright's Cadillac and we've been able to bring back enough food for a day or so, and the rain helped the water situation a great deal."

"We've even been feeding people in Hibiya Park—and the army finally showed up with some water carts."

Roger reached out and shook Hugh's hand, then bowed toward Tanya. "Well, please excuse me, I must get back to my duties. I'm sure I'll see you both again soon. Congratulations again Hugh. Wasn't it one of your folk writers who coined the phrase 'The reports of my death have been greatly exaggerated?' "

"Yes, Mark Twain."

"Well, whomever. Must have been a clever chap. Cheerio for now." He turned away into the crowd.

"Please come with me," said the Major. "I'll show you around a bit and then get you some food. No doubt you saw the big cooking pots on your way in."

Hugh and Tanya agreed that they had.

"The residents of the ruined embassies are set up here—we're in the north wing—people are spread all over, some with and some without their organizations.

"Who had charge of the casualty list?" asked Riordan.

"I honestly haven't the slightest idea." He noticed Tanya taking Hugh's hand at that moment. "Anyway, I'm overjoyed you were able to cross out your name. Oh yes, here is the banquet hall—pretty well filled with Tokyo newspaper operations. Careful, the floor has dropped a bit. Please, sit here and I'll get some rice for all of us."

Even with the large crowd, they soon had rice, and the Russian girl sweet potato. "Hugh told me you especially liked sweet potato." They smiled at that, then fell to using their chopsticks.

"Tell me Major, is their any news from Yokohama?" asked Tanya.

Faymonville looked thoughtful as he pushed the moist rice into his mouth and chewed. He coughed once. "Well, the little specific news we've heard has been pretty bad. Yokohama apparently suffered worse damage and fire than we did. I'm awfully sorry. I remember you said you had many friends there."

"Yes," said Tanya, wiping a few tears away with a tiny handkerchief.

"Good Lord, the problems here in Tokyo are enormous," observed Phil, "Food, water—there's a trickle in the unbroken mains—sanitation, the injured, the homeless, the thousands of bodies. I'm glad the crown prince declared martial law."

"I'm happy to hear it," seconded Hugh. "We've been out of touch, but that should be a great help."

"We Americans are trying to get a relief ship in here." He paused a moment, considering. "Well, you both should try to stay here. There's a private women's section—food and water assured."

- "No, no, thank you, Major," Tanya shook her head, "If I can't get to Yokohama, I must get to my hotel where I have clothes and jewelry, and personal things."

"Well, let's see—where was your hotel? Honjo—no, Hongo, wasn't it?"

Tanya nodded.

"I'm afraid it's nothing but ashes now. It'd be crazy to try to get through."

"No, no, I simply must!"

Faymonville held out his hands in helplessness. "Can't you stop her Hugh? You can both live here—water, food, sanitation. Who knows what you'll run into out there—poor souls maddened by thirst, people who haven't eaten in days. And, you two dressed for the theater—you'd be crazy!"

"No, no Major, we must go!" insisted Tanya.

Faymonville thought for a moment, slowly shaking his head. "You know who's staying here—Monsieur Côte, the Director of Athenée Français, your school—he asked if I had seen you. You could have nice conversations with him. I'd bet many friends of you both are here."

"They most likely are, but we must go."

Phil turned to Hugh, "And what about you, war hero? Can you talk some sense into our Russian friend's head?"

Hugh began relating again how he had visited Tanya's hotel looking for her and it had seemed in pretty good shape then.

"Yes, I remember—but, that was a couple of days ago. So much has burned down and crumbled since," said Phil, now more exasperated. He stood up, "I'm sorry. It's really none of my business. You certainly survived your walk here from Shinjuku and I've only been out of the Imperial once, but we keep getting reports of terrible perils outside."

When they got to the entrance, where the rice was still boiling, Major Faymonville paused and asked, "Say, can you give me some money? The hotel's receipts for the month were banked on Saturday, just before the quake, and we have to pay cash when we buy provisions up north."

Hugh gave him a bunch of five yen notes and Tanya found a few one yen notes and some coins.

"This is terribly embarrassing," apologized the American, holding the money. "I wish you both Godspeed, and I'm sorry I got out of line." He extended his hand to Hugh who shook it warmly. "Thank you for all your care and concern, Phil."

"I don't want to lose my Russian teacher," he said, lightly embracing Tanya.

"Thank you, Major Faymonville."

*   *   *

The weather was hot and sunny, no doubt contributing to the awful stench of the bodies. Many of them were cooked and blackened, bloating now where they had fallen.

Tanya and Hugh avoided Tokyo's great central shopping area, Ginza, because they'd overheard people at the Imperial Hotel talking about the destruction there. They preferred to recall strolling past its charming shops during happier times.

It would also have taken them some distance from the Central Station where Tanya wanted to check for herself about trains to Yokohama. There were none. They guessed that perhaps some service could be resumed in a couple of weeks.

Bodies had been cleared away from the palace area. They walked by the moats at the southeastern part. "Why do you think the palace didn't crumble during the shocks?" questioned Tanya.

They both stopped to see, as much as was possible over the moat and through the trees. "I've heard the palace buildings are on an eminence—or a higher piece of solid ground, basically a huge rock. You know most of Tokyo is built on filled in ground that is known to move quite easily in a smashing earthquake."

"My, aren't you smart," remarked Tanya, squeezing his hand.

"Well, I've studied Tokyo rather thoroughly."

"And, are there more of these 'eminences?' " asked Tanya.

"Yes, I believe Kudan Hill, and Ueno Park are similar." he answered.

The pair crossed Kandabashi Bridge without incident, appreciating the fact that few bodies were in evidence. The remains of a brick Catholic school drew their attention. Most of the walls had collapsed, and those remaining bore scorch marks from the flames that had gutted the inside. In front stood a golden statue of Joan of Arc, still proudly holding her flag on high, unaffected by the chaos around her.

"I know you're Roman Catholic, Professor. Does this re-confirm your faith?"

"I don't know," replied Riordan thoughtfully. "Here in the midst of all this horror surrounding us I guess it wouldn't hurt to offer a prayer to St. Joan."

They proceeded up Nishikicho heading roughly toward the northeast. Most structures in the area were burned out, but there were comparatively few bodies. These were arrayed on horse-drawn carts, managed by the army, which obviously wanted to get corpses away from the palace environs. There really weren't many carts, but those that passed headed toward the bordering canal.

The massive Russian Orthodox Cathedral loomed up before them. They went to the front door but it was locked. Hugh told her about seeing it on his search through the city, and that the huge golden cross was not visible even then. It looked relatively undamaged, though its foundation had risen a few feet on one side.

With the hope they could cross at Suidobashi Bridge, they decided to try to reach it by following the canal. On this, the palace side, were piles of abandoned clothes, carts, furniture, and household items. Across the canal a vast number of bodies were being cremated, under the direction of soldiers. They were dragging mud covered dead from the water, then lifting them onto pyres where they too could be consumed. Even with a westerly breeze the stench was overwhelming.

Tanya muttered some Russian prayers and looked away. She recalled doing that a number of times today. Hugh took her arm as they headed for the bridge. "Well, we know it has to be done, but it is awful. I'm afraid there'll be a lot more."

The canal widened slightly as they continued to follow along it. They discussed the shallowness of the water, and Hugh conjectured that the earthquake must have created a large hole somewhere, causing the water level to drop so much.

"But, where could the hole be?" asked Tanya.

"Probably in Tokyo Bay."

Now, they approached Suidobashi Bridge. People moved over it in both directions. As they crossed, Riordan remembered the impassable tide of refugees that had kept him from going this way before. He took Tanya's hand. "Welcome to Hongodori Avenue."

The area was devastated, but no bodies were being burned even if there were quite a number close by. Grimly, they made their way, stepping carefully through debris. Suddenly, two men, obviously drunk, barred their way. They were dressed in dirty cheap kimonos and tied around their heads were headbands bearing kanji characters.

"Stop, you are Koreans!" one bellowed.

Both brandished swords.

"Greetings," said Hugh, deciding not to bow. "I am an American, and this lady is a Russian."

Tanya closed and fastened her parasol.

One of the men roared, "You Koreans destroyed our city with your explosions!"

"I'm an American," insisted Hugh.

"Then she's a Korean," exclaimed the other drunk, "look at her clothes."

"But, she's a Russian. She wears a white dress because it's cooler. Not all . . . "

Hugh sidestepped the unskillful blow from the heavy sword and moved closer to deliver a stiff-handed judo chop to the fellow's neck. The assailant dropped to his knees. Hugh kicked the point of his chin.

With a roar, the other man raised his sword above his head and approached Hugh from a different angle. Tanya drove the sharp point of her parasol into his face.

He staggered with a yell of pain. Korean women didn't do such things.

Two soldiers arrived on the scene. One advanced on the thug felled by Tanya who raised his sword toward the infantryman. The soldier easily deflected it with his bayoneted rifle. He then pivoted around and smashed his rifle stock against the luckless fellow's skull.

While the soldiers apologized for the behavior of the two drunkards, a truck pulled up. They threw the bodies in the back, bowed, and jumped on the running board. Hugh bowed, shouting thank you to each soldier in turn.

Tanya shouted thanks, too, but her voice was lost in the noise of the truck engine as it pulled away. She sat down on a piece of broken masonry and reopened her parasol. "I can't believe it. I've never had any trouble with a Japanese man before—never—but to be attacked with swords!" she shook her head with incredulity.

"Well, they were both drunk." Hugh removed his suit jacket, in the steamy heat. "Before we left, Heise warned me about some Koreans having been attacked."

"But, why?"

"I don't know—but, we're living in strange times—and, we can be thankful *we're* alive." He began fanning himself with his straw hat.

"You were very good," complimented Tanya. "What did you do to that fellow?"

"Well, luckily I wasn't up against a trained warrior. He was only a drunken lout."

"But he had a big sword!"

"Yes, well I hit his neck with a judo strike."

"Isn't there a judo school very close by?"

"That's right, Professor Kano's. I've been a regular student there. He's my instructor. The Japanese are the best in the world at martial arts."

"Martial arts?" she questioned, rising to her feet.

"Yes, unarmed combat."

"I guess I'd better not pick a fight with you," commented Tanya wryly.

Slowly they started on the way once again. Hugh said, "If you do please make sure you're not carrying a parasol or an umbrella. You really surprised that rascal by jabbing his face. If only Professor Kano accepted female students."

Even in the heat, Riordan could tell Tanya was blushing.

They avoided the large cracks in Hongodori Avenue as they approached the corner where Atsui-san, the street vendor, had served his tasty food. "My Lord," said Hugh, it's hardly changed since I was here looking for you—except for more dead, more destruction, and the university is almost gone."

"I'm sorry," said Tanya, taking him by the hand.

Contemplating the damage, they stood just inside her alley. Buildings on both sides had burned down, or were merely shells.

Riordan recognized some of the bodies, but now there were more. The woman with the bloody head gash was still there, but now horribly bloated. He also recalled the young man crushed on the hood of his car by the telephone pole.

"Poor Mr. Fuji," commented Tanya tearfully.

"You knew this man?" asked Hugh.

"Yes, he was my pupil. He was going to drive me to Yokohama that day."

"My, I didn't know you were that crazy about new motor cars," remarked Hugh with jealous disdain.

"I had to get to Yokohama, and he offered to drive me," she retorted. "Besides, you're being terrible! She surveyed her former home. "Let's go inside."

From the exterior it looked about the same as Hugh remembered, only slightly more damaged. He followed her, squeezing through the entrance as he had before.

When their eyes adjusted to the sunless interior, Tanya exclaimed, "the stairs!" Three days ago the stairs had been negotiable. Now, the first step was about five feet off the floor. A ladder leaned against the initial step so at least an agile person could use the twisted staircase.

Evidently, some had, because there were four pair of sandals in the lobby corner. Tanya slipped her shoes off and Hugh began untying his shoelaces.

"What are you doing?" questioned Tanya, astonished.

"I'm taking off my shoes. You know," he replied somewhat surprised, "it's an old Japanese custom."

"You're not going to my room," she announced emphatically.

Hugh continued taking off his shoes. "Of course I am. You probably can't even get up the ladder."

"Yes, I can, thank you very much. This is my home. I'm staying here."

"No, damn it," he said angrily. "Don't be stupid. You're going back with me to Shinjuku! Heise expects us!"

Saito-san appeared, and bowed deeply, smiling. "Mademoiselle Lunskaya, I feel great joy at your return."

Both Riordan and Tanya bowed, she saying, "I feel great joy to see you, and the Matsunami."

"Riordan-san," he bowed again, smiling.

"Saito-san," said Hugh. "It must have been very difficult for you."

"Yes, it has been difficult, but we must do our best."

"Do you have water?" asked Hugh.

"Yes, we've had a little. The gods smiled on us with the rain last night. We saved as much as possible."

"Do you have any food?"

"We ran out of everything yesterday," he smiled sadly.

Hugh turned to the Russian girl. "You'd better go to your room and pack. I'll give Saito-san our rice cakes. Can I boost you up the ladder?"

Her eyes flashing, Tanya replied, "Don't you touch me."

While she was packing, Riordan shared a canteen with the innkeeper, gave him two rice balls from his knapsack, and two five yen notes. "I don't know what they'll buy now, but something eventually."

Saito-san thanked him profusely.

When Tanya returned at the top of the ladder, Hugh took her red wicker suitcase and helped her down.

As she assured Saito-san she would be back, he handed her a note. Her anxious expression turned to one of joy.

"It's from Klavdia. She's staying with her friend Midori."

"That's wonderful news, I'm so happy for you," said Hugh.

Farewells were exchanged, and the couple began their return journey to Shinjuku.

Outside, Hugh put her suitcase down and moved to attempt to remove the pole from Mr. Fuji.

"Don't you dare," squealed Tanya.

"Why not?" asked Hugh. "Poor man's been here for days."

"Because," declared Tanya, "you smell bad enough already, Professor."

"Well, I'll be," exclaimed Hugh, grabbing her case and pretending to struggle with it. "How many rooms *did* you have at the Matsunami? Don't worry, I'll be happy to let you help me. You can carry it as many times as you wish on the way back to Shinjuku," he said in response to her disapproving look at his having taken her case.

The Kiss

Most of his students and some of his acquaintances would have said Dr. Heise possessed a withdrawn, somewhat sullen disposition. Certainly, the middle-aged German professor was not known to be a gregarious sort of fellow. Yet, he had always considered himself a man of the world with a sense of humor, and this necessarily included a streak of compassion for his fellow man.

Though the front of his rambling foreign house had caved in during the earthquake and had not been repaired, there remained plenty of room. He remembered promising Hugh a *sauerbraten* dinner on September first, and it bothered him that the dinner had never been held. Although many terrible events had intervened, he felt a sense of obligation to honor his friend as he had originally planned.

So today, some six weeks after the disaster, he told Hugh about his proposed dinner. Riordan politely objected saying it would be too much trouble, especially since conditions were still unsettled.

"Now Hugh, you know we Germans are great planners. The earthquake upset our dinner last time. And we have more reason than before to celebrate. We are still alive, and I am able to get some good meat and the rest of the necessities for a nice dinner."

"I don't have many friends, and my family won't return for two weeks, so why don't you and Fraulein Tanya invite some people and we can make it a kind of 'earthquake survivors party' along with the delayed celebration of your anniversary."

After a little more urging, Riordan agreed.

The following Saturday evening, the survivors gathered to enjoy an incomparable dinner. Food had been fairly scarce and very basic over the past weeks, and initially they concentrated on its savory goodness, rather than on the amenities of conversation. Heise sat at one end of the table with Hugh at the other. Tanya was to Hugh's right with Klavdia beside her. Next came Toshi Sugawara to Heise's left. To his right sat Kojuro Nabashima, then Paula, who had recently arrived from Yokohama in leg casts, and finally, in full dress uniform—Major Philip Faymonville. Tanya wore the superbly beautiful blue and red kimono presented to her by the family of Viscount Nabashima.

Goko-san, smilingly saw to it that everyone had enough food.

They all expressed to their unusually genial host their sincere compliments on the meal, especially the delicate flavor of the meat.

"Yah," agreed Heise, "the secret is in marinating good beef for at least three days. Anything less is a waste of time." He wiped his lips with his napkin. "Well, shall we retire to the living room for a bit of extra good taste?"

They got up, the gentlemen helping the ladies. Klavdia had some difficulty because her pregnancy was becoming more evident, slowing her movements. Sugawara helped her into one of the wider more comfortable chairs.

Heise poured a light "Saar" after-dinner wine, explaining the bottles had been stored in his personally designed, and now proven earthquake resistant, wine case, where the racks were protected by a sturdy metal framework.

"Like all of us, this wine is a survivor of what could likely go down in history as the world's greatest natural disaster. I suppose I should say in recorded history, but, this wine, unlike some of us, has a definite and immediate future. Let us drink to our survival and to the future, whatever it may bring—*Prosit!*"

Heise added to the toast. "Happy anniversary in Japan Professor Riordan."

They all sipped the fruity wine.

Hugh stood and bowed, saying, "Thank you." Then he paused and announced in a more serious tone, "Let us drink also to absent friends."

Most nodded in agreement.

"Yes, of course, we'll never forget them or the earthquake." Faymonville drained his glass with a gulp. "But, my experience at the hotel was much different than yours, Professor, or many others."

"The worst was the feeling," Hugh began, "the sense of betrayal—suddenly you can no longer trust the ground under your feet."

The Major agreed, continuing eagerly, "Yes, suddenly you can no longer trust the solid ground—the basis of all that is sure in this world."

Heise, enjoying this analysis added, "If the earth shakes—man loses faith in everything around him and is likely to become panicked." He drank deeply.

"Please forgive this opposite side of your theorem," began Nabashima. "Those of us with absolute faith did not panic."

"Your unquestioning faith, and your protection by the Goddess Kannon is really stupendous," complimented Hugh.

Everyone murmured agreement.

"As I watched Kojuro," confirmed Toshi Sugawara, "my faith returned to me and became stronger minute by minute until finally I saw the light of true devotion once again."

"It's just my luck my future in Russia hasn't been affected by the earthquake, said Faymonville. "Although I gained a greater admiration for the Japanese people because of it. There's a lot more behind those courteous smiles than I had imagined." He extended his glass to Heise for a refill. "I also learned the value of being in the right place at the right time.

"I do hope the fresh air in your new post does not prove

too cool for your comfort, Major," commented Nabashima.

Faymonville, drinking his second glass more leisurely replied, "It may turn out to be a refreshing change after all the warm weather here."

"We Japanese have learned to tolerate many natural inconveniences, both large and small, because of where we live. We must tolerate them—after all we have no choice in the matter—but we are not defeated by them."

Klavdia shook her head saying, "I can't remember seeing a single Japanese cry after the earthquake—not a single one—and some of them had lost entire families, or at least . . . "

"Stoical calm in the face of calamity is part of our heritage," explained Nabashima, "Just as we accepted the inevitability of the earthquake's coming, so we must accept the changes it has brought about. We have survived many disasters over the centuries, but our spirit has enabled us to grow stronger as a people whatever the personal sacrifice or tragedy."

Tanya observed, "Perhaps it *is* these natural disasters which have also united you and kept you from any serious internal strife such as we Russians have experienced."

"But, much of the pressure for your Russian Revolution came from outside influences," Hugh pointed out.

"Yes," she admitted, "I suppose that is true, but more of us should have resisted those influences.

"Many of those influences came from within my fatherland, I'm sorry to say," added Heise. "May I pour you some more wine?" He got up to refill a few of the glasses. "Let us drink a toast to the reopening of school next week, eh, Hugh?"

"I'll be glad to," Riordan responded, "although I wonder how many classes we'll be able to hold in those temporary barracks."

"Yes, no doubt there will be problems," mused the German. "But I have been too long up here in Shinjuku, looking into my beloved city, now and then feeling gloom and despair." He turned abruptly to the Major. "You have your headquarters in the Imperial Hotel. Please, tell us some good news, Major Faymonville."

"Well, only if mein host insists." There was a light smattering of applause, as Phil rose to his feet.

Nabashima and Sugawara immediately stood up, too. Bowing, Nabashima spoke first. "Before you speak, let me say that we Japanese owe supreme gratitude to the United States of America for sending well-provisioned naval ships so quickly."

Sugawara continued, with the grateful tone of his friend. "The ships of the United States of America helped for ten days until those of the Red Cross began to arrive."

"The American admiral has received our message of sincere appreciation," announced Nabashima. "You Americans have created a miracle."

Both bowed deeply and sat down.

The Major bowed in return. "Thank you gentleman. We Americans were honored to be of help. We even got a destroyer into Tokyo harbor and a load of Ford trucks from Yokohama. I hope all this will bring our nations closer together."

Faymonville looked over his small audience. "Professor Heise you've got me making a speech and I'm really not prepared." He paused, thoughtfully. "What is going on at the Imperial Hotel? What can I say that might interest you? Well, most of the legations are there—as are the wire-services; newspapers; relief agencies—and water from the Yodobashi Reservoir is running well now. Tatiana Alexandrovna, Hugh and I were happy to find Paula in Yokohama," he touched the maid's shoulder gently, "and as you can see she's mending nicely." She looked up at him and smiled, but there were tears in her eyes.

"Many European papers have come out saying the Imperial Hotel is the only structure left standing in Tokyo. Well, we're grateful, but we know that's not true. I brought along, however, a print of the message sent to Frank Lloyd Wright by Inumaru and Baron Okura." He withdrew a neatly folded length of paper from his uniform pocket. He read it aloud, "Hotel stands undamaged as monument to your genius. Hundreds of homeless provided for by perfectly maintained service. Congratulations. Okura."

"Now, my dear friends, with your permission, I'll sit down and drink to Frank."

There was a bit of light applause.

"Danke, Herr Faymonville," said Heise filling his glass.

"How about your future, Paula?" asked Faymonville, abruptly gesturing with his newly replenished glass. "I'll be going to Moscow in a few months. I've been meaning to ask you, since you're alone now. Would you consider a position as a cook in the embassy there?"

Paula gasped, then crumpled her napkin nervously. "Oh no, I couldn't."

"You'd be safe, you know. The Embassy is privileged territory."

"I do miss my country, but I'm not sure I could go back, not the way things are now."

"You could probably become an American citizen, eventually."

"No, sir, thank you, I'm a Russian," she declared emphatically.

"Well, please consider it while you're mending. We can talk about it some more after you're getting around under your own power."

"Anyway," he said finishing his wine, "It has been a wonderful evening, but I really should be getting the car back. The dinner and the company and the wine were all delightful."

Hugh got up saying, "We'll help Paula into your car. Certainly glad you could get a car so she could join us."

It was not an easy task. Faymonville and Hugh had to carry her to the rear door of the automobile and lift her while

Sugawara maneuvered the leg casts inside. They all waved as the car disappeared along its bumpy course toward the Imperial Hotel and what remained of downtown Tokyo.

Soon after, the two Japanese men bowed to each of them, and departed.

Since the earthquake, like other people, they had gotten into the habit of retiring early. There were no theaters playing, and few restaurants serving supper, turning night into day. Perhaps, sleep was the best way of shutting out the awful charred odor of the burned out city.

Klavdia complained of stomach cramps, and Heise made her lie down on a large sofa with her head on an overstuffed pillow and brought a glass of water.

Tanya said, "We don't have to leave until you are feeling better, dear. Just rest a while."

"Ach, don't worry about her," assured Heise. "I know what to do. After all, my wife has been pregnant many times. Besides, you ladies can stay here tonight. Why don't you wait until morning? You can sleep across the street as you did before. "Now," he said gesturing toward Hugh and Tanya, "why don't you two go out into the garden and get some air. I'll watch over Klavdia."

They protested mildly, but he insisted saying, "The breeze is blowing toward the city, the fresh air will do you good— enjoy it."

Tatiana and Hugh stood hand in hand in the garden silently gazing down the hill into blackened Tokyo. The twilight is brief in Japan. Already the night was velvety, with the starlight and moonlight transfiguring the doll's house architecture of the Japanese home across the road.

They were surprised at the number of lights and colored lanterns peeping from below. Still they said nothing, for between them now there was the incomparable joy of not having to say anything. The only sound came from a chorus of crickets and frogs.

Finally, Hugh cleared his throat. "How are you and Klavdia getting on together in your tiny room?"

"Well, we don't have much space, but the most difficult thing is for her to climb the ladder to the second floor. I have no idea when the stairs will be repaired."

"I think we should try to find another place for her when her time gets nearer."

"Yes, I suppose so. I don't think she can climb up much longer. I *do* want to take care of her though."

"Of course, we'll both do that," he assured her.

"I want to be with her when she has her child."

"I understand your concern for her—I rather feel it too. But, what about you?"

She looked away, into the middle of Tokyo, but really saw nothing. "Oh, I expect I'll get along, once school begins again, and . . . "

"You know I love you, very much. I have for quite some time."

"Yes."

"Tanya, will you—will you, marry me?"

"Yes. I love you, Hugh."

They embraced lightly, then passionately, for quite some time. At the height of their kiss a substantial tremor shook the earth beneath their feet. Startled, Tanya gasped, "was that another earthquake?"

He did not let her go, but held her reassuringly and smiled. "No, I don't think it was an earthquake. I think it was our kiss."

ABOUT THE AUTHOR

Lee Riordan grew up listening to his parents' vivid recollections of the Great Kanto Earthquake. Tatiana and Hugh Riordan passed on to their son not only a sense of the tragedy that befell Tokyo on September 1, 1923, but also an admiration for the Japanese people and their ability to pull together in times of trouble.

Lee Riordan has written seven books, and received the Mary Roberts Rinehart Foundation Award for "writing excellence." He has also worked as an editor at a leading New York publishing house, taught writing at three prestigious universities, and was once a scriptwriter for television.

The author now lives in Milwaukee, Wisconsin, and maintains contact with the offspring of the friends his parents made while in Japan, thinking of these individuals and his parents' memories of their time in Tokyo as his "Japanese treasure."